Randall Collins grew up in country New South Wales before moving to Wollongong to begin working with BHP at its Port Kembla steelworks as electrical engineering cadet. He spent more than 17 years in various departments before leaving and crossing the continent to live in Perth, Western Australia.

For the last 17 years, he has worked with identification systems.

He now lives in Rockingham, South of Perth, with his family and enjoys the coastal lifestyle that the city offers.

To my wife, Jo, my biggest fan. You knew I could do it.

Randall Collins

TIMESLIP

AUSTIN MACAULEY PUBLISHERS™
LONDON * CAMBRIDGE * NEW YORK * SHARJAH

Copyright © Randall Collins 2023

The right of Randall Collins to be identified as author of this work has been asserted by the author in accordance with sections 77 and 78 of the Copyright, Designs and Patents Act 1988.

All rights reserved. No part of this publication may be reproduced, stored in a retrieval system, or transmitted in any form or by any means, electronic, mechanical, photocopying, recording, or otherwise, without the prior permission of the publishers.

Any person who commits any unauthorised act in relation to this publication may be liable to criminal prosecution and civil claims for damages.

This is a work of fiction. Names, characters, businesses, places, events, locales, and incidents are either the products of the author's imagination or used in a fictitious manner. Any resemblance to actual persons, living or dead, or actual events is purely coincidental.

A CIP catalogue record for this title is available from the British Library.

ISBN 9781035804757 (Paperback)
ISBN 9781035804764 (ePub e-book)

www.austinmacauley.com

First Published 2023
Austin Macauley Publishers Ltd®
1 Canada Square
Canary Wharf
London
E14 5AA

Where does one even start to identify the depth and variety of support that goes into reaching your dream of becoming a published author. Thank you to my family and friends. I feel so blessed to have had degrees of care, encouragement and, of course, love from so many.

Thanks to my wife Jo for her encouragement and constructive criticism. Thanks to my friend Sue Allen, my sister Katie and her husband Gerard, my brother Peter, editor Laura Dobra and the people at Austin Macauley who all made me feel as though I wasn't wasting my time.

Thanks to everyone who had anything to do with editing the book. It is much better for your efforts.

The best is yet to come.

Prologue

Arizona desert, USA, 2017

When the countdown reached zero, there was a bright flash of light from within the dome and Lieutenant Emery Dean of the United States Army ceased to exist.

Thirty minutes beforehand, two heavily armed men in army fatigues stood guard outside a small concrete building which was the lone man-made structure for as far as the eye could see. The desert sun beat down on them mercilessly but if they felt any ill effects from the heat, they certainly didn't show it.

Their eyes were constantly scanning the surrounding countryside as if they were hoping that somebody might intrude on their space. In truth, though, there was enough electronic surveillance of the area around the pillbox to make their jobs redundant. Cameras, and motion and infra-red detectors covered the area far better than the two soldiers. Still, the army was not taking any chances in the security of this installation and cameras and motion detectors weren't able to shoot at a possible threat.

One soldier raised his eyebrows then gave a slight nod to his colleague who, after a moment, replied in kind as the noise became audible to him as well. Within a few seconds, the cause of the noise appeared—a helicopter, rapidly increasing in size. The two soldiers remained in their positions but gripped their weapons a little more firmly as they were finally able to make out the AH-64 Apache.

The sudden noise from the small speaker mounted on the wall behind the soldiers startled both men but a casual observer wouldn't have noticed. 'Take it easy, boys. We're expecting them,' said the voice of their supervisor, who was comfortably seated in the air-conditioned security control centre a number of floors below ground level.

The helicopter stopped its forward progress about fifty metres in front of the pillbox and slowly descended to the ground, throwing out dirt and sand far enough to reach the two soldiers. A slight squinting of the two sets of eyes was the only sign of any discomfort.

The helicopter door opened and two uniformed men stepped down. The first was very tall, at least four inches over six feet in height, while the other was almost ten inches shorter.

The shorter, stocky man walked quickly towards the pillbox like a wrecking ball that intended to knock it down. Both guards figured he was in his late fifties as they could see the closely cropped grey hair peeking out from beneath his cap and jowls hanging down, giving his face the look of a bulldog.

The taller man hunched over somewhat in an unnecessary involuntary posture to keep clear of the chopper blades as he hurried to keep up. Once out from under them, he rose to his full height and stretched out his powerful frame, effortlessly keeping pace with the shorter man. A slight smile, or was it a smirk, appeared on the young, handsome face. He looked thirty years younger than the older man, no grey in his short, sandy hair. Deep, brown eyes stared back at them. Maybe he was a bodyguard. The soldiers recognised that type of relaxed walk from their years in the army and knew that he was capable of exploding into action. He was a dangerous man.

As they came closer to the two guards, their rank became clear. The smaller man was a general while the oak leaf on the taller man's uniform identified him as a major. Neither guard released their weapons to salute as they glared at the two officers.

With a pneumatic hiss, the door in the pillbox slid open.

A cliché from old science fiction movies stepped out. The white dust coat and thick glasses proclaimed the man as an academic but the wild shock of white hair, as if he'd stuck his finger in a power point, screamed "mad scientist". The man's face was so pale it looked like he had never been in the sun, which made it hard to determine his age. The major thought he looked a bit pudgy. *Typical office worker. Too many desserts and not enough exercise.*

'Welcome, General Morgan,' said the scientist, completely ignoring the major.

'Thank you, Professor Windsor. Now, how about we get this show on the road.'

The doors hissed closed. Neither the general nor the professor seemed interested in small talk, so the major was able to observe his surroundings without distraction. They had travelled down a short staircase and come to the elevator door. Instead of a button on the wall there was a pad on which the professor had placed his palm. After a brief flash of light from the pad, the elevator doors had opened.

The major was surprised when he looked at the number of buttons on the control panel. The professor reached out and pressed a button and after a few moments the elevator came to a stop on floor number seven. According to the numbers on the panel, there were still five levels below them. The doors opened onto a stark corridor and the three men stepped out. After a short walk past a number of unmarked doors, the professor stopped in front of one with another pad next to the door lock. He placed his palm on it and after another brief flash of light there was a loud click and the professor turned the handle and walked in, followed by the two uniformed men.

They entered a massive room. It was packed with about twenty consoles with a person sitting at each one. They were all dressed similarly to the professor. The only soldiers here were two guards near the door, who scanned the newcomers as they walked in. Video displays on each console showed bar graphs and circular readouts that fluctuated constantly. The major was reminded of scenes from the movie *Apollo 13* with all of the scientists buzzing around, trying to bring the crippled ship back to Earth.

The far wall was free from any banks of computers or other equipment and seemed to be covered by steel shutters. The major noticed that the consoles were all facing that way. What was hidden behind there?

The general finally spoke. 'I've been with this project all along, Professor, but Major Carmichael is new to my staff so why don't you give him the executive summary.'

Giving the first indication he knew that the man was there, the professor turned towards the major and squinted. 'How technical do you want it to be?'

'I'm a soldier, Professor, not a physicist.'

'Indeed. Well, you are in the largest facility of its type in the world. To put it simply, this is a particle accelerator. We fire two sets of particles in opposite directions, through vacuum pipes, around a circuit some sixteen miles long. When they are practically at the speed of light, we steer them into each other—'

The major interrupted the professor, 'How do you steer particles like that in a big circle?'

As if he was a university lecturer answering a silly question, the professor replied, 'We have over one thousand superconducting electromagnets creating the magnetic field we need to bend and steer the particles, and others to focus and then direct the two streams into each other.'

Impressed by the scale of the project, the major asked another question. 'What happens when the two streams collide?'

The professor sighed and turned to the general. 'You haven't hired this man for his technical ability, General.'

'No, Professor. Major Carmichael has expertise in other areas which are also important to this project.'

Clearly sceptical, the professor turned back to the major. 'When the two streams of particles collide, we create conditions very similar to that which occurred during the Big Bang, on a much smaller scale, of course.' The major's eyes widened at this statement. The professor continued. 'There are many areas of research that physicists want to observe from this, such as the creation of the fundamental particles that we understand today. Others would study the nature of antimatter. We have teams here to look at these issues, but the main purpose of this installation is to harness what is referred to as dark energy.'

'What the hell is dark energy?' asked the major.

Now the professor was warming to the topic. 'Think of all the stars, planets, gases and everything that you know of. What percentage of the total mass in the universe do you think those things make up?'

The major shrugged. 'One hundred.'

'Five. Five per cent. The rest is made up of dark matter at around fifteen per cent and dark energy making up the rest. What you can't see is many times more abundant than what you can see.' The major looked unconvinced. Disappointed, the professor tried to dumb it down. 'You are aware the universe is expanding?' The major nodded so the professor carried on. 'But are you aware that the rate of expansion is accelerating?'

'How can that happen? I mean I can comprehend that a body in space will keep moving at a constant rate without friction to slow it down, but you'd think things would slow down if anything, with different bodies having a gravitational attraction to each other. How can the expansion still be accelerating?'

The professor snorted. 'Well, at least now you're thinking, just as others have been for some time. Now I have unlocked this mystery.' The major felt like a first-year college student at a lecture on the teacher's favourite subject but found that he was intrigued as to what was coming next.

The professor continued. 'There was a tremendous amount of energy released at the time of the Big Bang and not all of it was as heat and light. There is still a force pushing the universe apart and it is dark energy.' At this point, the professor smiled. To the major, it gave the man a more crazed look than he already had. 'The dark energy created gravity waves which spread from the centre of the universe like ripples in a pond from a dropped stone. If an object is riding the downslope at a particular point on the wave, then it will accelerate.' The major nodded his understanding and the professor continued.

'So, I have discovered the optimum point on the gravity wave and a way to harness it and use it, albeit in miniscule amounts, to achieve our ultimate goal.'

'And what is that?' asked the major.

'Temporal displacement.'

'What's that?'

The professor rolled his eyes. 'You might understand better if I said time travel.'

'Time travel? You've invented a time machine? You can't be serious,' said the major, looking back and forth between the general and the professor.

The professor started again. 'We are quite serious. Simply put, it is like a surfer catching a wave on the ocean. He is propelled forward in time by it. In fact, we have achieved this goal already.'

'What? How?'

'We have sent solid, inanimate objects into the future,' stated the professor.

'What! How can you possibly know that?'

'Apart from the physics and mathematics being irrefutable, we have observed the phenomenon. The selected object ceases to exist in this time and reappears a short time later.'

'How short, Professor?' asked the general.

'Up to an hour, depending on the mass of the particle streams and the object. The length of this period is something we hope to refine at a later time but the purpose of today is the first demonstration of temporal displacement of a live subject. It is not something that I wished to do at this stage of the research, but the army is keen to see results of, what it deems, a more useful nature.'

The major was startled at this disclosure but before he could ask any further questions the general queried the professor again. 'Who is it?'

The professor checked a clipboard on the desk in front of him. 'Lieutenant Emery Dean has volunteered to have the honour of being the first human time traveller.'

The professor pointed to one of the men standing nearby and then waved at the far wall where the shutters were situated. The man pressed a button on his console. The shutters opened like a venetian blind and then retracted into the ceiling. They had concealed a window overlooking a huge, brightly lit room.

A number of large pieces of equipment crossed the space. Each was about five metres across and four metres high and roughly circular in shape with a series of ribs running around the circumference. Thick electrical cables dropped down from the ceiling into large junction boxes mounted at the front of the machines. Each had a label attached to it, announcing them as "Magnet 1027" to "Magnet 1034".

A massive metal cylinder emerged from one wall, crossed the room between the magnets and disappeared into the wall on the other side.

The major's attention was quickly drawn to the central feature of the room. On a raised platform, in front of the cylinder, was a large glass dome criss-crossed by metal bands. Inside the dome was a naked man, presumably Lieutenant Dean.

It was impossible not to notice the strong physique of the soldier, who was standing there looking embarrassed to be on display. The major smiled at the lieutenant's discomfort.

The general looked away from the glass dome and asked the professor, 'When do we start?'

'General, we have started already. We have fired the streams of particles and have been accelerating them for approximately six hours. But the final result will be in…' And he pointed to a digital display on one wall.

Both the general and major looked up to see the display count down from "00:02.00" to "00:01.59". The professor turned away and started looking at various consoles. The other people in the room were engrossed in their displays. The major looked at the general, whose concentration was focused on the man in the dome. He was reminded of a snake he had seen at a reptile park as a child. The snake had stared at a mouse, seeming to hypnotise it before striking.

When the display showed thirty seconds left, the professor spoke up. 'Status?'

He was answered in turn by six people seated at consoles monitoring different parameters. 'Normal.'

'Proceed,' said the professor.

The display continued to count down.

Finally realising these people were serious, the major asked, 'How far into the future do you intend to send Lieutenant Dean?'

'We have calibrated the levels for approximately five minutes,' the professor replied.

All attention in the room now focused on the glass dome containing the naked man. The major looked up at the display to see it "00:00.02" and then turned back to the dome in time to see a bright flash of light from within the dome.

Then Lieutenant Emery Dean ceased to exist.

Unfortunately for him, though, it was not as the professor had predicted. Instead of disappearing, to materialise some five minutes in the future, he had become a mass of blood and bone and gore splashed about the inside of the dome.

'Holy shit!' exclaimed the major. 'Next volunteer.'

'Perhaps you'd like to step up,' snapped the general, glaring at the major, who clamped his mouth shut. 'Well, Professor,' he said turning to face the shocked academic, 'this has turned to crap. If you want to continue in this line of work, I'd say you had better come up with some answers. Instead of celebrating the success of this project, I'll have to write a letter to the man's family telling them how he died a hero, trying to defuse a road side bomb in Afghanistan. How else are we going to explain that he looks like roadkill?'

The general turned towards the door and started walking. 'Let's go, Major.'

Chapter 1

Professor Windsor stared at the whiteboard as he had for most of the last two months, ever since the embarrassment of the live trial of what the impudent major had christened "the Time Machine". What a stupid term for a project that he had devoted such a large portion of his life to. Unfortunately, it was a catchy title—the type that the uneducated masses seemed to focus on—and it had stuck.

The professor thought again about the events of that day. The fact that a man had died was irrelevant. The only bad thing, the professor thought, was that it hadn't been Major Carmichael inside the temporal displacement dome.

He had told the general that they weren't ready for a live trial, but you could only keep the men footing the bills quiet for so long and then they had to have their way.

He stared again at the whiteboard. He had started his calculations from first principles for the tenth time in in the last two months and ended up with the same result each time. He was sure he had made no mistakes. What had gone wrong?

The professor threw up his arms in frustration and let them drop to his head. Unconsciously, he grabbed a handful of hair with each hand and pulled, leaving his hair standing up in a more bizarre fashion than usual, which only added to his eccentric look.

He turned and walked out of the laboratory, deciding a cup of coffee might stimulate his flagging energies. He would have loved to light up his pipe. Like the one man in history he looked up to, Albert Einstein, he thought a pipe calmed the mind and stimulated rational thinking. But the facility was a non-smoking zone, so instead he worked his way through the complex, heading to the mess hall. On his approach, he passed the recreation room where several army security personnel were watching some senseless sport on satellite television involving two teams beating each other up over a ball. They cheered wildly at some particularly brutal contact, which made the professor shake his head. He wondered why they were excited over something so trivial when they were on the verge of being involved in something so monumental and important.

He entered the mess hall and walked over to the coffee machine and poured himself a cup. He sat down at a table, sipping the coffee, trying to relax, but he could still hear the cheering coming from the next room, which only served to increase his frustration. He thought to himself that he would love to shut them up. Maybe he could interfere with the signal somehow.

The professor sat bolt upright. Anybody watching him might have laughed. He looked like a character in a bad sci-fi movie that had been shot with a freeze ray by an alien. Despite his comical appearance, however, there were some serious calculations going on behind the glasses.

'My God. Can that be it?' He jumped up, the chair flying backwards across the room and coffee spilling all over the table, but he didn't notice any of those things. He ran out of the door to the room and back towards the lab.

Chapter 2

Special Agent Cathy Owens walked through the fourth-floor corridor of the FBI headquarters on Pennsylvania Avenue, Washington DC. Cathy was a tall, attractive, fair-haired lady in her mid-twenties. A hint of makeup highlighted her Nordic features, which assured her of second glances wherever she went.

Cathy's father had instilled into her a sense of justice and it was only a matter of time before she had followed in his footsteps and entered into law enforcement, despite his protests. He had visions of his daughter becoming the first female president and had tried to nudge her in that direction but she had ideas about being the first female director of the bureau instead.

She had excelled during her training at Quantico and since then had performed well in each of her postings. She had only recently returned to Washington after an undercover stint in Florida where her work had been important in the breaking open of a drug importation ring. Now after a week of debriefing and report writing she was eager to move on to her next assignment.

She knocked on the door of her boss, Special Agent in Charge Arnold Wilson. 'Enter,' boomed the voice from behind the door.

She looked at the slightly balding African-American man behind the desk. He was huge. At six and a half feet tall and well over two hundred and eighty pounds, there was nothing small about him. It was legend among his co-workers that Wilson had never had to fire his gun in anger and that he had, on a number of occasions, physically intimidated suspects into surrendering by stepping into plain view and demanding that they drop their weapons.

He looked up at Cathy. 'Special Agent Owens,' the voice rumbled out. Cathy gulped involuntarily but was immediately reassured by the friendly smile from the other side of the desk. The large gap between his front teeth drew Cathy's attention, as it always did. She tried not to stare.

'Yes, sir.'

'I had something else planned for you, but this has just been handed down from above. Sit down and take a look,' he said as he passed over a folder to Cathy, who sat in the chair opposite. Wilson studied Cathy as she looked through the file. The way she flicked her hair out of her eyes absent-mindedly as she read reminded him of his own daughter and he couldn't suppress a smile as she did it again.

When she had finished reading, she looked up. 'So, six weeks ago, two scientists die in a helicopter crash while working on a top-secret project for the army. That's it in a nutshell?'

'That's right,' responded Wilson, 'but there are a few more things. These were the only two casualties from the helicopter crash.' He pointed at two photographs. 'The pilot survived. Something which is deemed highly unlikely.'

'So, some sort of set-up then?'

'Finding that out is going to be your responsibility.'

'Well, sir, why us? I mean the army has its own crew to sort this out.'

'That's true,' said Wilson, 'but they've had six weeks and this is what they came up with.' He gestured to the report. 'One of the dead men was the son of Senator Parsons from Indiana, who's an old college buddy of our revered deputy director and he has called in some favours. This is to be kept as quiet as possible. You have till this evening to give me a list of resources you think you'll want on this case. Any questions?'

'No, sir,' said Cathy, standing.

'Go get 'em.'

Chapter 3

Perth, Western Australia, 2021

Matthew Fraser ran hard along the footpath in Kalamunda, a hilly suburb, some twenty kilometres east of Perth, Western Australia. He had been running for fifty minutes and was heading towards home. Now that the strong, early morning, easterly winds that regularly swept through the suburb had died down, the heat was already becoming stifling and he was looking forward to a cold drink.

With a long athletic stride, he looked as though he would be hard to keep up with as he had indeed proven many times. It was not a long-distance runner's body though. He was tall, at a couple of inches over six feet, with broad shoulders and a strong body indicating he could do a lot more than run. He had been sought after by the local football clubs as his athletic abilities became well known but his dreams had lain elsewhere.

Matthew cursed as a car travelling in the opposite direction turned the corner in front of him without indicating. He was forced to stop suddenly to avoid the car, locking his knee, expecting a sudden stab of pain. Happily, though, there were no problems. He was only recently recovered from an injury that had happened when a careless motorist had, almost identically, turned a corner without giving way at a pedestrian crossing, hitting him and causing severe damage to the ligaments in his right knee.

The subsequent operation and recovery had shattered his hopes of representing his country at the Olympics in the triathlon because he had not been able to compete in the selection trials. It galled him to watch the Olympics on TV, to see people he had beaten, racing instead of him.

After a few tentative steps, Matthew picked up the pace and decided to set a record for the rest of the way home, all the way cursing drivers that didn't know what an indicator was for and for his bad luck in general. *Tomorrow I'm going swimming instead*, he thought to himself.

An hour and a half later Matthew rode his bike through the gates of Harmon Brothers, the courier company he had recently joined. He loved the ride down from the foothills even if it meant that he had to really put in an effort to get back up the hill when his shift finished.

Matthew had suffered a double blow when, along with the knee injury, sponsorships had dried up. Major companies expected some level of success for their corporate dollars and now with no chance of competing, let alone winning, they had deserted him. His meagre savings had allowed him some recovery time, but they had eventually run out.

Now that he was forced to work, Matthew had decided, this wasn't too bad. The flexible nature of the job allowed him plenty of time to train and driving around Perth listening to the radio wasn't a bad way to spend his time. *Anyway*, he thought to himself, *only three more years till the next Games.*

Matthew entered the office and said hello to Kate Preston, the company receptionist. She had recently finished high school and this was her first job. She was a pretty, young blonde and was obviously, to everyone but the object of her affections, enamoured with the tall, dark, athletic Matthew.

As he walked towards the job board which showed which drivers were doing what runs, Matthew saw that there was nothing next to his name. Perplexed he turned towards Kate. 'Bob asked if you could see him when you came in,' she explained, smiling broadly. 'It's nothing bad. I heard him talking about some special job today.'

'Thanks, Kate,' he replied, oblivious to the feelings of the young girl, and turned down the corridor towards the supervisor's office.

Matthew knocked on the door marked "Robert Harmon" and after a mumble from inside opened the door and walked in. 'Hi, Bob.'

Bob Harmon was the son of the eldest of the two Harmon brothers and was about the same age and height as Matthew but carried a lot more weight as a result of being office bound during the day and couch bound at night. Still, he was friendly and a fair boss and Matthew liked him. 'Hi, Matt,' Bob said, giving a slight wave.

'Kate said to come and see you,' said Matthew.

'Yeah. I need a favour and normally I'd get Jim to do it, but he has something on tonight. It's an overnighter up north. You ever been to Murchison?'

Bob was referring to the Shire of Murchison, which was located about six hundred and fifty kilometres from Perth. The shire's area of roughly 50,000 square kilometres was made up almost entirely of pastoral leases. Referred to as "the Shire with No Town" it was the only shire in the country to have this distinction. The population of the shire was something less than two hundred people.

'Not too many triathlons up there,' replied Matthew.

'Suppose not. Anyway, there's a farmer up there who needs a bit of equipment by tomorrow and I'm hoping you can do the trip.'

'Yeah, sure,' said Matthew. 'What's the plan?'

'Great. Grab the van, drop past your place and get whatever you need then head out to Rockingham to pick up the gear. We've booked a room at a motel in Mullewa for tonight. Drop the stuff off at the farm tomorrow morning and then head home.' He handed Matthew a written itinerary while he spoke. 'The address is on there. I'm told it can be tricky to find but the GPS in the van will show you the way now that we've had it fixed. Oh, and mobile phone reception around there is rubbish, so grab the sat-phone before you go. You've used it before, haven't you?'

'Yeah. Once. I don't think I'll have any trouble with it. Well, I'd better get going then, I've got a long drive.'

'Thanks, Matt. I appreciate it.'

'Sure,' said Matthew, turning to leave the office.

An hour's drive north of the Murchison settlement was the cattle station known as Armison Flats. The locals, not that there were a lot of them around, wondered why the foreign investor had bothered establishing a dairy farm in an area that wasn't really suitable, but he seemed to have more money than sense and he obviously had plenty of the former, judging by the number of trucks that had been coming and going for the last few years. They had heard rumours of a new breed of cattle that was very hardy in drought conditions. Maybe the benefits would flow to the rest of the region.

Standing outside, enjoying the early morning sun, Major Carmichael strolled back to the elevator, the entrance to which was hidden in what was an actual working milking shed or whatever the hell was the right expression for it. The major was not at all interested in farming and his men had learned not to correct him if he used a name that wasn't quite right. Shovelling cow shit for a few hours helped remind a man to keep his mouth shut.

He was walking back to his office when he was approached by the communications officer. 'Sir, we received this during the scheduled communications window.' The officer handed over a piece of paper.

The major read the message while walking away. *So, it's all coming to a head*, he thought to himself. Time to see Professor Windbag.

Professor Windsor turned as the major walked into his office. 'When does the general arrive? Now that we have successfully performed our inanimate tests in the new location, I would like to proceed with the live trial as soon as possible.'

'I've just received word that he'll be here later today. I hope for your sake that the results are worth the money we spent moving this whole facility from the US to this Godforsaken backwater in the middle of the outback. I mean, we were very lucky finding a farm for sale in the area and then dismantling the whole operation, transporting it here and reassembling it in secret, all in four years. It has been some achievement. But it won't mean spit if it doesn't work.'

Major Carmichael did indeed have areas of expertise useful to the project as General Morgan had told the professor. Logistics and security for the project relocation had been a huge undertaking and he had performed admirably over the period. As far as they could tell there was no hint that ASIO, the Australian Security Intelligence Organisation, had any idea that the facility was there. Now that it all was done, the main worry for the major was maintaining an operational farm on the surface so there wouldn't be any reason for suspicion from the locals, as few of them as there were. He had been able to select some men from the ranks who had ranching backgrounds and put them to work maintaining the façade of a working cattle farm.

The professor glared at the uniformed man. 'Yes, well, this is hardly the outback, less than a ten hours drive to a capital city. Need I remind you that once I determined that ambient radio and electromagnetic noise caused the failure of the previous attempt, the search for a quiet zone became all important? The lack of any significant sources of interference in this entire locality has made it ideal for us. I'll put the final preparations into place and we should be ready for the test at nine o'clock tomorrow morning.'

The area in which the farm was located was indeed a dead zone as far as electromagnetic interference was considered. It had few people, which was a bonus in terms of privacy but was invaluable to the operational success of the project. The area had also been earmarked for the international Square Kilometre

Array (SKA) radio telescope project. Radio telescopes collect radio emissions which have a longer wavelength than light waves. As such, the area of the telescope, the array, has to be larger to get a similar resolution as an optical telescope. In this case, as the name suggested, it is one square kilometre. Lack of interference from nearby radio sources is critical with such devices. The research already conducted by the international scientific community on the SKA had saved Professor Windsor valuable time in finding a new site.

The major nodded but the professor had already moved his attention to other matters, so he turned and left the office. After working with the professor for the last four years, he had mixed feelings about the results of the test tomorrow. On one hand, he hoped everything went smoothly and the United States Army achieved their goal of controllable time travel, giving them a huge advantage over potential enemies. On the other hand, the professor had been an insufferable prick for the entire time and he would love to see the smug look wiped off his face. *I guess we'll see*, he thought to himself.

Chapter 4

Matthew had stayed overnight in the local hotel in Mullewa. As with many country towns the hotel was the centre of all local activity. He had enjoyed a counter meal and watched some of the townsfolk showing their prowess on the dartboard, not something that he was very good at. Judging by some of the physiques on display, a high level of fitness wasn't required for success in hitting the bullseye when needed, so Matthew left them to their fun and retired early.

Before the sun was up the next morning, he felt the need for some exercise and since his preferred swim session was no longer an option, he decided to go for a run. He ran for half an hour and the few locals he saw at that early hour looked at him like he was from another planet. He thought to himself that they must have had other means of keeping fit, even the ones with a belly hanging over their belt buckles.

After a shower and a quick breakfast, he was ready to hit the road. Given the lack of facilities further north, Matthew stopped at the local service station to top up the van and grab a couple of snacks that might be able to serve as lunch a bit later on. He kept the receipts, knowing that Bob Harmon was a stickler for details like that.

According to his itinerary the farm was about a three-hour drive north, so Matthew put the details into his GPS and after a brief, one-sided conversation with the unit he drove off along the Carnarvon-Mullewa Road. *At least this section of the road is sealed*, he thought to himself, knowing that he would be using dirt roads later in the morning. Matthew didn't even bother trying to find a local radio station, knowing it would be a waste of time, instead hitting the button on the CD player. The sounds of Cold Chisel filled the cabin and he drove on, foot tapping in time with the music.

The scenery barely changed during the drive. Mile after mile of fields full of brown grass passed by with only slight bends in the road relieving the monotony.

Matthew cursed himself for forgetting to bring along some of his own music. He hadn't gotten around to loading any tunes on his new mobile phone yet. Cold Chisel had given way to Slim Dusty, which was the only other CD in the van. He had never been a country music fan and was a bit surprised to find that he knew the words to some of the songs, but all the same he didn't know if he was having a beer with someone or if the pub had run out of it and the fields didn't look like any rain had tumbled down lately. With some relief, the last song finished and he hit the eject button and reloaded the Chisels.

He passed through Murchison Settlement after two hours; if he hadn't been paying attention, he would have missed it. He drove along for another half hour and a quick scan of the itinerary showed that the next landmark he needed to find was a sign pointing to Number 20 Well. *Maybe there'll be signs to the other nineteen wells leading up to that one. Or maybe not. Let's see what the GPS thinks.* He looked at the GPS unit for the first time in a while to find that instead of displaying the road that he was on, it was showing a map of suburban Perth.

'Oh, great,' Matthew said to himself. He slowed the van down and pulled to the side of the road. He reached for the GPS, pulled it out of the cradle stuck to the windscreen and switched the unit off. After a few seconds, he turned it back on, but the screen remained blank. He tried switching it off and on again but once more he was left with a blank screen. 'Good one, Bob. I thought you fixed this bloody thing.' He checked the Maps app on his own phone but he didn't have internet access and it wouldn't connect. 'Oh well, let's try the old-fashioned way.' He opened the glove box to look for a map but only found an owner's manual and the registration papers for the van, plus a few empty lolly wrappers. Matthew sighed in exasperation.

Now he was faced with a choice to either go back half an hour to Murchison Settlement to try to get a map or to push on, following the directions on the itinerary. No brainer, he decided. Full speed ahead. He put the van back in gear and pulled back onto the road. 'Now, where's that sign?'

Despite his pronouncement of speed, Matthew drove along at only eighty kilometres per hour, not wanting to miss the sign he was hoping to see. He hadn't seen another vehicle since he had passed through Murchison Settlement, so he wasn't worried about holding up traffic.

In another ten minutes, Matthew saw a sign in the distance. Slowing down even further he moved up the road towards the sign. It was quite faded but he definitely could make out the word "WELL" on the sign. He checked his itinerary again. *OK. Next right and then fifteen kilometres and I'm there.* Unfortunately for Matthew a closer inspection of the sign would have shown him that it once read "POWELL RD".

One kilometre further up the road and Matthew came to a right-hand turn. The sealed road gave way to gravel and Matthew kept to a steady speed, as he didn't drive on unsealed roads that often. He checked his odometer, so he would know when the fifteen kilometres was up. 'Thanks Bob. I made it despite your best efforts.'

After fifteen kilometres without seeing the entrance to the farm, he was looking for, Matthew was starting to regret patting himself on the back. 'Bob, if I ever find this place and actually get back, don't ever ask me for another favour.' Jimmy Barnes, the lead singer of Cold Chisel, was starting to grate on his nerves so he stabbed the off button on the CD player and drove on with only the road noise to accompany him. Finally, up in the distance he could make out a large gate. About time.

Matthew slowed the van as the road finished at the gate. He was expecting the name "Peabody Downes" to be on the gate and was surprised to see "Armison Flats" and in even bigger letters "KEEP OUT". He shook his head. Oh well, he'd give them a call. He reached for the itinerary and located a telephone number. He picked up his mobile phone but as he expected there was no signal. 'OK, Bob. Last chance. The bloody sat-phone better work, or I might never find this place.'

Matthew checked his watch. It was nearly nine o'clock. He picked up the sat-phone and stepped out of the van to make the call.

General Morgan strode into the control room. His stocky, powerful frame dominated the setting. He had believed Major Carmichael when he said that the newly located facility was all but identical to the one from the old location but now, he saw, it really was.

In his younger years with the army, it had never been an issue, but now a case of jetlag reinforced the fact that he was in another country. Still, he was the general and he wasn't about to show any of these youngsters any weakness. 'Good morning, everyone.' There was a muted chorus of returned greetings from around the room.

The general found Major Carmichael looking at him. It was a knowing look. 'Smart boy, that one,' he said to himself. 'Won't be a major much longer.' The major had excelled in getting this facility up and running. As far as he was concerned the major was the best officer to have ever served under his command.

With a nod to the major, the general turned his attention to Professor Windsor. Now there was a strange bird. A brilliant scientist, he seemed to be able to do complicated calculations in his head as fast as the computers the rest of the staff relied on. This whole facility was based on his theories and if details of the project were ever released, something the general would try to ensure never happened, he would go down as one of the greatest minds in history. Sadly, he lacked any social skills. Normally the army wouldn't care about that sort of thing, but the professor was a civilian, dealing with civilian staff as well as members of the military. His abrasive manner constantly irritated people. He expected others to be able to think like he did, which meant he was disappointed most of the time, so people had to get used to working without any praise or encouragement.

Still, staff turnover was a minimum on this project. The scope, the budget and the potential history all combined to keep the staff engaged and loyal. Apart from that, they had all signed non-disclosure contracts, which ensured they would never be released from prison if any hint of the project came to public attention.

There had been a regrettable situation after the last live test, with two scientists wanting to go public about the truth of the volunteer's death, but the major had kept a lid on things. The threat of prison hadn't seemed to be enough of a deterrent for those men and a more immediate solution had been required. The general had left the details of their demise to the major's imagination and as far as the rest of the staff knew, their late colleagues had died in a helicopter crash while on the way to some talk-fest. Morgan wanted this to be an army-only operation and any outside agency involvement was to be avoided.

The general had been present at the old facility for other tests and from what he could see this one was progressing much the same. He looked into what he thought of as "the dome room". He was sure there was an actual term for it but he didn't really care. A naked man stood in the dome. Lieutenant Johnson. He was a fine specimen, about six feet tall, with a strong body and a friendly, contagious smile. He looked confident. The general knew he had only heard about the good results from the new facility not about the previous live test. Hell, he wouldn't be looking so confident if he'd heard about that one. The prospect of exploding all over the place would definitely make a man nervous.

The general looked at his watch. It was a couple of minutes to nine. The clock on the wall reached the two-minute mark. The professor was moving around the control room checking various displays.

At the thirty second mark, the professor asked 'Status?'

The senior people sitting at the various consoles called back in turn, 'Normal.'

'Proceed.'

The clock proceeded to count down. The general focused his attention on Lieutenant Johnson, who was now looking a lot less confident. Three, two, one…

Matthew dialled the number for the farmhouse at Peabody Downes and waited for the call to go through. After a few rings, there was a click on the far end. 'Hello?'

Matthew's world became a sudden burst of light which exploded in his head. He was smashed to the ground, pain threatening to rip him apart. He couldn't see, couldn't think. Pain was his entire world. Then blackness descended on him.

…zero.

The general had been holding his breath for the last few seconds. He was expecting a flash of light within the dome. Nothing. He looked at the clock. It was now counting up. Lieutenant Johnson was still in the dome looking somewhat bemused. 'Did it work?' The lieutenant's voice came over the loud speakers mounted near the ceiling. The general looked at the major. He seemed to be smirking in the direction of the professor. The professor was standing still, staring at the dome containing the naked man.

Suddenly the professor spun around and started talking to the staff at the consoles. 'What happened? Did particle stream collision occur or not?'

The man at the console nearest the professor spoke up. 'Yes, sir. Collision occurred. According to my readings everything went according to procedure.'

'No, it didn't,' replied the professor. 'Now let's get busy and find out what went wrong.'

Matthew slowly clawed his way back to consciousness. He was totally disoriented. 'Where am I?'

He found himself lying on his back on a dirt road, next to the van. 'Oh God...' He rolled onto his side and was violently ill. He wiped the back of his hand across his mouth and spat, trying to get the taste out of his mouth.

Slowly, realisation came back. 'What the hell happened?' he mumbled to himself.

With nobody to give him answers, Matthew got to his hands and knees and after a few seconds, when it didn't feel as if the world was going to fall on him again, he slowly stood up. He badly needed something to drink so he stumbled over to the van and grabbed one of the soft drinks he had bought earlier. He ripped the top of the can and downed it quickly. Feeling a little better, he took stock.

He decided he was still alive at least. He was also covered in dirt. Matthew brushed off the worst of the dust and used some of the water from a bottled drink to rinse off his face and hands.

His gaze fell to the sat-phone lying in the middle of the dirt road. *Surely, I didn't get some sort of electric shock from that*, he thought to himself. He took the few steps over and squatted down next to the phone. Tentatively he reached out, and with the back of his hand, touched the phone. Nothing happened. He picked it up and looked more closely. The phone was either dead or switched off.

Matthew stood up and walked back to the van. He tossed the sat-phone onto the passenger's seat. He climbed in. *I still don't know where I am but I know I'm not staying here.*

Matthew turned the van around and headed back down the road.

For the next five minutes, General Morgan watched the professor and his staff moving around and consulting various monitors and displays but at the end of that time decided he wanted some answers. He walked over and asked, 'Well, Professor, what happened?'

The professor turned around looking ready to snap until he saw it was the general. 'It appears everything worked as we expected, up until particle stream collision. But instead of the gravity wave being directed at the dome it was directed somewhere else.'

'Where?'

'We're still trying to work that out.'

'And what effect will this energy have in this other location?' the general persisted.

'Something similar to what we expected here would be my theory but without more time to establish the facts, it's only a guess.'

Both men were distracted by the major's voice. He was pointing at the dome where a naked Lieutenant Johnson was tapping at the glass, shoulders raised in a questioning shrug. 'Can someone get him out of there?'

Chapter 5

Matthew reached the end of the gravel road and turned back onto the sealed section. He was physically recovered but still wondered what had happened. He felt maybe he had been struck by lightning but found it hard to believe as there wasn't a cloud in the sky and there hadn't been one all week. Another disconcerting possibility was that he had imagined the whole thing. Surely not. But the thought nagged at him.

Trying to put it behind him, Matthew pulled off the road. *I still have to find the right farm,* he thought. He looked at the sat-phone sitting on the passenger's seat. Tentatively he picked it up, switched it on and stepped out of the van. After checking the number, he dialled again but immediately after dialling held the phone at arm's length. 'No point being stupid.'

The phone rang a couple of times and then there was a click. 'Hello?'

Feeling a bit silly now, Matthew brought the phone up to his ear. 'Hello. I'm after Joe Carson.'

'Speaking.'

'Joe. It's Matthew from Harmon Brothers Couriers. How are you?'

'I'll be good if you're close by.'

'I guess I am,' replied Matthew, 'but I'm having a bit of trouble finding your property.'

'Well, if you can tell me where you are now, I can guide you in,' said Joe.

'I just got back on the main road after a detour to a property called Armison Flats.'

'Oh yeah, some American guy bought that place a few years back. Never met him though. Not very sociable. Anyway, that was Powell Road.' Matthew silently cursed himself on hearing the name of the road. 'The one you want is up the road about ten k's. There's a sign on the left for Number 20 Well and then about 2 k's past that is a turn on the right. Sorry the sign got wiped out by a road train and we haven't got around to replacing it yet. Don't hold your breath waitin'. My place is at the end of the road. Think you'll be right?'

'Thanks, Joe. I'll be fine. See you soon. Bye.' Matthew pressed the stop button on the phone. He gently tossed it back onto the other seat and started the van. 'Alright, let's go.' He pulled onto the road.

One minute further up the road Matthew's attention was drawn by a lone tree in a paddock near the edge of the road. It was leaning over, growing almost horizontal, similar to some he had seen earlier in the trip. Just beyond the tree he saw some movement and found it was two emus walking around, obviously looking for food. 'Now there's something you don't see every day.'

Matthew turned back to the road. 'Shit!'

A large kangaroo had just jumped out of the paddock on the other side of the road, right into the path of the van. Matthew slammed on the brakes and swerved onto the shoulder of the road but once he hit the gravel section the wheels lost traction and the van went into a spin and he could feel it about to flip over.

Then Matthew felt a blinding stab of pain in his head. He lost contact with his surroundings while the pain continued for what felt like a few seconds and then suddenly the sensation stopped and he was conscious of the van once again. He started to wrench the steering wheel over, trying to compensate for the skid and then realised he was back in control but on an unsealed section of the road.

He thought that he must have luckily steered onto a side road even though in the commotion he didn't remember seeing one. Much better than a fence or a ditch.

Matthew felt like he had been in a triathlon. His heart was racing and he was breathing like a winded horse. Fighting the reaction, he slowly applied the brake and pulled over to the side of the road again.

Matthew reached for the water bottle and had a long drink. After a few seconds, he started to relax. *Get me back to the city. It's too dangerous out here.*

Matthew gave himself a few minutes to recover but felt time pressing on him again. He should get going. He slowly pulled the van back onto the road and drove off. He turned the corner onto a sealed section of road. 'That was some skid. I could have been decorating that fence.'

As he drove on, Matthew looked at the scenery around him. 'Everything in this place just looks the same.' Then he spotted a tree in the paddock. It was leaning over just like the one he had seen a few minutes earlier. Then, open mouthed with surprise, he saw two emus.

Almost unconsciously, Matthew put his foot on the brake, slowing the van dramatically and when he turned his attention back to the road, a large kangaroo jumped out of the paddock on the other side of the road. Fortunately, though, this time the van was going slowly enough that the kangaroo had plenty of time to get clear of the road before the van reached it. Matthew breathed a heavy sigh of relief. 'Phew. Major déjà vu.'

A short time later Matthew pulled up out the front of the Peabody Downes farmhouse. Two men came out to greet him. They were unmistakably father and son, one around fifty-five and the other looked like the same man but twenty-five years younger. They could have been carved from the local granite boulders that dotted the area. They were big, strong-looking men, though their faces were open and friendly. The older man stuck out his hand for Matthew to shake. 'G'day. Joe Carson and this is my son, Ted.'

Matthew shook hands with both men. 'Hi. Matthew Fraser.' His hand felt like it had been squeezed in a vice twice by the time he was finished, but he didn't want to appear soft to these friendly folks and he refused to wring out his hand afterwards.

'Have any trouble finding the place?' asked the elder Carson.

'Not after we spoke on the phone. Your directions were spot on.' At this, Matthew noticed the two men give each other a strange look and wondered if he had offended them somehow but decided against saying anything. Maybe it was a farmer thing. 'So where do you want this gear that I have in the back of the van?'

Ted answered while pointing. 'Just pull over near the shed and we'll unload it for you.'

After the crushing handshakes, Matthew wouldn't have been surprised to see either one of the Carson men throw the load over their shoulder and carry it over to the shed even though it had required a forklift to get it in the van. Instead, Ted wheeled out a hydraulic lift and they used a sling to lift the load, some sort of large drive shaft, and then wheel it into the shed.

Matthew asked Joe Carson to sign the delivery docket and they all shook hands again and he climbed back in and left the other two men staring at the van as he drove away.

Joe turned to his son. 'Strange bloke, that one. Don't know what made him think we spoke on the phone.'

'Must be all that pollution down in Perth, Dad.'

'Reckon that's it, son.'

Chapter 6

General Morgan had given the professor as much time working things out as he was going to get without getting some answers. One hour was as long as he was willing to wait. He strode back into the control room closely followed by the major. The staff were buzzing around like the flies that infested the outside area of the base.

The general was about to yell at the professor but before he could a young, fair-haired lady in a lab coat spoke first. The general didn't remember seeing her before, but he wasn't in charge of recruiting. She was a little stocky for his tastes but if she lost a few pounds, she might be attractive. She was standing in front of a computer monitor on the opposite side of the room to where most of the activity was taking place. 'Professor Windsor. I've found an anomalous reading I can't explain.' She seemed quite nervous as the attention of the room suddenly focused on her.

'Well, what is it?' The professor snapped, once again demonstrating his lack of social skills. He was annoyed to have had to stop whatever he was doing.

'Uh, we have passive radiation monitors around the base.' These were dotted around the base and its perimeter as a precaution against accidents rather than against attacks of any kind.

'Yes.'

'I've checked the log of the detector next to the main entrance to the base and there was a sudden spike in the reading at the time of our experiment.'

'Go on.'

Everybody in the control room was now hanging on her every word. 'It's not a dangerous level but seems to be of the same wavelength as we expected to have as a result of the live trial. The level stayed steady for a couple of minutes and then slowly decreased. It could be the level was just dropping or it could be that it was moving away.'

The major asked. 'Did any of the other sensors pick anything up?'

The fair-haired lady pressed a few buttons and from where he stood the general could see the display change without making out the detail. 'The one just to the south has a lower reading at the same time as the first sensor, and as the first sensor reading decreases the second one increases for a short time before fading away. To me this indicates the radiation source is moving away from the main entrance.'

The major pointed to the woman. 'What's your name?'

'Jean Williams, sir,' she gasped out, going a bright shade of red now that she was in the spotlight.

'Great work, Jean,' said the major. 'Now I need you to work out a way to make one of those sensors portable. Use whatever resources and people you need. And I want it to be directional. Go.'

The woman nodded. 'Yes, sir.' She was relieved to be able to stand up and leave the control room.

The major walked over and picked up a phone hanging on the wall. He pushed a button. 'Call up video footage from camera one for 0900 and send it to the security monitor down here.'

The general moved towards the monitor. The display came on but showed only snowy interference. The major spoke into the phone again. 'Is this thing working? OK. Rewind to 0858 and play.'

The display flickered for a second and then a clear picture came through showing a van driving towards the gate. The van stopped and after a few seconds a man stepped out and looked to everyone like he was going to make a phone call. The picture dissolved into the snowy interference again.

The general walked over to the professor. 'Well, Professor, what does all this mean?' he asked, pointing at the monitor. 'Has someone infiltrated the project or is this some freak accident?'

For once, the professor had no answers.

Jean Williams walked towards the engineering workshop on the base. It was a small but well-equipped room with an expert staff who were expected to be able to repair just about anything that might be needed for the running of the facility.

Jean was a pretty girl who didn't really know it. She pulled her fair hair back in a ponytail and never wore makeup on her pale skin. She didn't socialise with the other people in the facility that much, preferring her own company.

Jean was one of about one hundred of the civilian personnel who worked on the project and lived in the accommodation wing of the facility. It was built closer to the surface than the control room but still underground, not that it bothered her that much. She took a little bit of time out on the surface but was happier at her workstation.

She was happy to be on the good side of the major because he scared the shit out of her.

Jean had been thrilled to be working on such a momentous project despite the secrecy and the threat posed by the non-disclosure contracts. Not many people ever got to work on something this important.

She had been involved with this project for five years since being recruited not long after finishing university. As well as the career opportunity, there had been an added bonus for Jean. She had met the man who was to become her lover, Don Campbell.

Don had been her direct supervisor and over time she had come to a gradual realisation that her feelings were becoming more than professional. His dedication to the job, friendly personality and charming smile had combined to win her heart. After a while, she knew that he felt the same way too.

Not long before the first inanimate trial at the original site they had started a secret affair, afraid that it would seem inappropriate in front of the others.

One night about a week after the failed first live test they had been in bed. She was cuddled up to him, her head on his chest. She could feel his heart racing and knew that something was bothering him. 'Don, what's wrong?'

He was silent for a few seconds. 'I can't get over the death of Lieutenant Dean. He just exploded. I don't know how they can just cover it up like it never happened. People should know the truth, but the army isn't going to let it happen.' He was silent again, absent-mindedly stroking her hair. 'Ray Parsons and I are going to confront that new man in charge of security. He saw what happened. Maybe he'll do something.'

Ray Parsons was a colleague of Don's. She had heard he was the son of some politician but apart from that didn't know a lot about him. The new man in charge of security was, of course, Major Carmichael.

'Oh, Don. Please don't. Please just let it go. Let the army deal with it,' she pleaded.

'Someone has to do something,' he had answered.

That was the last time they had been together.

According to the official story both men had died in a helicopter crash the next day while on their way to a symposium on quantum physics. Jean knew that Don wasn't going anywhere that day other than to confront Carmichael. She was sure that Don and Ray had been killed by the major to keep them quiet, but who could she tell? And she didn't have any proof. She thought it was lucky that no-one else knew about their affair or maybe she wouldn't be here either.

Jean had her chance a little while later when FBI agent Andy Burgess had come to the base to investigate the deaths, but she had choked. She couldn't bring herself to voice her suspicions. She was so scared and didn't know what to do. She had been left a card and had looked at it many times, only to put it away again.

Now here she was helping the man she suspected of killing her lover.

A few hours later the portable detector had been put together by the engineering team, following her directions. It looked somewhat like a bull-horn with a digital display where the mouthpiece would be.

Jean tracked down the major to explain the operation of the device. 'It looks a bit of an odd shape,' he told her.

'That's because radiation isn't linear, and we've had to come up with a design to give us direction.'

'Are my men going to be able to adjust it or repair it in the field?' he had asked.

Field? What field? Jean thought to herself. 'Uh, maybe not,' she said.

'Well, then, I'm going to need you to come with us.' He gave her a smile which chilled her to the bone.

Chapter 7

Major Carmichael had been busy after viewing the video footage from that morning. The pictures didn't allow them to view the side of the van to see any signwriting, but they had a clear view of the number plate and they were also able to print out some pictures of the driver.

The major decided to keep the detective work simple and called the Mullewa police station. He told them that a van had backed into his car and left the scene but a friend had managed to see the number plate. The police had provided him with the company name, Harmon Brothers.

Now, at two o'clock in the morning, here they were outside the company compound in Kewdale, a light industrial suburb, south of Perth City. The black Hummer rolled to a stop on the road on the eastern side of the compound, while the other two Hummers kept driving around the area so as not to draw undue attention to the group.

The major loved the Hummers. He thought of them as trucks rather than, as the Australians called them, a four-wheel drive. *What a pity they aren't being made anymore.*

He looked at the driver and then the man in the rear seat. 'You two know what to do. You've done it before. Keep it simple. Get in and get the information and get out quickly. Don't leave any traces. We need to know where this guy lives. Any questions?' he asked. Both men shook their heads. 'Good. Go.'

The two men exited the trucks. They threw a thick blanket over the strands of barbed wire and were over the fence in seconds. The blanket came down quickly and they disappeared into the night in the direction of the office.

'Should we be doing this?' asked Jean Williams nervously from the back seat.

The major smiled at her, though Jean didn't see any sign of warmth in his eyes. 'Jean. Really. Let me remind you. This man may have, either intentionally or accidentally, had some sort of effect on our multi-billion-dollar project. We need to establish just what happened and where this man fits in. So, yes, we should be doing this.'

In fifteen minutes, the men were back in the truck with a piece of paper which one of the men handed to the major. He reached over and punched the information into the military specification GPS unit. 'Call the others on the radio. Give them the address. All approach from different directions. Let's go.'

It was late that night when Matthew arrived back in Perth. He drove the van directly home as he was sure the gates to the compound would be closed and he thought he would just drive it to work the next day. In truth, Matthew knew he wouldn't have driven in to the compound even if it was open all day.

He had hardly noticed the scenery on the way back and certainly didn't feel up to a Slim Dusty sing-along. He was on edge, constantly looking out for kangaroos waiting to jump out in front of the van. So, it was with some relief when he pulled up in his driveway.

After a light meal, Matthew felt a bit better. He thought he had eaten too much junk food while on the road and a home-cooked meal, no matter how simple, eased his conscience somewhat.

He tried to lose himself in a TV show which did little to show how much talent Australia actually had and the performers only irritated him, so Matthew decided to burn off some frustration and headed out to the garage which served as a home gymnasium. He was still troubled by the events earlier in the day and thought pumping some weights might take his mind off it all.

It proved to be a forlorn hope. It was all he could think about. Had he been struck by lightning? He must have been. That was all he could put it down to. Then another thought occurred to Matthew. Maybe he had a brain tumour. That might explain the sudden, blinding headaches that he had experienced twice that day.

After a shorter than usual workout, Matthew gave up on the weights. Too many unpleasant thoughts intruded on his concentration. He went back inside for a quick shower before climbing into bed.

The Hummer with Major Carmichael in it slowly approached the address programmed into the GPS unit. It stopped fifty metres down the street and the major surveyed the surroundings in the illumination cast by the overhead street lights. He pointed to the house. 'Can you detect any trace of the radiation from here?'

In the back seat, Jean slowly brought her makeshift radiation detector up to the window. She asked herself for the thousandth time what she was doing sitting in the car with this psycho. She couldn't contain herself any longer. 'You're going to kill him, aren't you?' she blurted out.

'Now, Jean,' he replied, turning to stare at her, 'why would we want to do that? How would we ever find out anything if we just went around killing people? Of course, we aren't going to kill him. The idea is to detain this man and then to see what he knows about our little project.' Jean couldn't hold the major's gaze and turned towards the window. 'Now, let's try again. Can you detect any radiation?'

Jean flicked a switch on the side of the detector and pointed it at the house the major had indicated. 'There's a slight trace. It's barely registering.'

'Could it be background radiation?' the major asked.

Jean pointed the detector in the opposite direction. 'Nothing at all in that direction.' Then she added reluctantly, 'I guess whatever is causing the radiation is in that house.'

'Let's get a closer look,' the major said to the driver. The Hummer slowly advanced along the street until it was parked outside the house next door.

Matthew's place was an older single-storey house with a tiled roof in the middle of a row of houses, on the high side of the street. A garage under the main roof was on the left-hand side of the house with small gates on either side up to the fences that bordered with the neighbours. There was a row of houses behind those he could see in front of him, so he wasn't going to be able to easily advance on the house from all sides.

The major considered his options. He activated the on switch for his throat microphone. 'B-team, move to the road running behind this street and take up a monitoring position. C-team, enter through the front door but take all necessary precautions. We don't know who it is we are dealing with here. And remember,' he turned to Jean at this point, 'we want this man alive and mainly healthy, so bean bags at ten paces.'

While the driver from C-team remained in the Hummer, the other three members of the team exited the vehicle and approached the house. Despite the street lights, they were nearly invisible in their dark clothing. They held shotguns modified to take bean bag rounds. These rounds containing bags of lead shot pellets left the muzzle of the shotgun at around 90 metres per second and for the most part delivered a non-fatal but debilitating blow to the target. A shot to the stomach knocked the fight out of anyone. Each of the men carrying the weapons had, in fact, been shot with these as part of the major's training program and none were keen to go through it again.

The first man, Corporal Crimmons, climbed the stairs and stepped onto the wooden porch. The boards creaked under his weight causing him to stand completely still. 'Dickhead,' said the man behind him, inaudible to anyone more than a metre away. All three men froze, waiting to see if the noise had given them away.

Matthew was sleeping only fitfully that night. Dreams of brain tumours wearing boxing gloves beating him up had woken him a number of times. Then he heard the squeak from the front porch. Someone was out there. He wondered if it was someone after his bike. As a competition model, it was very expensive and he couldn't afford a new one if it was stolen. As quietly as possible he rolled out of bed, dressed only in the pair of shorts he wore as pyjamas.

He slowly made his way to the wardrobe, eased open the door and reached in to grab the cricket bat he knew was in there.

Matthew tiptoed his way into the living room.

The three soldiers at the front of the house hadn't heard anything after a minute and had mutually decided to proceed. The second two men avoided the squeaky board when stepping onto the porch as Crimmons moved towards the front door. He gently placed his shotgun on the floor and extracted a set of lock-picks from a pocket in his jacket. He thought to himself that the major's training program was unconventional for a soldier but it was going to prove useful tonight.

Matthew heard faint scratching sounds coming from the front door. *Shit. Someone's trying to break in*, he thought to himself as he stepped lightly towards the door, raising the bat to shoulder level, ready to swing. He reached his left hand towards the light switch not quite believing his eyes when the door slowly started to open. Matthew pressed his back against the wall, the cricket bat in his right hand and his left at the light switch.

A shadow slowly crept into the room. Matthew waited until he was two steps in and flicked the switch. Despite being ready for the light to come on and expecting the intruder to be disconcerted by the sudden brightness, Matthew was shocked by the speed with which the man spun around, bringing a gun of some sort to bear on him.

Not giving him a chance to line the gun up, Matthew swung the bat with all he had and collected the intruder in the head with a sickening thud. The man, dressed all in black, dropped to the floor. Matthew stepped over to him. The man had a pinched face, small, pointy ears and no chin, and now a big lump on his forehead.

'Psst,' Matthew heard behind him. Startled, he turned around to find two more men standing there with guns pointed at him. Reflexively, Matthew started to lift the bat again when the first man fired his weapon. Instantly he dropped the bat and collapsed to the floor in agony from the almost point-blank shot to the stomach. Matthew felt a blinding stab of pain in his head.

Gasping for breath, Matthew sat bolt upright in his bed. He reached out for the lamp, knocking over the glass of water he had left on the bedside table. Unaware of the spill, he looked down at his stomach, expecting a big hole to be there. Nothing! It didn't even hurt.

What the hell was going on?

Matthew felt as though he was going crazy. That hadn't been a dream, had it? It had seemed so real.

Matthew knew that he wasn't getting back to sleep that night, so he climbed out of bed and quickly threw on some clothes. He needed to get out of the house and find somewhere that he could calm down and think.

He picked up the keys to the van and was heading out the door but turned around, opened the wardrobe door and grabbed the cricket bat. 'Just in case,' he said to himself.

'You're going to kill him, aren't you?' blurted out Jean Williams.

'Now, Jean,' Major Carmichael replied, turning to stare at her, 'why would we want to do that? How would we ever find out anything if we just went around killing people? Of course, we aren't going to kill him. The idea is to detain this man and then to see what he knows about our little project.' Jean couldn't hold the major's gaze and turned towards the window. 'Now, let's try again. Can you detect any radiation?'

Jean flicked a switch on the side of the detector and pointed it at the house the major had indicated. 'Nothing.' She moved the detector slowly from side to side. 'I can't get any readings at all.'

'Well, we'll have to assume he's in there anyway.' He activated the on switch for his throat microphone. 'B-team, move to the road running behind this street and take up a monitoring position. C-team, enter through the front door but take all necessary precautions. We don't know who it is we are dealing with here. And remember,' he turned to Jean at this point, 'we want this man alive and mainly healthy, so bean bags at ten paces.'

A few minutes later there was a voice in his earpiece. 'Crimmons here, sir. Negative on the target. Repeat, he's not here.'

'Fuck!' he exploded. 'Any signs he has been there at all?'

'There's a glass of water that's been knocked over on the lamp stand that looks like it's only just happened.'

The major considered that. 'I don't know if he's lucky or clever. Everyone back to the vehicles.' He looked at the other men in the Hummer. 'We'll have to try to acquire him somewhere else. B-team, go south and see if you can spot him. C-team, go north. We'll go west, back down the hill. Everyone knows the van that he's driving. Report in if you spot it.'

Chapter 8

One of Matthew's favourite places in the entire city of Perth was only ten minutes from his house. The Zig Zag Scenic Drive had many spectacular views of the city. As the name suggested, the road zigzagged down from the hills hundreds of metres till it met the coastal plain of Perth.

Matthew loved to bring any visitors to the state here to show off the city, and at night he considered the sea of lights shining from below to be one of the most beautiful sights in the world.

Tonight, as he sat in the front seat of the van, he couldn't take in the vista below. All of his thoughts were on what he had just experienced. The dream had seemed so real that Matthew would have sworn it had actually happened.

He thought back to the incident from the day before while he was driving. He knew that wasn't a dream because that incident had started while he was wide awake. Matthew wondered if he had suddenly developed ESP or the ability to see the future. If that was the case, then who were the men who were going to break into his house?

Maybe there really was something wrong with him, like a brain tumour. That seemed more likely than seeing into the future.

Either way, both thoughts were very disturbing. He could see into the future and people were trying to kill him or he had a brain tumour and it was trying to kill him. Matthew made his mind up to make an appointment to see his doctor later in the day.

He was snapped out of his ruminations when he heard another vehicle driving towards his vantage point over the escarpment. He had had enough surprises over the last day or so to last a lifetime, so he turned to watch the road. The headlights of the approaching vehicle were incredibly bright, turning the night to day. He held his hand up to his brow to shield his eyes from the light. Whatever the vehicle was, it sounded big.

Due to the curve in the road, the headlights of the vehicle swept over and past his van, which was stopped in the carpark of the viewing area. There was a screech of tyres on the road and the vehicle stopped. From where Matthew stood, it looked like a Hummer or some other large four-wheel drive. It had enough spotlights on it to light up the field for a game of day-night cricket. It just sat there. Matthew's eyes never moved away from the vehicle.

The Hummer slowly backed up so that its lights were shining on his van. Matthew was getting a very bad feeling about this. He reached out with his left arm to pick up the cricket bat from the passenger seat.

With another screech of tyres, the Hummer accelerated towards his van. Shit. Matthew reached up and made sure the interior light was switched off.

He opened the door and leapt down to the ground. Thinking quickly, he kept the van between him and the approaching vehicle and jogged towards the small wooden fence at the edge of the viewing area. There was sufficient ambient light for him to see there was only a short drop down to the ground below. He climbed down and made his way through the scrub to stand behind one of the many rocky outcrops dotted throughout the region.

Above him he heard the Hummer skid to a halt. Doors opened and he heard multiple sets of footsteps running. There was one voice. 'Fuck. He's gone. Spread out.'

Matthew was in no doubt now that he was in serious trouble. He tightened his grip on the cricket bat.

Corporal Crimmons smiled to himself. He had done this type of thing many times before, moving quietly through the terrain, looking for enemy combatants and taking them out. Unfortunately, this time, the subject had to be taken alive, which added to the difficulty factor but sure made things more exciting.

He crept past some bush that stabbed him painfully in the face with its spiky leaves, narrowly missing his eyes. *Fuck this place. As if it's not enough that the spiders or the snakes are having a go at you, even the trees are trying to kill you.* He moved past the plant towards a big rock that looked a likely hiding spot.

Got you now, he mouthed silently to himself as he slowly rounded the rock, suddenly jumping forward ready to fire his weapon. Shit. Nobody there. He lowered his weapon.

Matthew heard the slight rustling of the nearby bushes. He hoped the snail hakeas were giving whoever these guys were lots of trouble. As a young boy, he had had many painful encounters with the native plants with each leaf having as many as twelve to fifteen needle-like projections on them. Smart people learned to stay away from them.

He moved as carefully as he could around the rock, away from where he thought the other man was coming.

The man leapt forward, creating what seemed to Matthew to be a lot of noise. Matthew took three quick steps around the rock and there was the man from his dream, one of the men who had broken into his house.

Matthew didn't have time to take this thought any further because the man exploded into action, spinning and bringing his weapon to bear.

Matthew swung the cricket bat as hard as he could, connecting with the man's head with a sickening thud. He went down noisily. He looked down at the man. He was the same one from his troubling dream. The pointy ears and lack of a chin were unmistakable. He looked like a soldier of some sort. Matthew wondered what soldiers were doing chasing him through the hills of Perth. Whatever it was they had against him, he decided that discretion was the better approach and it was time to get out of here.

Matthew's head exploded in pain and he fell to the ground unconscious, alongside the soldier.

The other soldier looked down at Matthew with the stock of his weapon poised, ready to deliver another blow if required. 'Good move, kid,' he said. He looked over at his fellow soldier lying on the ground next to the subject. 'Dickhead.'

Chapter 9

Dr Ahmed Barazani stared out the window of his office in the Pakistan Atomic Energy Commission (PAEC) headquarters building in Islamabad. A large park across the road meant the view was a pleasant one filled with grassed areas and trees and it never failed to lift his spirits.

The buildings on the other side of the park showed the typical Islamabad style of architecture—modern buildings, many with colourful Islamic murals and designs covering the walls.

Ahmed was a short man just starting to put on a few extra pounds as he grew older. A neatly trimmed moustache highlighted a kindly face. He reached for his lighter, lit up a cigarette, then exhaled with satisfaction.

He was winding down after another long day, which was typical for the vice-chairman of the PAEC. Today, meeting after meeting had left him worn out and he was grateful that he had this small amount of time to himself before he left work to go home.

As he watched people strolling along the footpath that bordered the park, Ahmed reflected on his long and distinguished career. With retirement age approaching, he doubted he would get to enjoy years of playing with his grandchildren the way that others would. He still had so much to do.

He had been fifteen and still at school when the disastrous war with India broke out in December of 1971. Up until that time Pakistan had consisted of two "wings". There was West Pakistan, which the world knows as the current Pakistan, and there was East Pakistan which is known now as Bangladesh. The two wings were separated by the world's seventh largest country, India.

Governance of East Pakistan by the western half of the country was made extremely difficult by the vast distance between them, both physically and culturally. From the late 1960s, the Bengali majority of the East pressed the West for independence but after this was rejected, a campaign of civil unrest was established. Eventually the West sent in the military to quell the riots and a brutal crackdown began, targeting the dissidents. In the subsequent turmoil, hundreds of thousands were killed and millions of refugees fled to India.

India viewed the unrest not only as a humanitarian crisis but as a financial disaster that it was being forced to pay for by setting up and maintaining refugee camps. In order to pacify her own military, the Indian prime minister ordered them to draw up plans to end the conflict in East Pakistan. The Indian military mobilised but before any action was taken, Pakistan launched pre-emptive air strikes on air bases in North-West India on 3 December 1971.

India considered this a declaration of war and launched its own air strikes later that night and then proceeded to implement massive air, sea and ground campaigns that crushed their Pakistani opponents in less than two weeks. East Pakistan gained its independence and eventually became Bangladesh.

Ahmed's father was a colonel in the Pakistan army that had been sent to East Pakistan to establish control. His older brother was in the Pakistan navy, serving on a destroyer based in Karachi. His mother struggled to find what had become of them after the shameful surrender but both had been killed within two days of the war starting. Their bodies were never recovered.

After this humiliating blow to the national psyche, the Pakistani government and military sought to ensure that such events would never happen again and they launched their own nuclear program. To the world they proclaimed it was a program designed to bring it self-sufficiency in power and they built a number of nuclear power stations throughout the country, with the assistance of many Western nations. In secret, though, their primary goal was nuclear weapons.

Due to his outstanding academic record at school, the Pakistani government granted Ahmed a full scholarship to university and his choice was nuclear physics at the Pakistan Institute of Nuclear Science and Technology (Pinstech) in Nilore. To him this was Pakistan's future.

Ahmed graduated at the top of his classes in almost every subject and at the end of his study he started work at the PAEC in the Design Directorate. While purporting to be designing nuclear power stations, this division was secretly designing Pakistan's first nuclear weapon. Ten years later he was the head of the Directorate.

By this time, the world had become aware that Pakistan's nuclear program was not what it had seemed and they deserted en masse.

Pakistan developed their devices but never carried out a critical test until 1998. They detonated five devices in a single day as a response to the testing of a similar number of nuclear devices by India. Pakistan had become the world's eighth nuclear power.

Ahmed's direction in life changed dramatically a short time later. He was in his favourite café not far from where he worked, finishing a cigarette and the last few sips of coffee after lunch, when he was approached by a man who turned out to be a member of the al-Qaeda network. They were planning attacks on the West and they were certain that if nuclear weapons could be obtained, they would have an impact that would be felt for generations.

Ahmed listened carefully. He felt the man sitting opposite was delusional if he thought the world would stand for Sharia law but his thoughts crystallised and he realised that here was an avenue to achieve something he had dreamt about for a long time.

While his father and brother had both been killed in the short war with India, Ahmed didn't blame his South Asian neighbour. Pakistan and India never saw eye to eye on anything but at least it was an honest relationship. Who he really blamed was Pakistan's closest ally at the time, the United States.

Despite claiming friendship, the US had stood idly by while his country had been torn in half. Just a small effort on their part could have made all the difference. His family could have survived. His mother would not have wasted away before his eyes, dying long before her time, her heart broken by the loss of her husband and son.

Ahmed convinced the al-Qaeda representative that use of nuclear weapons had to be a well thought out, long-term strategy, years in the making. The man, while disappointed, had agreed and then hinted at some other plan to deliver a crushing blow to the US. America would be brought to its knees. They had parted on good terms with methods of remaining in contact.

Two years after that fateful meeting, Ahmed knew what that plan was when he had seen the World Trade Towers collapse.

It was after that meeting Ahmed decided that he needed to be seen to be anti-nuclear weapons, so he switched to the Nuclear Power Directorate, all the time carefully maintaining his contacts within the weapons program.

Ahmed's public face was now one of publicly championing the peaceful use of nuclear power and condemning its destructive side.

It was close to two decades since that fateful meeting in the café and the years of careful planning and execution were about to bear fruit. Components that had failed quality control tests, carried out by men loyal to him, were reportedly destroyed and then gathered together in a secure workshop. Gram by gram the required quantity of fissile material needed for the fuel had been accumulated.

Under his supervision, three devices had been assembled and using the al-Qaeda contacts he had arranged separate transport of each device to a location in the US.

Soon they would learn the price of their treachery.

Chapter 10

Matthew climbed out of the darkness very slowly. His head pounded and he felt like he might be sick. No. He was going to be sick. He saw a rubbish bin on the floor and grabbed it just in time before he was violently ill.

With that out of the way, Matthew tried to take in his surroundings. He was in a small room that contained a bed, which he had been lying on, a desk and chair, some sort of built-in cupboard and the rubbish bin-cum-sick bucket.

Very unsteadily he stood up, grimacing at the pain that shot through his head. He felt dizzy and held onto the wall for support. The sensation passed after a few seconds.

He walked slowly over to the desk. There was nothing on it or in any of the three drawers. There were power points near the desk but there was nothing plugged in. He turned his attention to the cupboard. It was full of clothing, lots of lab coats and the like but enough skirts, blouses and shoes to tell him that it was a woman's wardrobe.

The room was lit by fluorescent lights recessed into the roof. There were no windows. Two air conditioning vents about thirty centimetres square were installed in the ceiling in opposite corners.

Matthew looked for a way out of the room. There was a door in the middle of one wall and he made his way over to it. He tried the handle. Locked. No surprise there. He banged on the door with his fist. 'Hey, let me out of here!' he yelled, instantly regretful as the pain in his head stabbed through him again.

Matthew walked back over to the bed and sat down, holding his head between his hands, trying to let the headache subside. He looked up as a he heard a key in the door lock. A man in a military uniform entered carrying a glass of water. He was quickly followed by two other men. The latter arrivals held the same type of gun that he had seen before. Was that last night?

'Hello, Matthew,' said the first man through the door. It was obvious he was the one in charge. He reached into his pocket and pulled out something small and tossed it to Matthew, who looked down to find it was a blister pack of tablets. 'For the headache,' said the man, smiling at him. 'You've got a nasty bump there.'

'What's going on? Why am I here?' Matthew blurted out.

'Both very good questions,' said the man moving over to the chair and sitting down. He put the glass down on the desk. The other two men stared intently at Matthew as if inviting some kind of attack from him. 'Questions to which we both want answers.'

The man continued to regard Matthew with a faint smile on his face but the look in his eyes was anything but humorous. 'Time for introductions. I am Major John Carmichael of the US Army and you are Matthew Fraser of...?'

Matthew had been alarmed and puzzled before, but this took it to a whole new level of bewilderment. What was the US Army doing chasing him around the hills of Perth? He shrugged his shoulders at the major, not quite sure what to say. 'Harmon Brothers transport company.'

The hint of a smile vanished from the major's face. 'We know that bit, Matthew, but we want the rest of it.'

Matthew looked around at the other two men but they were staring at him just as intently as they had been before. 'There isn't any more. That's it. I drive a delivery van around Perth.'

'We'll see.' He turned to one of the soldiers. 'Get rid of that,' said the major, pointing at the bin. He stood up and walked out through the door. The soldier picked up the bin, grimacing as the smell hit him, then turned and followed the major. The last soldier backed out, all the while keeping his weapon pointed at Matthew. The sound of the key in the door indicated he had locked it behind him.

Matthew stood up to move towards the door to test it and was punished by a bolt of pain through his head. He looked down at the packet of pills in his hand and popped two of them out and washed them down with the glass of water. He lay back down on the bed, hoping the crushing pain would disappear and that he would wake up from this nightmare back in his own bed.

Sometime later Matthew woke up feeling a lot better but unfortunately, he was still in the same room. He didn't know what time it was or how long he had been asleep. The room was a bit like a submarine, without windows and only lit by artificial light, so it gave away no clues. He was thirsty. There was still half a glass of water left so he drank it. As soon as the water reached his stomach it made him realise, he was hungry. He must have been here for hours.

He heard the key in the door and it swung open. One soldier stood there with a shotgun pointed at him. The soldier stood to one side and another entered carrying a tray of sandwiches and a cup of something. Matthew recognised him as the man he had bashed with his cricket bat. He was a corporal, judging from the two stripes on the uniform. He had a bandage wrapped around his head. 'If it was up to me, I'd let you starve,' he said as he put the tray on the desk. Matthew decided he was about the ugliest man he'd ever seen. The small, pointy ears and lack of a chin made him look like a weasel.

Matthew stared but said nothing as the men backed out of the room. He wondered how they knew that he was awake each time they had come into the room. He looked around and eventually found what he was looking for. There was a small camera tucked up high against the ceiling in one corner. They were watching him. He shrugged. Let them watch. He was hungry and he was going to eat.

After he had eaten the ham sandwiches, he tried the coffee. It wasn't what he was used to but he managed to swallow it. American coffee. With nothing to do in the room, unless he wanted to take up cross-dressing Matthew lay down on the bed to conserve his energy.

A short time later the door opened again. There was Major Carmichael with the original two soldiers flanking him. 'Hello, Matthew. Feeling better?' Matthew just stared at him. 'I hope so. I wouldn't want anything bad to happen to you before we get some answers. Please come with me.' The major stepped back through the door and held his arm out inviting Matthew to walk in that direction. The two soldiers each took a step back to give Matthew a path between them. He shrugged again and walked through the door.

It was like being in a hospital. He was in a corridor lined with doors on each side. The lighting was provided by fluorescent fittings recessed into the ceiling. Matthew couldn't see a trace of natural light. He somehow got the feeling that he was underground.

The four of them walked along until they came to a door that looked like it was an elevator. The major placed his hand on a glass panel to the side of the door. There was a flash of light from the panel and the doors opened. It *was* an elevator. They stepped inside and the major pushed a button. Matthew looked at the display. The numbers were counting up but they were definitely going down. They had to be underground.

The elevator stopped and the doors opened. The major strode out and turned right and Matthew trudged along behind him followed by the two soldiers. They went some distance down the corridor, past doorways with no markings and then the major stopped. He opened the door. No flashing lights on this one, just a simple handle.

'Please come in, Matthew. You two wait out here,' he said to the soldiers. Matthew walked in to find two men deep in conversation, but it stopped as soon as they noticed him. The man in uniform had to be a general. Even a non-military Australian could recognise what stars on the shoulders of the man meant. The other one was undoubtedly a scientist. Matthew could picture him trying to liven up the Frankenstein monster and probably succeeding.

'This is him?' asked the general. The major nodded back. The general stared at Matthew and he couldn't help but feel as though he was the main course at dinner, so intent was the man's gaze. 'So why don't you tell us who you are and just what you were doing at our facility yesterday?'

For a few seconds, Matthew had no idea what the general was talking about and then it occurred to him that they were talking about his trip to the Carsons' property. One look at the general convinced Matthew that it wouldn't do any good to protest against his current situation, so he started to talk.

'My name is Matthew Fraser. I drive a van for a transport company around Perth. Yesterday I delivered some machinery to a property in the Murchison area. Is that where I am now?'

He may as well not have asked the question. It was ignored. The general kept going. 'How did you interfere with our project?'

Matthew was perplexed. How had he interfered with what project? 'I don't know what the hell you're talking about.'

'Show him,' the general said. The major walked over to a computer and pressed a couple of buttons on the keyboard. The screen came to life. It showed the pictures of Matthew driving his van up to the gate, getting out and making a phone call. Then the picture dissolved into static.

Matthew had watched in amazement at the video. There was no doubt in his mind that it was him on the monitor, not that he had even noticed any video surveillance in the area. He was desperate to see what had happened to him at the end and was bitterly disappointed the picture had stopped. 'What happened next?' he practically yelled.

'There is no next,' said the general. 'Our video died right then. Now, once again, why don't you tell us what you know.'

Matthew shook his head in disbelief at his current situation. His natural inclination was to tell these people to go to hell but like them, he wanted to know what was going on. What had been happening to him since that moment just shown on the monitor.

'Alright. I'll tell you my side of the story,' he said, 'but I want answers from you as well.'

The general looked over to the major, who paused for half a second then nodded. He turned back to Matthew. 'Deal.'

Matthew looked at the two men and decided that he didn't trust either of them, and the other guy looked way too weird, but his urge to find out anything about what had happened to him overcame his caution.

'Right at the end, when the video stopped, I felt like I had been hit by lightning. I was knocked out.' Matthew noticed the scientist was getting very excited by his story, taking notes. 'When I came to, I took a little while to recover and then I drove off to try to find where I was supposed to be.'

'I told you the gravity wave had been redirected,' the scientist blurted out.

The general glared at him and then turned back to Matthew. 'Go on.'

Matthew had no idea what the scientist could possibly be talking about, but the guy obviously thought it was important. 'A short time later, while I was driving, I had some sort of premonition. I was driving along the road and I was distracted by some emus and nearly crashed into a kangaroo. Five minutes later those exact events happened again except that I slowed down a bit and avoided the possibility of crashing.'

The scientist couldn't contain his excitement. 'This is amazing. Did you have any more instances where this type of thing happened?'

'Last night...I guess it was last night...I had a premonition that men dressed in black were going to break into my house and shoot me. I left the house to find somewhere to think and that's where your guys caught up with me.'

The scientist looked as though he was about to burst with enthusiasm. 'Are you sure these were premonitions?'

'Well, it did seem pretty real at the time. I was sure I could feel the pain of the gunshot but I woke up back in bed and I was fine.'

The general spoke. 'So, Professor Windsor, do you have any theories about what happened?' Despite the circumstances, Matthew smiled to himself. He had been correct about the crazy looking old guy.

'I believe that somehow this man has been affected by our experiment. Somehow, he has now become able to go back in time when put under situations of extreme stress. The trace radiation you have measured ever since he arrived must spike at those times, causing a reaction. Amazing!'

The general pondered for a minute. 'I'm not buying it,' he said. He pointed at Matthew. 'Major. Shoot him.'

The major smiled, drew his sidearm and fired.

Matthew felt pain.

There were three men with him in an elevator. The numbers were going up and the elevator was going down. *Shit, it's happening again*, Matthew thought to himself.

The elevator doors opened and the major strode out and turned right. Pushed from behind, Matthew reluctantly shuffled out the door and followed him along the corridor.

The major stopped in front of the same door. He opened it. 'Please come in, Matthew. You two wait out here,' he said to the soldiers.

Matthew walked through the door. Once again, the two men inside stopped talking and looked at him.

'This is him?' asked the general. The major nodded back. The general stared at Matthew. 'So why don't you tell us who you are and just what you were doing at our facility yesterday?'

'I just did,' replied Matthew.

'Don't be smart, son. You're already in a lot of trouble.'

'I'm not being smart, General. I'm deadly serious. This is the second time I've lived through the last five minutes.' Matthew saw the puzzled expressions on the faces of the two officers but he could see the gears turning in the professor's head. 'I told you about what had happened to me and Professor Windsor here said that some radiation in me spikes at times of extreme stress sending me back in time. I have no idea how but that's what he said.'

The general pondered for a moment. 'I'm not buying it.'

'Wait!' yelled Matthew.

'What?'

'You were going to tell the major to shoot me.'

The general scratched his chin and smiled. To Matthew he looked like a kid who was happy he had just pulled the wings off a fly. Major Carmichael spoke. 'He knew the professor's name, General.'

The general looked from Matthew to the professor. 'Is this possible?'

The professor's eyes came back into focus. 'I would have to do some major calculations here, but somehow this man might have been pushed down the backslope of the gravity wave, actually moving back in time. Imagine being able to go back and alter the way events have occurred. This is fantastic.' He stood up and practically ran out the door.

'You're a lucky man,' said the general. 'Major, I think we should make sure our guest comfortable. I think the accommodations back in our original facility in the States would be far more suitable and a lot safer for everyone.'

The major nodded.

Chapter 11

Matthew was lying on a bed in a huge underground facility somewhere in a desert region in the United States. He didn't know which of the states he was in but had seen enough in his few minutes above ground, after the plane landed, to know he was miles from anywhere with no idea how to get to civilisation.

He had just had a shower after going for a run of about fifteen kilometres through a huge tunnel buried beneath the ground. He had gone easy on the outward leg but really pushed it on the return trip. Soldiers ran with him in relays as they had realised early in his stay how fit he was. The soldiers who had run with him today on the last leg had staggered away after they left him with the guards outside his room. In a way, he felt some sympathy for the three men who ran with him as they carried extra weight with all of their army gear, boots and guns. But in the end, he had overcome that emotion and tried to break his own personal best for the distance.

Two weeks before, a soldier had told him that this was the original facility that had been stripped out, with all of the important equipment transported to Australia. The accommodation and office spaces had been left here so this could still be used as a training ground for the army. The accommodation wing was featureless. Three floors that looked like a hotel hallway with rooms running of either side. What was lacking was a view, with none of the rooms having windows.

The tunnel that remained was about an eighteen-mile-long circle. Matthew did a quick calculation in his head and came up with thirty kilometres. If he was here much longer, he would work his way up to that distance to keep up his fitness and be ready for any opportunity that presented itself.

Apparently, the US Army wanted him fit and healthy as well, as he could do pretty much whatever he wanted just as long as he was accompanied by at least two men. He ate in a mess hall, watched television or videos, worked out in a gym and ran as much as he wanted. The one thing Matthew couldn't do here was make any contact with the outside world. There was no phone, no email and no internet. So, he was in a prison of sorts but generally speaking, a comfortable one.

He would have liked a pool to swim in and a bike to keep up the training but these requests were greeted with a stony silence by Captain Klinger, who oversaw his security. Perhaps it was the name or the big nose and nearly bald head but Matthew had to stop himself from calling the man Colonel Klink, after the character in *Hogan's Heroes,* every time they spoke. Whatever the case, he was happier with Klinger than that cold-blooded major. That guy hadn't thought twice about shooting him.

He thought back over the journey that had brought him to this base in the middle of nowhere. A convoy of Hummers had transported him from the base in the middle of a cattle farm to some sort of military base near what he thought might be Geraldton, a few hours north of Perth, on the coast.

In fact, Matthew's guess was close to the mark. There was an Australian Signals Directorate facility at Kojarena, about thirty kilometres east of Geraldton, called the Australian Defence Satellite Communications Ground Station. The station intercepted communications throughout the region for analysis by the United States spy agency, the NSA. The Australian Defence Force was in charge of the facility but as part of the ANZUS treaty the US Defence Force had almost free rein to come and go as they pleased.

That morning it pleased them to roll up at the airfield and load Matthew onto a military transport plane and begin the leapfrog journey to their final destination. Two days later he had arrived here.

He had been treated well throughout the trip but had been watched very closely by men he thought would have no hesitation in taking him down if he gave them a reason. He especially felt the hostility from one man, the guy who looked like a weasel who he had whacked with the cricket bat. He made a mental note to be careful around that guy.

As he stared at the ceiling in his room, Matthew pondered why he was there in the first place. It was three weeks since he had been kidnapped by the US Army from where he lived in the Perth hills and now, he was somewhere in the United States. They thought it was possible that he had the ability to go back in time when subject to stress. Now that some time had passed, Matthew was finding it difficult to believe his own memories. They seemed more like dreams to him, but he was sure the mad professor was doing all he could to unravel the mystery.

Professor Windsor was indeed hard at work, back in Australia, trying to do just that. He had barely slept since running out of the room after the meeting with Mathew or, as he thought of him, "the subject". He stared at the whiteboard in his office. The door opened and his deputy director, Jeff Caldwell, walked in.

Caldwell stood a couple of inches under six feet, was of average build, with average looks and dark hair now going slightly grey, but he was an incredibly smart man who had graduated with the highest honours from the Massachusetts Institute of Technology (MIT). He had been headhunted by the army for this project and had been thrilled to accept the position.

To the professor, Caldwell was a barely adequate assistant.

'Can I help, Professor?'

With a hint of annoyance, the professor replied, 'I am trying to use my initial calculations as a starting position, going back through them to a point where the results diverged and I am recalculating for the other variables such as the satellite phone. I've done this a number of times and ended up at the same result. Why don't you try?' Caldwell nodded. 'I'm going to start from an assumption, the end point, that the subject had travelled back in time and try to do the calculations backwards.' Caldwell may as well have ceased to exist after that as the professor became engrossed in his work.

As Caldwell pondered the formulae on the whiteboard, the professor sat at his computer and started typing in figures. He thought that going forward had been the goal of the project but how valuable would it be to go back in time? The ability to alter the past and fix mistakes would give man God-like powers, metaphorically speaking. The professor hadn't been able to find an equation that proved God existed, so to him God was just a theory with no basis in science.

He turned his attention back to thoughts on the subject. He would work this out even if it meant killing him.

From his office in the Pentagon, General Morgan was also thinking the ability to go back in time would give a man God-like power. But not just any man. Him. That was why he was having the civilian treated so well. The general wanted him alive and well until he was sure that he didn't need him alive and well any more. Then, all bets were off.

The professor was still looking at a way to duplicate the results of the procedure, so he was still hopeful that they would get there eventually, even without the Australian.

In the meantime, the general wondered how he might prove that it was all real. Now, it was just the professor's theory that the man had travelled back in time but there had to be a useful way to prove it. A profitable way.

He had an idea. It would take some organising but Carmichael was good at that. The general would leave the details up to him. The major was still in Australia and it would be a lot easier to work out the details with him here. He reached for the phone.

Jean Williams was very happy when Major Carmichael left the Australian facility. She had been on tenterhooks since the night they had travelled to Perth and kidnapped that man and had half expected that she would be locked up or worse when they returned but to her relief, she had been able to go back to her normal duties. At least they hadn't killed Fraser, but what they did was wrong and she felt responsible for it.

She didn't trust the major and she was never going to do anything about the kidnapping with him lurking in the background, but with him gone she felt a lot more comfortable with what she planned to do. Finally, this was her chance to try to make up for her lack of courage when Don had died.

For the most part, the base personnel kept to themselves and remained on site but every couple of months they were given the opportunity to travel to the nearest large city for some R&R and act like tourists. They all knew better than to discuss their work with any of the locals. Jean had been happy enough with her duties on base and never felt the need before but this time she had signed up and had driven to Geraldton with three other people, two men and a woman. She was on nodding terms with all of them without being friends, but the others were all pretty chummy with each other. She shared a room in a hotel with the other lady while the two men did the same.

Today they were all going to go and do some shopping and after that a trip to the beach. However, Jean planned a little side trip which she didn't share with the others.

With the two men doing their own thing, Jean and the other lady, Kaye, walked along the city street, window shopping. There was a shop with some dresses in the window. Kaye grabbed her by the arm. 'These look nice. Let's try in here.'

As good a place as any, thought Jean. They walked in.

The single shop assistant walked over. 'Can I help you, ladies?'

'I've seen some lovely dresses in the window I'd like to try on,' replied Kaye.

Trying to appear as apologetic as possible Jean butted in. 'I'm really sorry but do you think I could use your bathroom.'

Obviously, the thought of the commission on the sale of several dresses made the sales assistant a little less cautious. 'Sure. It's through that door and down the hall,' she said pointing without even looking.

'Thanks,' mumbled Jean as she walked away. Once through the door all pretence of the bathroom was forgotten. Jean looked through the doors on either side of the hall. She entered the small office she found on the left and walked up to a computer. Thank goodness it was still on. A small screen next to the computer monitor showed Kaye pointing out which dresses she wanted to try.

Jean brought up the email program and brought out the business card that FBI agent Andy Burgess had given her years before. She checked the address and began to type. She was finished in less than a minute. She pressed the send button and then deleted the email from the Sent file, erasing any evidence she had been there. She walked back into the display room. 'Oh, Kaye, that one looks so nice on you.'

Chapter 12

Major Carmichael had listened to the general with growing disbelief. He had argued against the idea that the general had put forward but, in the end, he was never going to win, and he knew it. Now he had to develop a comprehensive plan to achieve the general's wishes involving Fraser. At least he was fit and strong, which would make that part that much easier.

The major made his way to Fraser's quarters to discuss what would be happening. He didn't bother knocking, just walked past the guards, opened the door and strolled in. This was to impress on Fraser who was in charge and who was going to do what they were told.

'Hello, Matthew. How have you been? Well, I hope.'

Matthew had been lying on his bed reading a book he had obtained from the lounge room bookshelf. He looked up. 'Oh, it's you.'

'Yes, it's me. Are we treating you well? From all reports, I hear you're having a great time, running around, lifting weights, watching movies. Living the life of Riley.'

'Oh yeah. I'm having a great time, alright. Nothing like being cooped up in some underground bunker to make a man realise how he'd been wasting his life away before, being outside in the sunlight.'

'Funny you should say that because that's exactly what I wanted to talk with you about.'

Matthew sat up. 'What do you mean?'

'We're going to give you some outside time, you know, let you work on that tan. You're starting to look a bit pale.'

To Matthew this conversation was getting a bit weird. He thought Major Carmichael was a psychopath, just like the general. Nothing good was going to come out of this. 'So, what does all that involve?'

'You're going to be doing some training with my men. Outside. Full combat gear. Apparently, you're giving the troops a complex, running them into the ground. Let's see how you go in the full kit with the sun beating down on you.'

'Do I get a gun?'

'Not a chance.'

The early morning sun was low in the sky but despite this it was still hot and Matthew was sweating profusely. 'I thought it was winter in the Northern Hemisphere,' he gasped to the man running beside him, Private Mitchell.

'Yeah, man, it is. You wouldn't want to be doin' this in summer,' panted the other man. He was an inch or so shorter than Matthew. Matthew was sure the good-looking, fair-haired, blue-eyed soldier was a hit with the ladies and wondered what had motivated him to join the army. He would have to ask soon.

Today, he was running along an obstacle course designed to test the stamina of the soldiers. Yesterday morning he had rappelled from a platform and later in the day from a helicopter. Matthew, as promised, was training in the same combat gear and carrying the same load as the soldiers but whenever the other men carried rifles, Matthew had a barbell from a weight set to haul around. He had originally found running in boots with a full back pack and carrying his pretend gun to be very uncomfortable, definitely not what he was used to, but he took to it quickly. His respect for the armed services had increased greatly apart from a few people he thought dishonoured their uniforms.

After two weeks of training with the soldiers, he was earning their respect and many were beginning to be friendlier, which is what Matthew wanted. Even though he could have gone faster, he wasn't trying to win against them, just settling for middle of the field so that he could be seen as "one of the boys". He wasn't sure what the soldiers had been told about why he was here or how many of them had been involved in his kidnapping but he was hoping to develop some allies amongst them. 'Hey, Mitchell, race you to the next wall,' he said, putting on a bit of a spurt to which the other man responded. Matthew smiled to himself as he was passed.

'Hah!' yelled Private Mitchell as he touched the wall just before Matthew. They high-fived and then used a buddy move to both get over the wall. Matthew cupped his hands to boost the soldier up to the top of the wall, who then reached back down to aid Matthew in climbing up and over. In seconds, they were running again.

The drill sergeant clicked his stopwatch as the men arrived at the finish. He yelled at the two men. 'My grandmother could have done it faster than that and she uses a walking frame.' Matthew and Mitchell smiled at each other and walked off to grab a bottle of water from the cooler standing nearby. 'Oh yeah,' added the sergeant, 'The holiday is over, so I hope you ladies enjoyed yourselves.'

'What's that supposed to mean?' asked Matthew.

'You guys are being assigned a mission.'

'Why the hell would I want to go on a mission?'

Major Carmichael looked at Matthew and smiled his humourless smile. 'I thought I might appeal to your sporting spirit. I looked at your bio and apparently you are very anti-drugs. That's the whole point of this mission, you know. Eliminating drugs.'

'I don't care enough about it to get shot at by drug lords.'

'But Matthew, you're invincible.'

'That's yet to be proven.'

There was that smile again. 'I'm sure we'll get there.'

'Forget it. I'm not doing it.'

'Matthew, you disappoint me.'

'Tough.'

'Oh well, I guess I was wrong. The general said you wouldn't do it willingly and I said you would. But he's the general and I'm only a major, so he ordered me to take out an insurance policy, and here it is.' The major pulled a phone from a pouch on his belt and pushed a couple of buttons. He tossed the phone onto the bunk next to Matthew.

Matthew looked at the picture on the phone. 'What the fuck is this?' he asked jumping up.

'Matthew, I thought you would have recognised your own mother. I bet she's your number one fan.'

'If you hurt her, I'll fucking kill you.'

'That's the spirit. Don't worry. She's fine. We're just keeping a friendly eye on her for the moment and she's oblivious to it all, but we really need you to cooperate. If you do this for us, your biggest fan won't even know we have a gun pointed at her head.'

'You prick.'

'Glad you see it our way.'

Chapter 13

The troop transport plane approached Tolemaida Military Base in Colombia, late at night. Major Carmichael wanted as few outside people as possible to know anything of the operation and had deliberately chosen the time of arrival to suit his needs. He contemplated the relations between this country and the United States over the past few years, since the Colombian Constitutional Court ruling that permanent foreign bases were unlawful. At present, the US didn't have the large numbers of troops there that it had planned for ten years previously, but it still had a significant number of men and assets spread around the country at facilities shared with the Colombians, ostensibly to support Drug Enforcement Administration (DEA) operations.

The plane landed and was in a hangar and the men in barracks long before the sun rose, but the major met with two men a few minutes after stepping off the plane. They both wore lightweight jackets that identified them as DEA agents. The first was in his mid-forties, tall, solidly built with silvery grey hair and a bushy moustache to match. The men shook hands. 'Smith,' he said.

'Jones,' murmured the other. He was a few inches shorter than Smith and a few years older, painfully thin, hair cropped so short it was hard to tell the colour. His dark eyes constantly scanned the surroundings.

The major smiled. 'Of course.'

'So how is this going to go down?' Smith asked the major.

'Well, your informant has told you that Hernandez has money offshore in the Cayman Islands—millions of dollars. Hernandez doesn't trust anyone with the account numbers, which he keeps in a ledger locked up in a safe. We need to get those account numbers. Thanks to your stool pigeon giving us plans to the compound we know where he hangs out. We go in, wipe out any opposition, including Hernandez, get the ledger and we split the profits. It's good for the US as it disrupts a pipeline of drugs into the country but even better for us because no-one, except for us, knows about the money. A real win-win.'

Agent Jones nodded his agreement. 'After years of this shit we might finally make enough to retire on.'

'Amen to that,' replied his fellow agent.

Matthew had competed in triathlons in countries throughout the world but never in Colombia. So, on arrival it came as a surprise to him that it wasn't as humid as he thought. He told Private Mitchell this as they walked to the barracks. His reply didn't bode well for the rest of the mission. 'Man, this isn't the jungle. This part of the country is civilised. Enjoy it while you can. It won't last.'

The men were allowed a few hours of sleep before being gathered into a meeting room to be briefed on the mission. There was a large monitor at the front of the room and the major stood in front of it surveying the people in front of him. All together there were eighteen men. Fourteen were from his unit, one of whom was Matthew, two were observers from the Colombian army and there were the two DEA agents.

'Okay, men. We are here to support a DEA operation. They're in charge of the objectives of the mission so I'll hand it over.' One of the DEA agents stood up and moved to the front of the room.

The situation was unbelievable to Matthew. He should have been riding his bike around Perth or swimming off Cottesloe Beach as part of his preparations for another shot at the Olympic Games. Instead, he was in Colombia as part of a DEA operation. He wasn't even sure what the letters in DEA stood for, except that "D" was probably "Drugs". How was he supposed to be of any use on a mission like this? He was going to get killed out there. He looked at the major as he sat down. *I suppose it's only a matter of time with that whack job in control*, he thought to himself.

The agent at the front of the room cleared his throat and began to speak. 'I'm Special Agent Jones of the DEA. That's Special Agent Smith,' he said pointing to his colleague. There were groans from the army personnel present and even Matthew rolled his eyes. 'This is the man we're after.' The monitor behind him updated to show a good-looking Latino man, black hair slicked back, looking for all the world like a model for Brylcreem hair products. The shot showed him walking through some sort of resort, a drink in one hand and a cigar in the other. The arrogance of the man showed even in the photograph. 'That's Mateo

Hernandez. Don't let the looks fool you. He's in charge of a major drug importation ring bringing coke into the US. He's ruthless and would think nothing of killing every man here and their families, just for having an idea about causing him trouble.'

Well, doesn't this just get better and better, thought Matthew.

Special Agent Jones continued. 'Our aim is to capture this man and get him to the US to stand trial for his crimes.'

'Why not just take him out?' asked one of the soldiers.

'Apart from that being illegal, we want to send a message to other drug lords that they will rot in a US prison if they bring drugs into our country. Taking him out is a last resort, only when we have exhausted all other options.' Jones stared down the soldier. 'We will split into two units. Each unit will consist of one DEA agent, one observer from the Colombian military and seven GIs. The call sign will be "Gravity". Gravity 1 will take a Black Hawk and circle around to this location.' The monitor behind the agent updated to show a relief map, which to Matthew looked nothing more than a lot of jungle. Jones tapped the screen. 'Gravity 2 will chopper in to here.' Another tap on the screen. 'We won't be landing. We'll rappel from the choppers and approach Hernandez's compound from two sides. It's approximately five miles from each drop zone to here. We will touch down while it's still dark, travel to near the target site, camp overnight and strike early the next morning.'

The monitor updated again this time to show a satellite image of a location which looked like a small village hacked out of the jungle. Matthew could see what looked like a small road leading to the village. 'We will locate any sentries. Our Colombian team members will give us the go-ahead to neutralise the sentries depending on them being armed or not.' At this were several guffaws of laughter from the soldiers. 'We will make our way to the centre of the compound to the main building and capture Hernandez.'

One of the soldiers put up a hand. 'Just how many men are we expecting to be up against?'

'We believe that Hernandez has up to thirty men there at any one time.' There were explosions of shock from the men. 'Look, said Jones, 'these men are thugs. They are not well trained. They have been given guns but they are nothing like any of you. You are the elite of the armed forces. They're a rabble.'

The others in the group seemed to take what Agent Jones said with rather more enthusiasm than Matthew. There were some 'Oh yeahs!' and high fives between some of them with many smiling and nodding. Matthew shook his head. *At least they have guns. What the hell do I get? Nothing!*

'As well as the site security forces there will also be civilians. These people are to be considered friendly unless they act otherwise. They're the ones who process the drugs but are treated little better than slaves, so go easy unless you can't avoid trouble. Once we have control of the compound, the choppers will land and we will evacuate the area. Any questions?'

Matthew had plenty of questions but didn't think he was going to get any answers.

The group was filing out of the room when Major Carmichael moved up beside Matthew. 'You may be sceptical, Matthew, but you're a very important part of this operation.'

Matthew looked at the major in disbelief. 'You've got to be kidding. I've been kidnapped from my home, flown halfway around the world, dropped into a war zone and not even given a gun. How the hell am I important?'

'You're our insurance.' Matthew continued to stare at the major. 'Inside that compound is a safe containing some very important information. It's your job to get to the safe and look at the journal that you'll find inside. I've assigned your old friend Corporal Crimmons, as well as Private Sanchez, to make sure that you get there safely and do what needs to be done. As soon as you've seen the information in the journal, you radio me and your part is done. Now, if anything does go wrong, you just keep letting me know that you have the information and we can wrap it all up. Simple.' The major smiled humourlessly at Matthew then strode off.

Matthew shook his head again. That major was one sick bastard.

He would have been even more convinced of this conclusion if he had overheard the major's next conversation.

Chapter 14

Most of the men grabbed a few more hours sleep in anticipation of the night-time insertion into hostile territory, then they had a meal in the mess hall. Matthew went with the others only because he had no choice. He certainly didn't feel like eating and where the other men seemed excited at the prospect of action, Matthew dreaded what was to come. He felt he was only a passenger in this trip to madness.

The men kitted up and made their way to the helicopters. Matthew had been assigned to the unit Gravity 1. Agent Jones was in the same unit as him, along with Crimmons and Sanchez, who looked to be good friends, a Colombian and four other soldiers.

Matthew took his assigned seat in the chopper. Agent Jones looked at him quizzically. 'Where's your weapon, son?'

Before he had a chance, Corporal Crimmons answered for him. 'He's on a special mission for the major. He don't need a gun.' He and Sanchez laughed.

Jones looked at the men. 'Keep him away from me then. I don't need a mad man anywhere near me.'

The helicopter came to a stop, hovering about ten metres from the ground. The drop zone had been carefully selected after satellite imagery had shown a relatively clear space in the jungle.

The only light came from a half moon and the stars when the chopper went dark. The passengers flipped night vision goggles down and the world became an eerie shade of green.

Two men stepped to the edge of the helicopter door and threw ropes out, reaching to the ground. The other ends were attached to a support on the roof of the cabin. The soldiers leaned back over the edge of the door with the ropes supporting their weight and then dropped into space.

Crimmons tapped Matthew on the shoulder. 'Our turn.'

A few moments later they touched down on the jungle floor and stepped to the side to wait for the remaining men.

In less than two minutes, they were all on the ground and the helicopter was gone.

With the down-draught from the chopper gone, the air became thick with all manner of insects. Matthew felt appreciative of the repellent that he had been told to smother onto any exposed flesh. The amount of noise surprised him as well. It seemed that every creature out here had a voice and was desperate to be heard. The first birdcall sounded like a single drop of water falling into a pond. Plonk. Then another, and another, until it was a tropical downpour.

It was still dark and no-one was keen to move through the jungle at night so they all looked for spots to get comfortable before they moved off. Matthew pulled the netting from his hat down over his face to keep away the mosquitoes willing to brave the bug cream and curled up on a waterproof sheet which he set on the ground. He hoped when he awoke the nightmare would be over.

It wasn't.

When it became light enough to see, Agent Jones called the men together. They consulted a GPS unit and established the direction to the compound. He pointed to one of the men. 'You take point.' Then he turned to Sanchez. 'You're on drag. The rest, fall in and let's go.'

Matthew did the conversion in his head—five miles was about eight kilometres; it didn't sound that far when they were in the conference room, but moving through the jungle was painfully slow. They seemed to be following some faint animal trail, but the man in front still expended a lot of energy hacking a path with a machete and so was regularly rotated back into the line. Vines as thick as a man's wrist snaked their way through the foliage. Leaves as big as elephant ears were pushed aside as the group moved past. The sunlight rarely reached the ground as the canopy was so dense and they walked in an eerie light as though the sun was setting. The group rested regularly and kept up their fluid intake. It was hard, hot, sweaty work and the noise never stopped.

During one break Matthew noticed a small orange frog. 'Hello, little guy.' It didn't seem afraid and so he reached out with a finger to scratch it.

'I would not do that,' said the Colombian soldier in his heavily accented English. Matthew looked quizzically at him. 'Poison dart frog. Very bad.' Matthew snatched his hand back.

'Why don't you give it a kiss?' Crimmons laughed.

Eventually, after consulting his GPS, Jones called a halt to the trek. 'This is where we stop for the night. Everyone get comfortable but keep it right down. We don't want to give the game away with any loud noise. First light tomorrow is show time.'

Despite the unceasing jungle noises, Matthew fell into an exhausted sleep.

Matthew had no issue with the focus of the mission. He was definitely against drugs. As far as he was concerned, they messed up people's lives. What he had an issue with was actually being there at the pointy end of the fight. Not only was he there against his will but he was unarmed, relying on others to keep him safe, and the man who was assigned to protect him had already expressed a desire to do him harm. On top of it all, that prick Carmichael had his own agenda and Matthew knew that whatever that was, it wasn't to his benefit.

Jones had gathered the men early for a final talk about the mission. They all had ear pieces and throat microphones so they would be able to communicate freely including with members of the other unit. Gravity 2 had approached from the other direction so they had the village covered from both sides. Matthew could see the village was situated in a small valley surrounded by low hills.

Jones said that he hoped that they were well rested because it was going to get busy very soon. He told the men to spread out and take vantage points, keeping a sharp eye for sentries.

Matthew, closely attended by Crimmons, found a position behind a fallen tree and lay down flat to wait. He nearly jumped out of his skin a short time later when his earpiece crackled into life. 'Hello, Matthew.' It was the major. 'This is a private channel, so it's just you and me talking. Any news for me yet?'

'We haven't even started yet.' Crimmons turned to stare. Matthew pointed to his earpiece to indicate he was communicating.

'Oh. Well, keep me informed. It's in everyone's best interest.'

What the hell was that about? Matthew thought. He tried to focus, knowing he needed to keep a cool head if wanted to get out alive. A few moments later he spotted some movement over to his left. It turned out to be a man, a sentry, in camouflage gear moving around. He was carrying what looked like some sort of machine gun. He was about to point the man out to Crimmons when there was a quick burst of movement from behind the sentry. A hand was clamped over the man's mouth and he was dragged down to the ground. After a short time, a soldier from Matthew's unit stood up with a knife in his hand. He wiped it off on his sleeve before sliding it back into a sheath on his belt. Matthew was shocked by how quickly it had happened. A life had been ended in the blink of an eye. He felt ill.

Crimmons had seen where Matthew's attention had been focused and nodded his approval when he saw what happened.

In quick succession, there were a number of calls over Matthew's earpiece indicating that enemy sentries had been found and neutralised. Matthew's unease about the mission continued to grow.

Jones' voice interrupted his thoughts. 'All targets have been located and eliminated. Everybody move in to the village.' Crimmons touched Matthew on the shoulder and gestured that they should stand up and move. They got to their feet and carefully started making their way through the remaining jungle towards the settlement.

A noise off to the left startled both men. Crimmons spun around, ready to fire, when they spotted a woman carrying a baby on her hip. She was poorly dressed, obviously one of the civilians they were told to expect. Crimmons held up a finger to his mouth. 'Shhhh.' And then pointed to the jungle. The woman took the hint and quickly disappeared into the overgrowth. Matthew wished that he could do the same.

They came to a timber building and Crimmons pressed his back to the wall. Matthew followed suit. They were joined seconds later by Sanchez. They reported their progress to Jones. Other men soon made similar calls and a short time after they were all ordered to proceed.

Sanchez stepped around the corner and that was when all hell broke loose.

He was instantly spotted by one member of the local security force who was leaning against a house, smoking a cigarette. Barely comprehending what he was seeing, the man started to lift his gun when Sanchez opened fire. The man was thrown back into the wall and collapsed onto the ground, dead.

That seemed to be the signal for every man with a weapon to start shooting. Matthew could hear shots from all over the village and he instinctively ducked at each shot. Crimmons had to shout to Matthew to make himself heard. 'Let's head towards the central building. That way.' He pointed with his gun.

The three men moved quickly from house to house using what protective cover they could. They stopped at one structure which appeared a little more solid than others. Matthew was peering out from the side of the building when there was a shot from behind him.

Matthew jumped when a man fell from the roof of the structure they were sheltering behind. He looked to where the shot came from to find Private Mitchell smiling from the roof of another building. Matthew gave him the thumbs up signal.

His relief turned to horror a second later. There was another shot and Mitchell pitched to the ground in an explosion of red mist. 'Fuck me!' yelled Sanchez.

Matthew reached out to grab the weapon from the dead security man in front of him. 'Oh no. You won't need that,' said Crimmons. 'Let's go.'

Somewhere in the distance there was a loud explosion. 'Grenade,' said Sanchez. 'Sometimes you need something a bit stronger when some ticks decide to dig in.'

Matthew felt that the sounds of the battle were diminishing. Perhaps the army units were winning the battle. He raised his head above a fence to try to see what was happening. He dropped to the ground with splinters in his right cheek when a bullet ploughed into the wood just inches from his head. 'Keep your fuckin' head down!' screamed Crimmons. He motioned for Sanchez to move off to the right and distract the sniper.

Sanchez stood and then quickly dropped to the ground. There was a shot into the fence above him. Crimmons saw the direction the shot had come from and quickly directed a burst of fire towards a window in the central building. A man slumped across the window sill.

'Come on,' he yelled and the three men quickly ran, in a half crouch, to the window of the building. This building was a lot more substantial than others in the village, being made of mud-brick.

Sanchez grabbed hold of the dead man's shirt and dragged him out through the window, dumping him on the ground into a position no live person could ever possibly achieve. He slowly raised himself to look inside the building. 'It's clear,' he said and lifted himself up and through the opening.

'You next,' said Crimmons.

Matthew was inside in seconds, closely followed by the other man. Sanchez had his gun trained on the doorway to the room.

They moved towards the door. Sanchez held up a hand indicating they should stop. Matthew thought he could hear someone walking towards the door.

Sanchez jumped through the door and opened fire. Matthew heard a body slump to the floor. 'Rabble,' said Sanchez as he started walking. Matthew was pushed from behind by Crimmons and he stepped into a hallway, following

Sanchez. He stepped over a dead man, one arm nearly separated from the body, not even bothering to try to retrieve the weapon.

At the other end of the hallway, a man stepped out ready to fire at them but Sanchez was quicker and the man fell back into the room with blood flying all over the doorway.

With Matthew and Crimmons close behind him, Sanchez stepped into the room and held his gun trained on a man sitting at a desk. Matthew was perspiring freely, but despite the heat, this man's hair was perfectly styled. He looked like a model about do a photoshoot. Matthew recognised him as Mateo Hernandez, the target of the mission. Now, with him captured, this madness could finally end.

Hernandez raised his empty hands and started to speak. 'Don't shoot. I'm unarmed.' An arrogant smile made its way onto his face. 'US Army, huh? I can make you very…'

Crimmons didn't bother to hear the rest. He opened fire on the Colombian drug lord and the man jerked wildly in his seat, red blossoms appearing on his torso, before falling to the floor, sightless eyes staring at the ceiling. 'Yeah, well, I can make you very dead.'

Matthew was stunned. Wasn't the whole purpose of the mission to capture this man and take him back to the US? Obviously Major Carmichael had other priorities.

Crimmons pointed his gun at Matthew and gestured to the seat with the dead drug lord in front of it. 'You sit down there and keep quiet.' He turned to Sanchez. 'Let's find the safe.'

The two soldiers started their search. They ripped pictures down till the walls were bare. 'Where is it? There's supposed to be a wall safe,' said Sanchez. They stood looking at each other in frustration.

Matthew now understood. There was only one thing that these men were interested in. The contents of the safe. This whole operation had been about that. So many people had died to get that information. He had to try to stop any more people from being hurt. From his seat at the desk, he looked around the room. There was only one place it could be.

In the corner of the room was a bar. A shelf full of bottles of liquor stood above a large mirror. He raised his arm and pointed.

Crimmons followed the direction of Matthew's finger. He smiled a victorious grin, raised his gun and shot out the mirror. The falling glass shards revealed the safe.

'Give me the det cord,' said Crimmons. Sanchez handed him a roll of the plastic tube filled with pentrite explosive from his backpack. Crimmons made multiple loops and stuck it to the safe door, leaving a trailing edge which he took out into the hallway. 'Get out here now!' he yelled.

Matthew realised what was about to happen and was very quick to rise from the chair, avoiding the dead drug lord, and exited the room. Sanchez was a step behind.

Crimmons held a device in his hand. He pressed a button on it.

Boom.

Even though he was expecting it, the noise still startled Matthew. He hadn't been that close to an explosion before and wasn't prepared for the intensity.

It was only seconds later, with dust still swirling through the room, that Crimmons ran through the doorway. He gave a victory whoop which indicated to Matthew that the pentrite had proved successful. Sanchez gave Matthew a push and the two moved into the room to find Crimmons rifling the safe.

Crimmons lifted a journal which was showing some signs of damage. He started thumbing through the pages. He found something that interested him. 'This is it.' He started to move towards Matthew when Agent Smith came charging into the room.

Smith was covered in dirt and breathing heavily. 'Fuck me. What a shit storm out there.' He saw the journal in Crimmons' hand. 'Is that it?' Greed was obvious in his expression.

'Yeah,' replied Crimmons. He threw the journal to the ground at Smith's feet. The agent eagerly bent down to pick it up but the smile on his face quickly disappeared when he rose and saw the gun in Crimmons' hands pointed at him.

'What…' was all he had time to say before half of his head was blasted away. He crashed to the floor, brains and blood oozing onto the timber.

'Less people to share with,' said Crimmons to Sanchez who nodded his agreement. Crimmons retrieved the journal, opened it again and took it to Matthew. 'Have a look at this.'

The whole situation wasn't making sense to Matthew but he had seen the lengths to which these two would go, so he took the journal from Crimmons and read what was on the page. It was a ten-digit number and a name, Diego Martinez.

Matthew had always had a good memory and could recall people's phone numbers for some time without having to resort to having someone text him just to get their contact details. He often laughed that some people didn't even know their own phone number. Knowing that the number on the page was important enough to kill for, Matthew made a more conscious effort to burn the number into his memory.

'Got it,' he said to the two soldiers.

'You sure?' asked Crimmons.

'Yeah.'

'Good. I don't know why the major wanted you to see it and I don't care, 'cause now I get to do this.' He raised his gun at a disbelieving Matthew and from point blank range started firing.

Matthew's world exploded in pain.

Chapter 15

Matthew found himself lying down behind a fallen tree. Shaken, he took stock. He was OK. But where was he? *When* was he?

He nearly jumped out of his skin when his earpiece crackled into life. 'Hello, Matthew. This is a private channel, so it's just you and me talking. Any news for me yet?'

So, that was it. The major had put him through hell just to get the information from the journal. He didn't care who was hurt in the process or how many people had to die so long as he got what he wanted. At least now, he had a chance to stop all the violence before it happened.

'Yes, I got it, you psycho prick. Now call this shit off.' Crimmons, who was lying next to Matthew, turned to look at him quizzically.

There was a soft chuckle in his earpiece. 'I knew I could count on you, Matthew.' There were a couple of clicks and the major started to speak again. This time it was obvious that Crimmons could hear as well. 'Gravity 1, Gravity 2, this is Gravity Base. Abort. Repeat, abort. Acknowledge.'

Matthew heard Jones respond. 'What the fuck's going on?'

'Radar has detected an aircraft heading towards the village. It appears to be Colombian military.'

'That's bullshit. We've cleared this with the military.'

'Apparently not all of them,' replied the major.

Matthew thought he could make out the sound of a helicopter approaching. Then he saw it pop up over the hill on the other side of the village. It must have roused the defences of the village as well. He heard shots as people started firing at it.

There were two streaks of smoke from the chopper as it fired missiles into the village and then a huge explosion as the main building and those nearby were obliterated.

Matthew's team made their way back to the original insertion point and were winched up into the choppers and flown back to the Colombian base. Matthew kept as far from Crimmons and Sanchez as possible on the return journey, and while moving he had plenty of time to think about his situation.

He was being used as a pawn in a game that only the general and major knew the rules to. He'd told the major that he had the information from the journal so Carmichael had arranged for the destruction of the village, meaning he wouldn't have to share whatever spoils were involved with the DEA agents and the two soldiers who had watched over him.

He thought about the extraordinary ability he now had and wondered how he might be able to use it to extricate himself from the clutches of the two madmen who thought it was their right to kidnap him and drag him to the other side of the world for their own ends.

Chapter 16

FBI Special Agent Cathy Owens sat at her desk; the phone pressed to her ear. 'Thanks for your trouble,' she said as she hung up. She glanced quickly at the only decoration in the office, a picture of her and her father which sat on her desk.

Frank Owens had been an FBI agent before his daughter was born and he had raised her pretty much on his own as her mother had died in a car crash when she was one year old. Work commitments ensured that bringing up a child as a single parent wasn't easy but Cathy didn't care. She loved her father deeply. Despite his protests, an FBI agent was all that Cathy had ever wanted to be and eventually, he gave up trying to dissuade her. The picture was of the day she graduated from the FBI academy.

Cathy looked past the bookshelf full of manuals of FBI procedures and policies, investigation techniques and criminal profiles, towards the clock on the wall. It showed five minutes after nine o'clock at night.

During any free time, she had been following up on the anonymous email that had been forwarded to her by Andy Burgess. He was one of the team that worked with her investigating the deaths of the politician's son and a co-worker nearly four years ago and he knew how much the case had meant to her.

The email had originated from a dress shop in the city of Geraldton, Western Australia. Before it arrived, she had never even heard of Geraldton, but she certainly knew where it was now.

According to the communication, it was all happening a few hours from there in the middle of the Australian bush, in a shire called Murchison. A shire. Sounded like something out of *Lord of the Rings*. Cathy thought that made perfect sense considering the email read like a fairy tale. Secret military bases in the outback, people being kidnapped by the army and, to top it all off, a time machine.

There were some things in the email, though, that grabbed her attention and made her consider that the contents may be genuine.

Firstly, was that it mentioned the two deaths in the helicopter crash on which she had led the investigation. The men were the senator's son, Ray Parsons, and his colleague Don Campbell.

This case had been closed, deemed an accident, but Cathy still considered this as a blot on her copybook, even if nobody else did. It was a case she hadn't been able to crack. She had probed the incident but had been stonewalled by the army and, in particular, Major John Carmichael. Now, his name was popping up again in regard to the two deaths and a number of other allegations.

Cathy had not been able to question the helicopter pilot, despite numerous requests, before he had been transferred to Afghanistan by his commanding officer, Major Carmichael. While other members of her team attempted to interview people at the site where the deaths had occurred, she had followed the pilot to Afghanistan. Unfortunately, when she landed, she was told the pilot had been killed in a training mishap. There was an accidental weapons discharge, a freak accident, the army investigator said.

Carmichael himself had never been available to discuss the case, which had infuriated Cathy. In the end, with no proof to the contrary, the deaths were declared accidental.

The mystery email had named Carmichael responsible for the deaths of the two men without actually giving any specifics or proof. Cathy knew she would need a lot more than an unsubstantiated, anonymous email before she would be able to lay any charges.

Cathy then tried to look into the revelation about the secret base in the Australian bush. Once again, the army proved adept at providing a blank wall for her to butt her head against. They denied knowledge of any such base and stated that it would be illegal to have such a facility.

The one thing that she could follow through was the allegation in the email that the army had kidnapped an Australian citizen. At least she had been given a name—'Matthew Fraser'.

Cathy had just been on the phone to the police in Perth and with a twelve-hour time difference between the two cities it was going to be another long night for her. Matthew Fraser was listed as a missing person and the van he had been driving had been found abandoned in a suburb near where he lived. It had been weeks since anyone had seen or heard from him. Yes, he had been to the

Murchison Shire in the week that he had been reported missing. His employer confirmed that.

This, at least, gave her something that she could take to her boss, Arnold Wilson, to try to get the case of the two dead men reopened. Cathy knew she would be grilled by the Special Agent in Charge and wasn't looking forward to it, but it was something that she had to do.

She stood up and walked towards the door. He'd still be in the office. Wilson always worked longer hours than she did.

Chapter 17

Matthew arrived back at the base in the desert. Many of the soldiers were frustrated that they didn't get to see real action, but Matthew knew that at least one man amongst them was lucky that he was coming back at all. The same couldn't be said of the people in the village. It had been almost entirely wiped out by the missile attack.

Matthew realised that he needed to be ready for any chance to escape because he was being used as a guinea pig by the general and the major. He also worried that they may decide to cut him open to try to determine out how his remarkable ability worked. As well as keeping physically fit, he needed to do whatever else he could, including trying to control the ability when he wanted to.

Up until now he had only gone back in time when subjected to life-threatening stress. It was time to experiment.

The first night back, Matthew lay on his bed staring at a book. To anyone watching on the cameras he hoped he would appear to be reading. He glanced at the clock on the desk. The digits showed 20:05. He would need a reference time to know if this worked.

Matthew tried to summon the feeling he first had when he was driving and nearly hit the kangaroo. He could feel the distress but nothing like he had experienced at the time. No matter how many times he went over it in his mind the clock ticked over one minute at a time and in a forward direction.

He moved on to the occasions when the soldiers had broken into his house and shot at him and when the major had tried to shoot him in the office. He replayed the incidents over and over in his thoughts but once again there was no result.

Matthew tried for about an hour without success before calling it quits for the night. There was no point getting frustrated and it looked as if he had time to work on it. He knew that all athletes had to train hard to attain success, it didn't come from just one session in the gym. He would try again tomorrow.

The next morning Matthew was back running around the obstacle course. At least there weren't any upcoming invasions being planned or else it was likely he would be getting some kind of specialised training as had happened prior to the last mission.

While Matthew was distracted by his thoughts, Private Mitchell ran past him, and called out, 'Hah. Too slow. I knew you wouldn't cut it here.'

'I'm just glad you're here at all!' yelled Matthew, remembering the soldier being shot while in Colombia.

'I know the breakfast here is bad but it's not that bad!' Mitchell shouted over his shoulder while clearing a series of wooden beams set at different heights.

Time to get back into the game, Matthew thought as he put on a burst of speed.

That night Matthew tried again at controlling his ability deliberately. The previous night it had been all about remembering recent incidents where people had tried to do him harm. This time he thought he would try to remember further back into his past. One example that came to mind was a triathlon where there had been a crash during the cycle leg. Three men had been taken to hospital and many others injured. Matthew had been thrown through the air and had been lucky to avoid injury after landing on a grass verge. That had been the most traumatic incident he could remember while competing.

Matthew looked at the clock, which was stubbornly moving forward. He was getting frustrated after two nights without success.

By the end of a month, he hadn't had a glimmer of success. He began to think that maybe he was never going to be able to deliberately travel back through time.

Matthew's level of frustration was low compared to Professor Windsor's at the facility back in the Murchison Shire. He had filled blackboards with equations over and over without making any progress. His trademark hair had been pulled and twisted so much that clumps had come out in his hands.

To a man used to solving any problem this was ego crushing. Throughout school and college his intellect and abilities had left his fellow students and colleagues far behind. Now here was a problem that he didn't seem able to solve.

He almost wished he had someone to share the problem with but that really would be admitting defeat. *It's no wonder nobody else is doing this work.*

He stood up from his desk and moved towards the door. Coffee was required to boost his flagging energy reserves. He headed to the mess hall and on the way back he passed the recreation room and decided to see if there was anything worthwhile showing on the television to distract him for a few moments. Now that there was no scheduled test, the men were again allowed access to the satellite television network and they were again watching sport. Being in Australia in summer there was basically only cricket or tennis available. *How could anybody watch either of them?* he wondered but sat down anyway. Today it was cricket. Someone called AB was talking to someone else called KP. They must go by their initials in this game. They couldn't afford whole names. He sniggered to himself.

A few seconds later, a technician sitting at a nearby table nudged his companion. 'Professor Windbag must be a real cricket fan. Look how excited he got when someone got out.' They could both hear the cheering man running down the hallway.

Chapter 18

Cathy Owens had a headache. The constant study of the last month was getting to her. She was used to training, but FBI training. Forensics and criminology, profiling and psychology. That was what she was used to. She practically ate the subjects up. The desire to be the best agent she could possibly be, spurred her on in her endeavours. But this. This was different. This was physics. And not just the physics that she studied at school—where the ball would land if thrown at a certain angle at a certain speed. This was relativity, string theory and particles.

Before this, she would have thought quantum foam was something used to wash your hair in the shower to give it extra bounce and lift. Now she knew it was something to be avoided at all costs.

There were agents of the FBI who were specialists in this field. The Counter-Terrorism Branch had nuclear physicists who knew how to build bombs and how to defuse them. Cathy had talked to their most senior man there, Eric Doppler, about the more technical aspects of the anonymous email and he had been beside himself with excitement about a possible undercover mission to a particle accelerator larger than the Large Hadron Collider at CERN (the European Organisation for Nuclear Research) headquarters in Switzerland.

Cathy had to tell him that he was too well known in the field to go undercover anywhere and that his task was to train her so that she could pass an interview, so that when a vacancy arose, she could step into the job.

She had convinced her reluctant boss that the investigation should be reopened and he had given her a small team who were working to uncover any project being conducted by the army using nuclear physicists and scientists. This was to be cross-checked against those who could be tracked down to working at facilities in the US. They could be eliminated as potential candidates to be replaced by her at a future time.

In the meanwhile, it was back to the books. Tomorrow, she had to explain to Doppler why a twin on a journey through space, travelling at nearly the speed of light, would be younger than the twin who had stayed behind, when the spaceship arrived back on earth.

Cathy groaned and groped through her desk drawer looking for the headache tablets.

Chapter 19

Life was in a holding pattern for Matthew at the desert base in the US. While he was still a prisoner, he was being treated well and he was pushing himself exercising, overcompensating for his failure to be able to intentionally move back in time. He could tell that the soldiers were much more relaxed in their treatment of him and he was sure that most of them had no idea why they were guarding him.

Despite that, there had never been an opportunity for him to escape and he really had no idea where he was or where to go even if he did manage to do it. He couldn't get any more information out of anybody and he had no access to emails or the internet. Matthew thought that the routine was never going to end.

Two weeks later he was flying in a military transport from the US, back to Australia.

Also on the plane was Cathy Owens.

Cathy's team had identified a number of scientists who were working outside the country and had found one who had just arrived back in the States. The normal passport requirements for overseas travel had not been met so it was assumed that the travel was done through military channels. The lady, Denise Overton, had been picked up from her home and taken to the local FBI office in Chicago.

She had been reluctant to provide any information, indicating that she had signed non-disclosure agreements that could mean years in a federal prison. She had been left to stew in an interrogation room for hours until Cathy had arrived to interview her.

Cathy walked in and sat down in front of the nervous scientist. 'Hello, Denise. I'm Special Agent Cathy Owens.'

Denise Overton was an inch over five feet tall. She was slightly built and quite ordinary looking with light brown hair and dowdy clothes. She was most comfortable when at work with people who carried out the same kind of tasks that she did. She had felt monstered since the FBI had come to her home and taken her away. 'I told the others that I signed a non-disclosure contract, so I can't talk about anything.'

'Oh well,' said Cathy standing up, 'if that's the case, then you'll be charged with obstructing a federal investigation and end up spending a long time in prison.' Cathy turned to leave.

'Wait!' Denise practically screamed.

'What?'

'Does anyone have to know it was me who talked?'

'Not if we can verify what you're saying.'

'What do you want to know?'

Denise painted a picture that confirmed the story that Cathy had received in the mystery email. The woman didn't personally know anything about the time travel experiment as she worked in a team calibrating and maintaining the instruments used throughout the facility, but that didn't stop her from chatting with colleagues who worked in that area. She was a little envious and wished that she was working in that department with them.

That suited Cathy just fine. She was still having trouble wrapping her mind around two twins aging at different rates, so if she had to replace someone then this seemed like the right person. Instruments measured discrete quantities. There was no mind-boggling thought required. How hard could it be?

Cathy and her team talked with the woman for hours, getting specifics on her duties, the types of instruments, her qualifications and how she was recruited to the project in the first place.

Once they had the information, the team then had to develop Cathy's cover story. Her team included a computer specialist who was able to give Cathy an almost identical background. Cathy wasn't sure if she should be hugely impressed at the lady's skill on the keyboard or dismayed that her colleague was so adept at hacking into educational institutions' databases.

So now Cathy's new identity was Rachel Black, Bachelor of Science.

They were worried about how to get her name in front of the recruiters for the project, but that part proved to be simple. They had Denise ring up her army contact to tell them that she had a badly broken leg and that she was out of action for a few months.

Captain Nathan Green had just had "that" phone call from his wife.

'It's time.' She was nine months and one week pregnant.

'But I've just started my shift.'

'I don't care. If you're not home in fifteen minutes to take me to the hospital, we will be at war.'

Realising this was a battle he couldn't win, Green tried to mollify his wife. 'Of course, I'll be there, baby. I'm on my way.'

Despite his assurances to his wife, he spent the next few minutes trying to call in favours to cover the rest of his shift. He hadn't had any luck when his phone rang again. 'Captain Green.'

'Captain, it's Denise Overton.'

'Who?'

On the other end of the phone, Denise wondered what she had to do to ever be remembered. 'Denise Overton, from the Australian project. Instrument calibration team.'

Green looked at his watch. 'Uh yeah, how can I help?'

'I'm in hospital with a broken leg and won't be able to go back there at the end of the week.'

Shit, he thought. It was going to take hours to sort a replacement. 'Can you recommend someone with your qualifications?'

Just like that, Cathy had a new job.

Chapter 20

The plane certainly wasn't what Cathy was used to, but unlike many army transport aircraft there were some comforts. It had some noise suppression and rather than benches up against the walls there were twenty seats, configured in five rows of two on either side of an aisle. There were even windows. A wall separated the passenger compartment from the freight area, which was a cavernous space full of crates of equipment. There were no stewards bringing around carts full of meals and coffee. Instead, a member of the flight crew came out and showed people where everything was stored and told them to help themselves.

Cathy walked up the stairs into the cabin and was immediately relieved that she had never met Major John Carmichael face to face because she saw him sitting in an aisle seat in the back row. She recognised him from his army file photo. In real life, he was more handsome than in his picture, but Cathy could detect a hint of cruelty behind a smile that didn't reach as far as his eyes. She turned away before he could make eye contact with her.

There were a number of civilians on the flight as well as army personnel. Cathy decided to try to sit near one of the soldiers, if possible, as she didn't want to be quizzed for the length of the flight by a scientist on the subject of her thesis or how important Planck's Constant was, though she did feel her skills on instruments would probably hold up to scrutiny after the crash course she had been put through in the last few days.

She walked up to a pleasant-looking soldier sitting in one of the aisle seats stretching out his long legs and asked if he would like some company during the flight. The man, who she later found out was Private Benjamin 'Call me Ben' Mitchell, was up in a flash, smiling, offering her the window seat. He looked as if he would go to war to make sure that Cathy sat next to him and not one of the other men.

Private 'Call me Ben' Mitchell proved to be pleasant if rather talkative company and Cathy felt that she didn't have to fear him finding out anything about her other than her phone number. For a moment, she considered giving it to him, but then was distracted by the next lot of passengers to enter the aircraft.

She instantly recognised Matthew Fraser from the Western Australia driver's licence photo that the police in that state had emailed her. What in blazes was he doing in the States? Fraser was accompanied by two armed, hard-looking soldiers and from their glares they were definitely not friendly with the Australian. He saw Private Mitchell and gave a friendly nod and briefly glanced at Cathy before looking up and then rolling his eyes. She guessed he was looking at Carmichael. Obviously, the two men were not the best of friends. One of the soldiers shoved Fraser forward. He turned and stared back at the man for a second but then walked down the aisle and found a seat near a window. Cathy noted that he was in army fatigues but with his shirt untucked and a few days of growth on his chin, he wasn't a poster boy for the military.

The two soldiers followed Fraser down the aisle but left him by himself and the two sat together a few seats away.

'What was that about?' Cathy quietly asked Private Mitchell. 'Who's that guy?'

'That's Matthew. Some sort of advisor to the major even though they don't seem to get along very well.'

Cathy thought to herself that this case was getting really strange. What was Fraser doing here? Was he a kidnap victim? What could he possibly offer the army as an advisor? She figured it was a long flight and she had time to think about those questions.

'Hey,' said Mitchell smiling broadly, 'What's the movie on this flight?'

Seven hours into the flight, the thrill was over. The seat had long ago ceased to be comfortable. Cathy was sure whoever had built the plane had deliberately sharpened the springs so they would stick through the covers into the people unlucky enough to sit in them. She looked around to see other civilians squirming just like herself. The army guys, though, seemed immune to any discomfort. Many of them were asleep, snoring loudly, adding their extra decibels to the droning of the engines. She wished she had earplugs. Ben, too, had drifted off but at least he was breathing quietly.

She needed to get up and stretch her legs, maybe use the bathroom and get some coffee. She unbuckled her seatbelt and manoeuvred her way past the sleeping soldier.

Matthew had developed a tolerance for discomfort over the preceding weeks, so the seats didn't bother him. He was looking forward to being back in Australia even if he was a prisoner. At least, he knew roughly where he was going to be. It was a lot closer to home than where he'd been lately.

A couple of people were at the front of the cabin getting themselves coffee and snacks. He saw the attractive lady who had been sitting next to Mitchell get up and start walking back towards the restrooms. He hoped she would get past Crimmons without incident but as expected an arm reached out and grabbed her by the wrist. The lady looked down and smiled, impressing Matthew with her self-control. He wondered what she thought looking down at the ugly mug leering up at her. He certainly wasn't good looking and even less so since the lump on his head from being smashed with the cricket bat had never gone down.

She indicated towards the restrooms and went to move off but the grip on her wrist tightened. Without thinking Matthew reached for his seatbelt buckle.

He hadn't even put his hand on it when the world dropped out from underneath him.

The pilot had no visual indication that they were near the edge of the jet stream, which most commercial and long-distance military aircraft travel along to increase their speed and fuel efficiency. The borders of the jet stream are subject to clear air turbulence so when they hit the downdraft, the plane dropped fifteen metres in half a second. People screamed. Anything that wasn't secured shot up towards the ceiling.

That included people. The civilians making coffee, those in their seats who didn't have their seatbelts secured, and Cathy, all went flying.

Matthew was held in securely by his seatbelt but watched, horrified, as the attractive lady rose through the air and smashed into the ceiling with a sickening crunch. Then his world dissolved in a blinding flash.

Matthew regained awareness to find the plane flying along smoothly. Had it just happened again? It seemed different to the other times. Previously his life had been in direct danger but this time it was much different circumstances. This time it was the girl in front of him in peril, though it was still emotional for him.

He was lost in thought for a few moments when he saw the lady sitting next to Mitchell getting up out of her seat. Matthew turned to Major Carmichael and screamed, 'You need to get everyone in their seats now.'

Matthew didn't think much of the man, but he liked how decisive he was. He responded instantly. 'Everyone sit down and put your seatbelts on. Now!'

The lady stared at him for a second then sat down. Those people at the front of the cabin looked at the major and seeing he wasn't joking, quickly returned to their seats. The army personnel, who were used to taking orders, all checked their belts.

A few seconds later one of the male civilians who had just sat down turned towards the major. 'Hey, what's uuuuuuuu…' he managed to get out before the plane dropped.

People screamed. Anything that wasn't secured shot up towards the ceiling, but this time it was only loose objects and not people.

The plane flew on unscathed but the people inside the passenger area were very badly shaken up. A voice came out of the loud speaker. 'Sorry about that, folks. Clear air turbulence. We'll move over a bit and hopefully stay clear of any more trouble.'

The lady sitting with Mitchell turned to stare at him. Her expression said it all: What the hell just happened?

Matthew shrugged and turned away.

While Cathy pondered about what just happened, Matthew felt some fresh hope about being able to control his ability. He looked at his watch. He didn't know which time zone he was in after so long in the air, but his watch showed him it was five minutes past two in the afternoon.

In his mind, he conjured up the sudden drop as the plane hit the turbulence. He didn't feel like anything happened and this was confirmed when he looked at his watch again. 14:06. Shit.

He then thought about the shock of seeing the attractive lady smash into the ceiling of the passenger compartment. It was like he had crashed into the ceiling himself; the pain was so intense.

Matthew shook his head to clear it. He looked at his watch.

14:01.

Matthew's response to the time on his watch was a typical Australian male's version of "Eureka": *You bloody beauty*. He smiled broadly and felt so excited that he could hardly contain himself.

For the rest of the flight, he practised intentionally moving back in time. After the initial breakthrough, it became easier for him to control the ability, though each time he still felt the pain, and at the end of the flight after a dozen occasions he was mentally and physically worn out.

He had averaged about five minutes each time it had happened. He had also tried what he came to think of as "piggy-backing"—moving back through time just after he had already jumped—but he had not been able to achieve this. *What a pity. I could have jumped my way back out of all this.*

Chapter 21

Dr Ahmed Barazani stared at his bedroom ceiling. He was too wound up to sleep. To calm himself he thought about the design of his bomb and the explosive process that would soon occur within it. The physics behind it was his form of counting sheep.

The device had been miniaturised so that it was smaller than a barrel of oil. His design was an implosion-type bomb, where a detonator triggers a series of simultaneous explosions around its spherical circumference. These explosions are precisely directed inwards onto a sub-critical mass of Uranium-235, creating enough force to increase the density of the mass so that it is super-critical or capable of sustaining an atomic chain reaction. This reaction occurs when a neutron strikes a Uranium-235 atom which absorbs the neutron but then becomes unstable and splits. More neutrons are released, striking more atoms. Each of these reactions takes mere billionths of a second and there are trillions of them happening.

Now that the core has become super-critical, all that is required is a source of neutrons to initiate the chain reaction. This is provided by a small pellet of Polonium-210 and Beryllium-9, separated by a thin membrane to stop them interacting. Polonium-210 decays radioactively, producing alpha particles which are easily stopped by the membrane but when it is ruptured, by the compression of the critical mass, the alpha particles strike the Beryllium-9, creating Beryllium-8 and a neutron. With millions of free neutrons now available, the chain reaction is self-sustaining and takes only around one millionth of a second to complete.

With a tremendous amount of energy released in each fission process, a nuclear explosion is almost unimaginable in its intensity.

Barazani contemplated his future. Things would happen very fast once the first device exploded. The Americans would be able to deduce from the nuclear residue where the bomb had come from and then they would launch an investigation which would quickly lead to him. He had no doubt about this and he had no regrets about his actions. He looked at his watch and counted down the minutes.

More than twelve thousand kilometres away from Islamabad, outside the port of Oakland, California, Captain Arthur Peters was waiting to dock on the Liberian-registered ship *Desert Star*. Oakland was the largest city in the East Bay region of San Francisco Bay and home to what was normally one of the busiest ports in the United States. Today wasn't a normal day.

After the accidental death of one of its members at work in the Port of Oakland, the International Longshore and Warehouse Union had brought the port to a standstill. For the last five days, no ship had been unloaded, costing the Californian economy an estimated one hundred and forty million dollars.

With the port management authority seemingly unable to resolve the conflict with the union, the governor of the state was set to enact legislation forcing the men back to work.

Until that happened, however, there were forty fully loaded container ships anchored between one and five kilometres off the coast of San Francisco, waiting their turn to have their cargo removed.

The *Desert Star*, which had last taken on containers at the Pakistan Deep Water Container Port, was thirty-third in line. Captain Peters was resigned to his delivery bonus being savagely reduced by the delay. The rest of the twenty-three-man crew were also extremely unhappy, many for the financial aspect of the delay and for the time they now wouldn't get to have ashore in San Francisco, one of the most fun cities on their globe-trotting itinerary.

The ship should have been unloaded by now and be steaming back for another run. The containers should have cleared customs and been transported to their final destinations.

Among the cargo was container SMIU573818, which was to be delivered to a casino in Las Vegas. Supposedly from Slot Machines International, the manifest showed it to be full of their products, going to enhance the experience of the gambling public with the catchy music and multi-coloured displays.

At this moment, though, while all of the other displays were dead, one remained powered up. This display certainly would not enhance the experience of any member of the public. Most would be filled with dread if they understood that numbers counting backwards from ten could only mean one thing.

When the countdown reached zero, the electronics in the timing mechanism sent the signal to the explosive charges around the circumference of the device. One millionth of a second later the temperature at the core of the device was one hundred million degrees centigrade, a fireball about fifteen centimetres across.

The fireball rapidly expanded, vaporising everything it touched. One tenth of one millisecond later the fireball was twenty-five metres across with a temperature of three hundred thousand degrees, cooling and slowing its expansion as it grew.

Captain Peters, who was the nearest of the *Desert Star*'s crew to the device, was obliterated instantly along with a large portion of the ship.

After one millisecond, a thousandth of a second, the fireball had expanded to eighty metres across and was still at twenty thousand degrees, still vaporising everything it touched, including thousands of tons of seawater, the rest of the *Desert Star*'s crew and the *Desert Star* itself. The incredibly hot fireball started to rise, taking with it all of the material it had reduced to molecules.

As it rose, there was a vacuum created which drew superheated material after it, making it look as if the fireball was rising on a column of steam.

One second after the countdown had reached zero, the fireball was four hundred and fifty metres across and at a temperature of three thousand degrees. As it rose, the cool air above pushed down on the fireball so that it curled at the edges, giving the explosion a distinctive mushroom shape.

A supersonic shockwave had moved away from ground zero, travelling much faster than the expansion of the fireball, at around three thousand kilometres per hour. The passage of the shockwave also heated the air it compressed and when it hit a freighter anchored four hundred metres away, the two sailors who were walking on deck, were mashed to a pulp against a container. The entire bridge crew was killed when the windows blew in, shredding them. There was extensive buckling of the ship's hull so that it was inevitable that it would be at the bottom of the ocean within half an hour.

A ship anchored a half mile from the *Desert Star* fared a little better, but only the ship itself. A member of the crew on deck on the explosion side had every internal organ damaged by the shockwave and was dead within seconds. The first officer, Mike Burns, was sheltered from the shockwave but was tossed around by the winds and had his left arm broken when he smashed into a container. Unfortunately for Burns, he also received a massive dose of radiation and died miserably two hours later from internal bleeding. Most of the crew also received high level doses of radiation but may have been saved if they'd had prompt medical attention. Since that didn't happen, they survived the initial blast only to linger between two and four weeks, their bodies slowly shutting down in front of the nursing staff in the hospitals they were eventually taken to. The chief engineer was the only long-term survivor. He was knocked unconscious, falling when the ship was buffeted by the shockwave. He had sufficient layers of iron between him and the blast to ensure he received only a mild dose of radiation.

There were three other ships anchored within a mile of the *Desert Star*. Half of the crew members died within six weeks from radiation poisoning. The rest were sick but since they received lower doses, recovered after several weeks in hospital. They were warned by doctors that ever-having children would be unwise.

The ships were heavily tossed by the shockwave and then again as the ocean rushed to fill the void left by the water vaporised in the explosion.

The captain of the *Occidental Dawn*, anchored about three kilometres from the *Desert Star*, was looking towards the other ship when it exploded and was flash blinded by the initial brilliant burst of the device, an effect which lasted the next few minutes. The ship was bow on to the blast and rode out the surge without major problems.

Of the forty ships anchored off the coast of San Francisco, thirty-eight remained afloat. Casualties among the members of the various crews totalled one hundred and one.

Chapter 22

At San Francisco Zoo, roughly five kilometres east of ground zero, a brilliant flash lit the sky. A few patrons were looking towards the explosion and were temporarily flash blinded. After the initial brilliant pulse, everybody turned towards the cause of the bright light. They were dismayed to see the fireball rising into the sky. A few seconds later the noise reached them. It was many times louder than a clap of thunder directly above.

Kaboooooom.

That was when panic set in.

One woman screamed, which seemed to be the trigger for a hundred more. People stampeded for the exits. In the tumult, there were scores of injuries including ten deaths, half of them children under eight. This type of scene was repeated at many sites around the city.

On the streets of San Francisco, there was chaos. There were hundreds of car crashes and rear-end collisions within seconds. Sunset Boulevard was instantly gridlocked. As the mushroom cloud grew people started tooting their horns longer as if that would somehow magically clear the road in front of them.

The television news stations had the story to air within minutes. They reported an apparent nuclear explosion a few miles off the coast. One station speculated that it was from a missile fired by North Korea that had either crashed by itself or been shot down by a US missile defence system. Another station said it was a naval exercise gone wrong. A third said it was a terrorist attack. They all found their own experts to discuss the matter with, but nobody had any sort of proof or details to back up the claims. What was not under question was the image of the distinctively shaped cloud spreading out on the horizon.

More than two hundred thousand people decided that where there was one nuclear explosion there might be more and there was a mass exodus, or at least an attempt at one. The roads were so choked that cars could barely move.

With so many empty houses and apartments, others took to looting, prompting the governor to call for the national guard.

Hospitals were overflowing with the wounded, from stampedes, car crashes, acts of lunacy on the roads and by the police and national guard as they tried to protect people and property from the suddenly lawless.

Despite San Francisco not having been seriously affected by the blast, more than four hundred residents died that day from its indirect causes.

Forty-five kilometres west of San Francisco lie the Farallon Islands. These islands, for the most part, are barren lumps of rock, uninhabited except for South East Farallon Island, where a few members of the US Fish and Wildlife Service have a base.

The islands are part of the Farallon National Wildlife Refuge, an area encompassing the islands and surrounding ocean. The refuge is an important bird sanctuary with a diverse range nesting there, including endangered species such as the ashy storm petrel. Apart from birds, the islands are also a breeding ground for a number of seal species. Whale watching cruises to the islands are popular during the migration seasons but the islands themselves, are off limits to visitors.

The chief wildlife officer stationed at the island was Lynn Johnston. Lynn was a tall, strongly built woman with mousy coloured hair and slightly prominent front teeth. Her best friend might have described her as plain looking. She lived for her job and just loved conducting bird counts. Recently she had been incredibly excited to see the rhinoceros auklet breeding on the island, a bird with a distinctive orange beak and a ridge of bone above it, looking for all the world like a rhinoceros horn.

Lynn was in charge of a team which included three other members. This morning they were about to head off to conduct a census of the Cassin's auklet on Middle Farrallon Island. This threatened species blends in well with the rocky outcrops it nests in, so the team expected to have their work cut out for them today.

A flash of lightning in the otherwise clear sky drew Lynn's attention. She turned around and was horrified by what she saw rising on the horizon.

Automatically, Lynn gauged the wind direction. There was an Easterly blowing, so it looked to her that they were in the path of any fallout that might occur.

Lynn ran back from the boat ramp to the building that served as accommodation and office. She yelled at the other team members, 'Drop everything. We need to get out of here now.'

The two men and one woman who were stationed with her instantly stopped what they were doing and looked at her. They saw someone who was completely serious.

'What is it?' asked her deputy, Karl Archer.

'There's been an atomic explosion. I can see the mushroom cloud from somewhere near San Francisco. The wind is heading this way and I don't want to be here when the fallout arrives.'

Almost on cue, a rumbling sound like distant thunder reached them. They all jumped at the noise.

All four team members quickly made their way down to the boat ramp and boarded the boat they used in their daily activities, a specially modified Sea Ray 300 SLX. The Sea Ray specifications told them that the boat had a top speed of thirty-eight knots or forty-four miles per hour. Lynn decided to see if they could do better than that today.

They pulled out from the ramp and guided the boat away in a Southerly direction, in a race for their lives, a race which they ultimately won.

The Farallon National Wildlife Refuge though, lost.

A million tons of seawater had been vaporised in the explosion. Prevailing winds pushed the mushroom cloud directly at the islands. The fallout pattern from the blast gave the bird sanctuary massive doses of radiation. For the nesting birds that stayed on the islands to tend the nests, the mortality rate was almost total. Death occurred within two to three days. The partners of these birds, who dived into the water regularly and washed off the fallout, fared much better. Predatory birds and scavengers who feasted on the dead and dying became sick and died themselves.

Some of the eggs hatched but genetic mutations were common.

The Islands' bird population would never be the same again.

Chapter 23

One and a half hours after the explosion off the coast of San Francisco, the meeting of the country's most powerful men and women began in the Oval Office.

Seated behind his desk was the President of the United States, Walter Bright. The former governor of New York had swept to power in a landslide at the last election. He was a tall, handsome man in his mid-fifties, with a ready smile and sincere eyes that dominated the television screens, inviting the electorate to trust him. At this moment, the man with the most power in the free world felt anything but powerful.

Bright had campaigned on being a peace-broker. He was going to do what no other person had yet been able to do: bring peace to the Middle East. Commentators had warned him that it was like trying to fill a bucket of water using a colander, but he had been undeterred. Recently he seemed to be having some success, bringing Iran into line on nuclear non-proliferation, but now he saw his dreams starting to crumble.

The president's chief of staff, Rebecca Smart, took her seat on his left. Due to her surname, people joked about the clever couple running the country and it was true. Rebecca controlled access to the president and was the only person on the planet capable of pushing him around. If she thought something was bad policy for the president, it died horribly.

Rebecca wasn't attractive at all. She was average height, had prematurely grey hair, thick glasses and was now starting to get a bit plump. But what she lacked in looks, Rebecca more than made up for in brain power.

They had studied law at college together and had been on opposite sides and the same side during many debates. Walter Bright respected her immensely and when he had become the governor of New York he had invited her to become his chief of staff. She naturally came with him when he stepped up to the White House. How could she not follow the man she loved?

The president's national security advisor sat on his other side. Timothy Scott was a former professor of Middle Eastern Studies at Harvard. A forty-year-old of average height, he was extremely good looking. The television networks loved to have him on to explain government positions. He had helped the president frame his foreign policies, including those on the Middle East, with a mind to bringing peace and stability to the region.

Also present were the Secretary of Defense, Andrew Croft; the Director of the CIA, Ash Connors; the Director of the FBI, James Benson; the Director of Homeland Security, Ed Turner; and the Chairman of the Joint Chiefs of Staff, General of the Army, Colin Risley. They were seated in a semi-circle facing the president.

The president glared at the men opposite him. 'What the fuck was that?' When nobody looked as if they were going to speak, he waited a few seconds, then, 'Anybody?'

The Chairman of the Joint Chiefs spoke up. 'Uh, Mr President, we believe the device was somewhere in the region of twenty kilotons.' General Risley was a couple of years away from retirement age. He very much looked the part of a soldier with the closely cropped, greying hair and ramrod-straight back, but it had been many years since he had seen a battlefield. His battles these days were political.

'Yes, but where did it come from?' This time the president looked at the director of the CIA, who quickly referred to his notes.

Connors was a bland-looking man, someone who would never rate a second glance on the street. Average height, average weight and an ordinary face. These were ideal characteristics for a security operative who had risen through the ranks of the agency. 'Mr President, from what we can tell there are two ships missing. One sunk after the event so we don't think that was it. The most likely candidate was a ship called the *Desert Star*, last stop was Pakistan. We assume the device was smuggled on there. It was supposed to unload in Oakland. We are trying to determine who built it, who sent it here and if there are more likely to be coming.'

'There's going to be more? That's just great. What's the damage from this one?' This time he was looking towards the director of Homeland Security.

Director Turner was a powerful-looking man. He had represented his country at the Olympics in weight lifting over twenty years before and still found time to visit the gym despite his punishing work commitments. 'Since it was a few miles offshore, Mr President, collateral damage is at a minimum. San Francisco itself has ground to a halt. The roads are jammed and it looks like half the city is trying to evacuate. We were lucky that the longshore union called a strike and the ships couldn't unload. If the device had exploded in the city, then it could have been tens of thousands killed instantly and more dying from radiation poisoning and nuclear fallout blanketing San Francisco.'

The president didn't seem to believe he was lucky. 'I thought we were able to detect nuclear devices on ships.'

'Mr President, we have detectors in the ports themselves but they are only partially effective. It depends on how well something is shielded and how close they come to the detectors. In this case, the ship didn't even enter the port so there was no way we could have picked it up.'

'Well, I want extra security, checking on any vessel entering our ports. If there's another bomb, I want it found and stopped. If something's here already, find it. Got It?' There were Yes Sirs and nods all around the room. 'Becky,' he said, turning to his chief of staff, 'that speech writer had better come up with something good. I need to get in front of the people and tell them everything is under control.'

'Yes, sir.'

The president turned back to the men sitting in front of desk. 'This is the top priority. Drop everything until we have this situation worked out.'

James Benson, the FBI director, gathered his notes. At forty-two, he was the youngest man to hold that position in the last fifty years, but at this moment he neither felt or looked that young. The bags under his dark eyes aged him ten years, despite the still dark and full head of hair. In an organisation that rewarded results, he had reached the top due to his hard work and outstanding intellect. Now he was going to have to demand even more of the people who worked for him.

After the meeting broke up, the men shuffled out of the room. Director Connors of the CIA walked up to the Chairman of the Joint Chiefs. 'A word, general.'

General Risley eyed the spy chief suspiciously. 'What's on your mind?'

'You guys might be in a position to offer more help than you know.'

'What's that supposed to mean?'

'Your research division under General Sam Morgan is working on something that might help.'

Risley found it hard to hide his surprise; first, that the CIA man knew that General Morgan was in charge of special projects and second, that he seemed to actually know what the project was, something that he, himself, tried to avoid knowing so he had plausible deniability. 'Oh, and what's that?'

'The time travel project.'

This time the general didn't even try to disguise his feeling. 'What the fuck are you talking about?'

The CIA boss laughed. 'You might want to have a word with Morgan. He's obviously playing his cards close to his chest, but something like this might help us out in a crisis.'

'Hmmm. I'll take it under advisement,' said the general turning to leave.

'You do that.'

The next day at the Pentagon, General Risley called his special projects director to his office. The general made the other man wait a few minutes after his secretary had announced his arrival.

General Morgan was used to the games people played, especially in this establishment, and he wasn't bothered at all by the delay. He figured that maybe he would be asked to develop something in response to the nuclear attack.

When he was eventually shown in, neither of the two men bothered with the formality of salutes. They shook hands. 'Colin.'

'Sam. Have a seat.'

'What's up?'

'You have a leak.'

'What do you mean?' gasped General Morgan.

'That CIA spook, Connors, told me yesterday all about your time travel project. I didn't even know what the fuck he was talking about. I looked like an idiot.' Risley glared at his fellow officer. 'How the hell did he find out?'

General Morgan thought hard for a few seconds. 'I don't know, but I'll find out. Don't worry.'

'Too late for that. If he knows about it, God knows who else does. I want it shut down.'

'You wanted deniability, Colin, so I kept you out of it, but trust me, this is going to be big. You are going to be very happy with what we are doing.'

'And just what are you doing?'

General Morgan really had wanted to keep Risley out of this. There was no telling what he would do if he was aware what the project achieved. Shit. 'We have managed to send someone back in time.'

The Chairman of the Joint Chiefs stared for a few seconds. Then, 'Seriously?'

'Yes, seriously.'

'And you can do this every time?'

'It hasn't been that simple, but we've finally ironed out the bugs and the next trial is going to succeed. We are going to have controllable time travel.' Morgan sounded confident but mentally he was crossing his fingers that he was right.

'When's the next trial?'

'In a few days.'

Risley pondered for a few moments. 'I want a report of how it goes on my desk the next day. If I don't like what I read, I'm pulling the plug. Do you understand me?' A nod from the other man. 'Do you think that we can somehow use this project to help protect us against a possible nuclear attack like Connors suggested?'

No fucking chance, he thought. 'I don't see how,' he told Risley.

'Come up with a way. Dismissed.'

Chapter 24

Matthew looked around the room. He had been given the same one he was in the last time he was in the facility. *Home sweet home. At least I'm in Australia. But I wonder why they brought me back here?*

Cathy was settling in her room as well in the accommodation level of the complex. There were guards sitting outside a room up the hallway. She wondered if that was Fraser's room and if he was a willing or unwilling participant here.

She had been promised an induction tour of the facility the following day. She was impressed by the scope of the project and was really looking forward to seeing it all, despite the list of crimes that they appeared to be committing just by being here. That was another question. Why were they in Australia at all? There was so much unpopulated land in the US. Why had they picked this whole place up and moved it across the world? Denise Overton, the woman Cathy had replaced, hadn't been able to shed any light on that.

Cathy stopped and forced herself to focus on why she was there. She was trying to find out what had happened to the two men who had died in the helicopter crash more than four years ago. If she was able to discover that, then the rest of this would be up to her superiors to decide. Now she had to try to discover who had sent her the mystery email.

Professor Windsor was deep in thought, contemplating the effects of the sun on the world. He didn't care about sunburn or skin cancer. He rarely went outside and wasn't likely to be bothered by the effects of sun on skin. Most of his time was spent working, with breaks for eating or sleeping. His thoughts now were turned towards the effect of the sun on the magnetosphere, the earth's magnetic environment.

To the professor, the sun was the most amazing celestial object. Like the earth, it rotates on its axis but as it isn't solid, material at the equator actually rotates faster than the material nearer the poles. A day for the sun, how long it takes to rotate on its axis, is about twenty-six days near its equator but more like thirty-three days nearer the poles.

This differential speed in rotation causes distortions in the sun's magnetic field. The distortions generally show up as sunspots, darker, slightly cooler areas on the surface of the sun. The magnetic lines of force are twisted and stretched like a cosmic sized rubber band, storing enormous amounts of energy. When they snap back into alignment, the energy is released in one of two ways.

The first is called a solar flare, which releases a huge amount of heat and light. Also released are streams of particles which can travel towards earth. These mainly have the effect of interfering with radio and satellite transmissions.

The second way energy is released is from the less well-known coronal mass ejection, known as a CME. Whereas the solar flare is mainly heat and light, the CME sends huge amounts of plasma hurtling into space, sometimes towards earth. The time taken for the effects of the CME to reach the earth is generally around two days. These clouds of plasma have their own strong magnetic fields which interact with that of the earth. This interaction is called a geomagnetic storm, the strength of which is given a Kp index number between zero and nine. If there is a geomagnetic storm with a reading above five, there is likely to be an aurora, a multi-coloured curtain of light hanging in the night sky. in the Northern Hemisphere, it's the Aurora Borealis and in the Southern Hemisphere, the Aurora Australis.

Professor Windsor contemplated the Kp index, the flash of inspiration he had received from watching the cricket game completely forgotten.

He had been able to look back through the records, to the day of the fateful test, and find the Kp number had been at a six. Aurora watchers had records that dated back years. He factored this new information into his calculations and as he had expected, the mathematics had worked out. He knew now if they repeated the experiment on a day where the local Kp index was a six, that they would get the results they wanted.

Since they were moving into the active part of the eleven-year solar cycle, they shouldn't have to wait too long, and they should get plenty of notice of when the next CME event of the desired size would occur.

Then he had a surprise for everyone.

Major Carmichael sat in his office. He had just heard about the explosion off the West Coast of California. He was livid but not about San Francisco. He didn't give a shit about that place, had never liked it. As far as he was concerned it was full of drug addicts and gays and he had no time for any of them.

He was angry that some foreign asshole had the gall to send a nuclear weapon to the United States, the country where he was born and raised, the country that he fought for. He knew he was no saint himself, but he still felt that everything he did was in the best interests of his country and if he benefited personally at the same time then, hey, everybody won.

Terrorists. He hated terrorists. Always in hiding. Never facing the enemy. What he wouldn't do for five minutes alone in a room with the man responsible. He would make the most of any chance.

Chapter 25

Salman Umrani wasn't going to waste any time waiting for confirmation from his bosses in the US that the nuclear device that had exploded off the West Coast had come from Pakistan.

As far as he was concerned, he had been given a huge head start in the investigation by the fact that they knew the ship had last stopped here. If the ship had been able to unload its deadly cargo and the bomb had gone off while in customs or at its final destination, it could have added weeks to the investigation while they waited for the analysis of fallout and residue to point them to the right source.

Salman was born and raised in the US by Pakistani parents. He grew up loving apple pie but just as much, biryani. He was multilingual, having learned Urdu and Balochi during his infancy from his parents, and since joining the CIA he had mastered all of the other regional languages such as Punjabi, Sindhi and Pashto. He was as home anywhere in Pakistan as he was in Los Angeles, where his parents still lived.

Salman was an even six feet tall and while at home in the US was always clean-shaven. Today he had a bushy moustache and was walking with a slight stoop, so a casual observer would think of him around three to four inches shorter. He was well built and extremely fit as he exercised regularly, but in the loose-fitting clothes he was wearing he was as ordinary looking as the man selling fruit and vegetables in the stall he had just walked past.

He had just received a manifest of the cargo on the *Desert Star* and was intending to work through it to see if there were any irregularities, but his first line of investigation was the Pakistan Atomic Energy Commission. He felt that, like any large organisation in Pakistan, there was bound to be corruption. For Salman, it was a no-brainer. Someone in this organisation was, in part, responsible for the nuclear attack on his country and he would make sure they paid for their crime.

Ahmed Barazani had been shocked that his carefully thought-out plan had gone so disastrously wrong. Instead of the widespread carnage he had imagined, the US had escaped relatively unscathed.

Still, he reflected, they would now be in a state of panic and scrambling to ensure there were no further attacks. It wouldn't do them any good.

Ahmed knew that the Americans would be looking for the source of the weapon and that their job had been made easier by the explosion being located off the coast rather than in port.

He was contemplating when he would need to disappear. He had money, resources and friends in al-Qaeda who would help him but if he left too early it would be a red flag, marking him as a person of interest. Still, it was time to make sure the plans would work. He would make some calls when he reached home tonight.

It had been a long day at work for Ahmed. All the talk had been about the bomb. He had meeting after meeting, with this as the only item on the agenda. It had been easy to blend in with the sympathisers with the looks of dismay on their faces because that was exactly how he felt as well but for much different reasons. He thanked heavens it was over.

Since Islamabad was designed and built around 1960 it had the benefit of being well laid out in almost a grid pattern, so it was a fairly straightforward drive from the PAEC headquarters through Blue Area to where he lived in sector F-11. He normally used the drive to unwind from the stresses of the day but that was impossible today, his mind constantly going over what had gone wrong.

Ahmed pulled up in his driveway, a bit surprised that the automatic light hadn't come on. After his wife had died two years ago, he was depressed about coming home to a dark house, so he had set up his lighting to switch on at dusk. He thought to himself that it was probably a blown light globe and he would see to it in the morning. Ahmed stepped out of his car, grabbed his briefcase from the back seat and then made his way towards the front door, reaching into his jacket pocket for the door keys.

His foot crunched on something on the paving. He took his phone out of his pocket and switched on the flashlight function, shining the light down to his shoes. It was broken glass. Now he knew why the light wasn't on. Kids had smashed the globe.

Ahmed looked up just as someone stepped out of the shadows near his front door. 'Peace be upon you, Dr Barazani,' said a voice that he recognised as one of his al-Qaeda contacts. 'I hope you don't mind too much about the light. I didn't want the neighbourhood seeing us meeting here.'

Ahmed was startled that this man would risk coming to his house like this, but he pulled himself together. 'And peace be upon you also. Of course not, Brother. I understand.'

'Good.' The man paused for a moment, again putting Ahmed's nerves on edge. 'Though it was still a blow against the Great Satan, we were disappointed with the results of the first explosion.'

'I completely agree. It was not what we foresaw at all. It was unfortunate that circumstances conspired against us on this occasion but that will not happen again.'

'Oh.' With one small word, the mocking tone the man used sent a chill down Ahmed's spine.

'No, Brother. The devices are already in place. The Americans will use all of their resources searching the ports but there is nothing to find in any of them. The outcomes are inevitable.'

'That is excellent news. So, apart from our commander, you are the only one who knows where the devices are? Nothing else can interfere with our plans?'

'That is correct. Nothing.'

The other man thought for a moment but even in the fading light Ahmed sensed that he had come to a decision. Ahmed's heart was racing and he felt sick.

The man spoke again. 'Then I am sure you will live happily in paradise.' He started to raise his hand and Ahmed could see an abnormally long gun.

Ahmed threw his phone at the man who flinched. Desperation lent him strength and holding his briefcase in front of him, he charged.

He connected with the man solidly, sending him flying back. There was a discharge from the gun. Somewhere in the back of his mind, Ahmed was surprised that the silenced gun was still that loud. He had thought that he wouldn't be able to hear it.

The man landed awkwardly, striking his head on the step up to the front door. He didn't move.

Ahmed dropped his briefcase and checked himself. He didn't feel any pain. The shot had missed. He looked down at the other man. He still hadn't moved.

Ahmed looked for his phone and found it against the wall, the flashlight function still on. He was surprised that the screen was still intact. Good. He would be able to use the contact list stored in it.

He walked over to the man lying on his front step and felt for a pulse. Nothing. The man was dead. Ahmed felt sick. Despite the damage caused by the bomb, he had never personally killed a person before.

Choking back bile, he stood up and moved to the front door and unlocked it. He looked around and was happy to see that he hadn't attracted any unwanted attention from his neighbours. He bent down and grabbed the other man by his shoulders and dragged him into the house. He felt there was no point leaving the man on display. Hiding the body might gain him some time. He closed the door.

He had expected the Americans to be chasing him very soon and had been prepared for that, but he hadn't anticipated that his allies would also want him dead just to ensure that their schemes went off without a hitch. That seriously disrupted his plans. Ahmed moved through the house to his bedroom and started gathering items to stuff in a suitcase.

It was time to disappear.

Chapter 26

Professor Windsor was contemplating the explosion of the nuclear device off the West Coast of the US but only from the perspective of what type of effect it would have on this facility. He decided that it was far enough away and of a small enough magnitude that it would have no effect at all.

He had already talked with Major Carmichael about it and they had decided to close communications down and try to keep the news from the staff in order to minimise distractions. The professor had little doubt that the soldiers would be full of nationalistic bravado, contemplating their opportunity at revenge, and the civilians would be worried about friends and relatives. Hopefully they had achieved a news blackout.

He logged on to the website of the Space Weather Prediction Center of the National Oceanographic and Atmospheric Administration. Finally, there was some good news. A coronal mass ejection had occurred and when it interacted with the earth's magnetic field it was expected to produce a geomagnetic storm of the appropriate size. In sixty hours, they would be able to carry out a successful procedure. He had no doubt about it.

The next volunteer in the temporal displacement dome would have the same abilities as the upstart Australian who had ruined the previous experiment. After that, they would have no further use for him.

The volunteer would have the power of a god. The professor was so confident of his work that he intended to be that man. Why not? It was his project after all. He should be the one to reap the rewards.

It was time to prepare. There was work to be done to make sure that everything went smoothly.

Matthew was going stir-crazy. He wasn't getting to do as much exercise as he wanted. His security was tighter and he didn't have as much access to the facility as he did when he was in the US. He figured that now that they were back in Australia, he was considered to be more of a security risk.

He was hoping to prove that true and was constantly looking for a way to escape but he wasn't having any success.

Since he was mainly confined to his room, Matthew tried to make the best of the situation and burn off some excess energy by doing some push-ups, sit-ups and any other exercise he could think of to do but it wasn't as enjoyable as any of the three disciplines of the triathlon.

My God. This place is for real, thought Cathy as she finished the induction tour. How in hell did they build this thing here without the Australians knowing? She had to stop her jaw gaping open in awe at the scope of the project, numerous times through the tour.

As it was coming to an end, her guide had received word that the head of the facility, Professor Windsor, had given the green light on the next procedure. Cathy had hoped to do a bit of poking around before her official duties started but it didn't look as though that was going to happen now. It was time for Cathy, in her guise of Rachel Black, to get to work.

She was heading to her workstation when she was spotted by the nice soldier from the plane, Ben Mitchell. He looked very upset, rather than the happy, smiling man she had experienced previously.

'Hello, Ben. You, OK?'

'Hi, Rachel. I just heard a rumour that there's been a nuclear explosion somewhere in the States but there's been a comms shutdown, so nobody seems to have the full picture.'

Cathy was stunned at the news. Surely this couldn't be true. She knew how hard the intelligence services worked to ensure that this type of thing didn't happen. 'Oh my God. Do you know where? Is there any other news?'

'Nobody knows anything else. The only ones who would know are the guys in the Communications Centre and the major and he's the one who initiated the blackout, so don't expect to get anything out of him.' He shook his head. 'Sorry, Rachel, I've got to get to my post. I'll see you later.' He gave her a half-hearted smile as he left her in the corridor.

Cathy was reconsidering her mission now. It paled into insignificance against a nuclear attack, but how could she possibly get out of here? The place had been shut down in anticipation of the next procedure and if she blew her cover, she had little doubt that Major Carmichael would cause trouble for her. He was a loaded gun waiting for something to aim at.

Reluctantly she headed towards the instrument monitoring section to start work.

Chapter 27

Two days later, General Morgan arrived unannounced at the facility in the Murchison Shire. He thought a surprise would shake things up a bit. Obviously, security wasn't as tight as he had thought if the CIA had wind of what they were doing.

Morgan had been embarrassed by General Risley calling him in and hauling him over the coals and now he was going to make sure that shit flowed downhill. Others were going to get their asses kicked.

Risley had asked if he thought that this project could help with the investigation into finding any information on the nuclear attack. Morgan had been aghast at the thought. His project was going to be used how he wanted it to.

The Chairman of the Joint Chiefs had initially wanted to shut the project down in case it came to wider attention and General Morgan had to argue to have the next procedure given the go-ahead. But that was the end of the guarantees. After that, the project could be shut down. He wasn't sure that even if he proved that it could work on every occasion, Risley wouldn't pull the plug.

If that was the case, then General Morgan intended to make sure that he was the one to benefit from the project's last hurrah. He would be the man with the power to travel through time.

One hundred and fifty million kilometres away, there were some tremendous forces being exerted on the sun. The differential rotation speeds of material at the equator and the poles was causing the lines of magnetic force to twist and stretch. One particular series was as contorted as any had been in the last two decades. Then, like a spark jumping from one point on a Tesla coil to the ground, the lines of force straightened. The sudden release of energy caused a massive coronal mass ejection, bigger and faster than had been seen in years. It started to speed towards earth.

General Morgan had checked in with security, telling them not to mention to anybody that he had arrived, then made his way to his quarters. As befitting his rank, his were the most comfortable in the facility. He unpacked and hung up some items in the closet. It had been a long trip, so he took a few minutes to freshen up. He looked at himself in the mirror. His face was becoming a little fleshier, but his stocky frame still had plenty of muscle on it. He mused that maybe it didn't have to get any older. With reflection time over, it was time to go and see the professor and get an update on how things were progressing.

The general made his way to the professor's quarters and pressed a button next to the door. He enjoyed the look of shock on the academic's face when the door had opened. Windsor had looked ready to tear strips off whoever had disturbed him, but that look had faded in an instant.

The general barged right past the other man and entered the room. 'So, professor, how are things going? When do we power up the hamster wheel?' He did enjoy pushing Windbag's buttons.

The professor looked at his watch. 'In a little under ten hours.'

'You are certain that this time the procedure is going to work? You have ironed out all of the bugs? We aren't going to end up with any road kill in the time machine?'

'I assure you, general, that there is no doubt about the success of the project. It is a mathematical certainty.'

'Glad to hear it.' Then despite already knowing the answer, the general thought he would toy with the other man a bit more. 'Who's the lucky volunteer?'

'Oh, um, er, it's the same man as last time. Yes, that's right, the same man as last time.'

General Morgan didn't become a general without being able to read other people well. He instantly knew that the professor was hiding something. What was it? It was time to turn the screws a little bit and really put the man on edge so that he would give up whatever secret he was keeping.

'You probably haven't heard yet, professor, but after this event our funding is being pulled. We're being closed down.'

'What? You can't do that! This project is history in the making.' The professor was livid.

General Morgan felt lucky to be out of the firing line. Spittle was coming out of the academic's mouth, he was so worked up. 'I don't have any say in the decision. The decision came directly from the General of the Army. If we had shown a process that was repeatable and of obvious value, then we would all still be in a job. As it is, we are lucky to have this last run at it.'

Professor Windsor stood there seething with rage.

The general moved in for the kill. 'Professor, since this is the last time, we get to do this, I have decided to be the man to undergo the process.'

'What? You can't do that! The instruments have been finely calibrated to suit the man who is already assigned.'

'I'm sure that you have enough people helping you to make sure that it's all set up properly in the time remaining. Make it work.' Bored now, the general turned to leave.

The professor could now see his carefully laid plans unravelling at the seams, his chance for glory quickly disappearing. Without thinking he picked up the one item on his desk that he valued above all others, an alabaster ashtray that had once belonged to Albert Einstein. He had paid a small fortune for it at an auction but since the non-smokers had nearly taken over the world, it was rarely used.

Today would be different.

With two large strides, he was behind the general with his arm holding the ashtray raised in the air. Too late, General Morgan sensed the movement and started to turn but the ashtray came crashing down on his head. He fell to the floor, unmoving.

The sudden act of violence drained the anger from the professor. He looked down at the general. Part of his skull had been crushed in the blow. There was no doubt that the man was dead.

Professor Windsor started doing some more calculations in his mind. If he hid him away, maybe nobody would find him until it was too late. It was only a few more hours. He tried picking the general up but the dead weight was too much for him. Grabbing the body by the boots, he started dragging it over to his closet. He opened the doors and rolled the body inside. He closed the doors again satisfied that it was hidden.

He looked around the room. There was no sign that the general had ever been there, apart from some blood on the ashtray. He carefully wiped the blood off with a tissue and put the object back in its proper place on his desk.

With that done, the professor dismissed the general from his mind and turned his attention back to the matter at hand.

He had history to make.

Chapter 28

Salman Umrani had a full list of employees of the Pakistan Atomic Energy Commission sitting on the desk in his hotel room. Headquarters had been able to obtain it for him and it had arrived just hours after he had requested it, sent in an encrypted file.

Salman had paid particular attention to those people currently working in the Design Directorate and those who had previously worked there. The CIA knew that department had been responsible for the designing and building of Pakistan's nuclear weapons, so it seemed a logical place to start.

No names had jumped out at him, so it had been a matter of working through the list. An obvious place to start was to see if any of the people were on holidays, away or absent for any reason. Any of those could be a sign that a person was on the run.

Salman was a reasonably adept hacker, but he doubted his skills would be good enough to crack the security of a country's atomic energy authority, so he had put in another request to headquarters and within an hour he had received a much smaller list.

Some of the names on that list presented possibilities. They included the supervisor in the SES, which provided engineering support throughout the agency. There was also the maintenance manager at the Karachi Nuclear Power Plant, the operations manager at Chashma Nuclear Power Plant Unit-2 and the vice-chairman of the entire agency. All of those people were likely to have the technical ability and contacts to have carried this off.

His next step would be to check on the names he had highlighted to see if there was an innocent explanation for their absences or if any of the four was likely to be the mass murderer he was looking for. Since he was already in Islamabad, he would start with the only person on the list who lived there, Dr Ahmed Barazani.

Later that evening, Salman parked up the road from the address he had been given for Barazani. It was a wealthy, tree-lined neighbourhood with a mix of modern and more traditional Pakistani architecture. He casually strolled along the road till he came to the house, a free-standing, double-storey structure, with a tall, white stone wall, bordered with darker bricks. It was a more traditional-looking house with white render, large arched doors and windows with patterned surrounds and upper floor balconies protected by stone column balustrades. There were no lights on. It was the only house in the street that was unlit.

His curiosity now piqued, Salman walked up the driveway. He was sure that the house would have an automatic light but if there was one, it didn't come on. Something crunched under his feet. Pulling a small flashlight from his pocket, he shone it down to see broken glass. Salman looked up and saw a smashed security light. Next to the light fitting was a small hole. A bullet hole?

He reached behind his back to the pistol tucked into his waistband, making sure he had quick access if required.

Not expecting an answer, he knocked on the front door. After thirty seconds of silence, Salman let go of his gun and instead reached into his pocket for a lock-pick set. Holding the flashlight between his teeth he pulled out a small offset metal rod and placed it in the door lock. Then he took a part which looked like a gun with a metal projection instead of a barrel. Maintaining pressure on the offset rod he squeezed the trigger a few times, causing the metal projection to move up and down. The whole exercise took five seconds before the door was unlocked.

As soon as he opened the door, Salman knew he had the right house. The smell was something he had experienced before, the sickly-sweet smell of a decomposing body. He brought a handkerchief up to cover his nose, breathing as shallowly as possible and stepped through the door, closing it behind him.

The body had been left a few feet inside the door, on its back. Salman didn't recognise the dead man, a task made harder by perhaps three days of lying on the floor. One thing he could tell, though, was that it wasn't Dr Barazani. He snapped a picture with his phone, sure that the analysts would be able to work out who it was. Hopefully, it was someone who deserved it.

He dialled a number from memory. When the call was answered, Salman kept the one-sided conversation short. 'It's Barazani. There's a dead body in his house. I'll send a picture for you to identify.'

In less than ten seconds, Dr Ahmed Barazani had become America's most wanted man.

With a few more keystrokes, he sent the picture through, then Salman worked his way through the house, hoping to find a clue to where Barazani had gone.

Chapter 29

More than a billion tons of material had been ejected from the sun almost ten hours previously. It had spread out as it sped towards earth, catching up with the previous CME, accelerating it and combining its energy. Now the massive magnetic field of the two coronal mass ejections blanketed the planet, causing a tremendous geomagnetic storm that was off the charts.

But apart from auroras being seen further north and south than had ever been recorded, most people on earth never felt the effects of the storm and never knew it had happened.

Major Carmichael walked into the control room. He was looking forward to the next attempt by Professor Windbag to bend time to his will. The previous efforts had been a source of amusement to him, but this time there seemed to be an air about the man that promised something more.

Once again, he was conflicted about the outcome. He wanted the United States Army to be able to do it. That would make them unbeatable. What he didn't want was the professor hailed as a hero. That would be unimaginable. Maybe there was a compromise, but he just couldn't think of it at the moment.

There was the professor now, hmm-ing and haa-ing over various monitors, making sure it was all running smoothly.

If the upcoming procedure went well, they wouldn't have any use for Fraser any more. He thought that was a pity. The major kind of liked the young Australian. He had performed well when out in the field, earning his respect, though that wouldn't stop him from doing what was necessary. Fraser had to die. He couldn't be released and he couldn't stay locked up forever. Sooner or later, he would use his talent and be able to escape.

The major looked up at the clock. It was just over thirty minutes to go before the next attempt in the time machine.

He wondered where General Morgan was. He knew the general was coming, he wouldn't miss the next live trial, but he hadn't been given the details. He smiled to himself. It was just like the old man to try to catch him out.

The major walked over to the closest desk and picked up the phone. He pressed a button on the base unit.

'Security,' answered the voice at the other end.

'Carmichael here. When are we expecting the general to arrive?'

'Uh, sir, um, he arrived about, let me check the log, about nine hours or so ago.'

'What? Why wasn't I informed?'

'Uh, general's orders, sir. He wanted his arrival kept quiet. Surprise inspection or something I guess.'

'You guess? Well, where is he now?' People in the control room were now looking at the major as he was getting louder, talking with the man at the other end of the phone.

There was silence on the other end of the line for a few seconds. 'Sir. We don't know.'

'Try paging him. Then I want a full security sweep of the facility. Find him.' The major slammed the handset back down onto the base.

Carmichael turned his attention back to the control room. The professor had gone and everybody else was at great pains to make sure they were busy. *Where the fuck is he?*

Twenty minutes later the major called security again. 'Have you found the general yet?'

'No, sir.'

'He is still here in the facility somewhere, isn't he?'

'Yes, sir. He hasn't logged out.'

The phone was in danger of breaking as the major slammed it down again. He turned to address everyone in the control room. 'Right. Everyone listen up. I want this shut down now. If the general's missing, we aren't going ahead.' He pointed at the man with the greying hair that he knew was the professor's deputy, Jeff Caldwell. 'Kill it now.'

The man pushed a few buttons on his console but when he looked up the clock was still counting down. He went through the procedure again and still the clock was moving backwards. 'Sorry, sir. It won't stop.' Three minutes to go.

'What do you mean "it won't stop"?'

'I'm locked out of the abort sequence.'

'What? Who has the authority to do that?'

'Only Professor Windsor.'

'Don't you have to give the system the go-ahead before it moves to the final stage?'

'I just checked. It's been set to automatic. I can't stop it.'

'Can anyone shut this down?'

People typed instructions into their consoles but the clock relentlessly continued towards zero.

At two minutes to zero, the shutters opened and retracted into the roof. Every eye in the room was drawn to the temporal displacement dome. The professor was standing inside, naked, his already pale body startlingly white under the lights.

The major was the first to speak. 'What the fuck is going on? What is he doing in there?' He picked up the phone again and pressed buttons.

'Security.'

'Get a team to the time machine now. Arrest the professor. If he resists, shoot him.' He had already hung up the phone before he had heard an answer.

Even though he knew the glass barrier in front of him was bullet and blast proof, Major Carmichael was still sorely tempted to empty his service pistol at the professor, but he knew all that would likely achieve was a ricochet hitting someone in the control room. He fumed as the clock reached ten seconds.

When the clock reached zero, there was a flash of light.

Chapter 30

With everyone focused on the upcoming experiment, Cathy found it easy to slip away from her workstation. She hoped to be able to get access to Matthew Fraser and get his side of the story. From her observations, he wasn't a willing participant in whatever was going on here.

Cathy still had no idea, if that's what had happened, why they would kidnap him, drag him halfway around the world and then bring him back.

The whole scenario made little sense to her. Apparently, the whole purpose of this facility was to build a time machine. One of the co-workers in her section had told her that they had achieved time travel but only with inanimate objects. Was that why Fraser was here, to live trial a time machine? It sounded ludicrous when she said it out loud.

What did she do if he was here against his will? Cathy's instincts and sense of justice told her that she had to help him get away. On the other hand, if he was here willingly, could she afford to divulge that she was an FBI agent? She longed for a straightforward case where the good guys wore white hats.

Cathy reasoned that if she was able to get Fraser out of this place and he was willing to testify against Carmichael, then at least she would have some justice and the major would end up in jail.

She made her way to the accommodation level. She arrived at her room and looked up the corridor. There was a guard sitting on a chair outside a door. She was sure it had to be Fraser's room. She was contemplating how to get access when three soldiers came running towards the man at the door. There was an exchange between the men, then all four of them ran past her towards the elevators.

Cathy stood there for a moment wondering what had just happened. Was there some sort of crisis? She decided not to look a gift horse in the mouth and walked up the corridor. She knocked on the door.

'What do you want?' came a voice from the room.

'Is that Matthew Fraser?'

'Oh, for God's sake. You know it is.'

'Matthew, are you being held here against your will?'

'What? Of course, I am. What a dumb question.'

'Matthew, my name is Cathy Owens. I'm a special agent with the FBI. I need to talk with you.'

'Well talk. I'm not going anywhere. The door's locked.'

'I'm a bit exposed here. If they catch me talking to you, I'll be in big trouble.'

'Look, lady, you're the one who wanted to talk with me. If you're too scared, then don't bother. Just go away.'

Cathy looked up and down the corridor. There was nobody in sight and she couldn't hear anyone nearby. 'Fine. Listen. I'm investigating the deaths of two men about four years ago. I suspect that Major Carmichael has something to do with it but I can't find any solid evidence against him.'

'I wouldn't put anything past that cold-blooded bastard. He's already tried to kill me more than once.'

'But you're still alive.' Cathy wondered how Fraser was still breathing if the major had attempted to do him in. The major struck her as being especially effective in that area.

'It's a long story,' yelled Matthew from inside the room. 'I'll tell you all about it if you get me out of this place.'

'Matthew, are you prepared to testify against him, that he kidnapped you and is holding you here? At least that way we can be sure he spends a long time in prison.'

'If it gets that psycho off the streets, I'll do anything you want.'

That was when alarm blasted out of the speakers in the ceiling. A few moments later the ground started to shake.

Chapter 31

The major looked from the control room to the time machine. The flash of light had died down. Unfortunately, the professor was still there and he was in one piece. The crazy academic was looking around, checking that his pasty arms and legs were in their correct places.

The loudspeaker startled the major from his scrutiny. 'Security for Major Carmichael.'

He picked a handset from the nearest console and pushed a button. 'Carmichael here.'

'Major. We've found the general. In the professor's quarters.'

'Yes?'

'Sir, he's dead.'

Shit, thought the major. That man had been his mentor for almost his entire military career. He owed his rise through the ranks to the old man, not to mention the sizeable chunk of money in a secret bank account.

He smiled to himself. At least there was one good thing. Finally, he could take out his frustrations on the old coot. The professor was going to pay for the years that he had made life miserable for everyone.

The heavy metal door to the room holding the time machine opened and four of his men, a sergeant and three privates, came through. The major reached for the intercom button on the console in front of him. Leaning forward he said, 'Arrest the professor.'

The sergeant nodded his acknowledgement.

Three of the soldiers took up positions around the dome, with their guns aimed at the professor. The sergeant walked to a control station and pressed a button and with a barely audible hiss, the dome started to rise, leaving the naked man standing there, staring at the soldiers.

Major Carmichael could see the professor talking with the men surrounding him. He leaned forward again to press a button to open the microphone into the dome room.

'I can feel the gravitons within me. Billions upon billions of them.' Professor Windsor lifted his right arm, looking at his hand as he wiggled his fingers.

The major looked at Jeff Caldwell. 'What is he talking about? What's a graviton?'

'Uh, in layman's terms, a graviton is a hypothetical particle responsible for generating gravity, but they are incredibly weak. So, it takes a massive object with lots of gravitons to have more than a negligible effect.'

'So how can he feel them?'

'I'm not sure. You shouldn't be able to feel them. I know they're looking for gravitons at CERN in their Large Hadron Collider. Maybe we've caused some sort of effect here with our own particle accelerator.'

The professor raised his other arm so that they were both above his head. The sergeant took this as a sign that the other man was surrendering and moved forward to take him into custody.

The major watched the professor turn his gaze to the sergeant, who suddenly started to lift off the floor. 'What's happening to me?' he screamed.

'Shoot him!' yelled the major.

All three of the soldiers fired, but incredibly the bullets stopped about a foot in front of the professor and just floated there. A second later they dropped to the floor.

The professor waved a dismissive hand at the men and they flew backwards to crash into the nearest wall and then fell to the ground. The sergeant, who had almost reached the roof, dropped like a stone, then lay unmoving.

The professor looked up at the control room. 'Close the shutters, quickly,' said the major to Caldwell, who reached out to press a button. Before he could make contact, he started to rise out of his chair towards the ceiling.

A woman next to Caldwell screamed.

That signalled a rush towards the door as the people in the control room tried to get away from what was happening in front of them.

A cackling filled the room from the intercom speakers. The major could see the professor standing naked in the dome room with his head thrown back, laughing. 'I can feel the power in me. Dark energy is mine to command.'

The major spoke to the few people still at their seats. 'Time to leave. Everybody out.' He walked over to the wall, punched out a little glass panel and pressed the evacuation alarm button within. He looked up at Jeff Caldwell, who was stuck against the ceiling, waving his arms and legs frantically.

'Help me!' the man yelled.

The major considered for an instant, then climbed up on a console. He reached out to Caldwell, who grabbed his hand. The uniformed man pulled at the scientist but wasn't able to move him down from the ceiling. The man seemed stuck.

There was a scream from the loud speakers. The major looked to see the professor clutching at his head. The windows in the control room started to bow in and out. He jumped to the floor. 'Sorry, Jeff.'

'Wait. Don't leave me!' he screamed but one second later he was by himself in the control room as the major went out the door. The windows exploded inwards, sending razor sharp shrapnel flying though the room. Caldwell was struck by hundreds of pieces and was dead in an instant.

Small objects such as pens and coffee cups started vibrating on the desks. The glass shards on the floor joined them rattling around. The objects started inching along the ground. The smallest pieces lifted off the floor and started floating towards the dome room, picking up speed as they moved. Larger objects in the room also started to vibrate and inch their way towards the shattered window.

Within moments, any object not secured to the floor was flying through the shattered windows, including the unfortunate Jeff Caldwell.

Then the whole complex began to shake as though struck by an earthquake.

Chapter 32

Cathy was standing outside the door, trying to maintain her balance as the floor vibrated beneath her. The alarm was still blasting out of the speakers. Matthew called out from inside the room. 'If you're going to get me out, now would be a good time.'

Cathy looked at the door handle. *I might as well try*, she thought. The door was locked. She looked around. 'Okay, I see something. Hold on.'

'I'm not going anywhere.'

Cathy shuffled up the corridor, holding onto the wall. She reached a fire extinguisher and lifted it from its bracket. She made her way slowly back down towards Matthew's room. Once there she lifted the extinguisher above her head and brought it down onto the door handle. *Tough*, she thought as the door showed little signs of damage.

She lifted the extinguisher again and smashed the handle as hard as she could. The handle sheared off. Cathy drove the extinguisher into the door near the lock and the door swung open.

'Knock, knock,' she said as she saw Matthew holding onto the end of the bed to maintain his balance.

'Oh, it's you,' Matthew said. 'The lady from the plane.'

'That's right. We weren't introduced. Cathy Owens, FBI.'

'Matthew Fraser, no fancy initials. So, what's with the alarm?'

'Luckily, I've just done the induction tour of this place. That's the evacuation alarm. Something serious must have gone wrong. We need to get out of here.'

Matthew let go of the bed, struggling to stand as the shaking increased. 'No kidding. Lead the way.'

'Follow me,' said Cathy backing out of the doorway. As Matthew followed her out, she said, 'Once the evac alarm sounds the elevators are disabled and door locks on the stairs turn off to allow a fast exit. We need to get to the stairs. There are some at both ends of this corridor. Quick, this way.'

Cathy started to move off to her left but stopped when she saw what was happening at the end of the corridor. The walls, floor and roof seemed to be warping as if they were elastic and being stretched. The effect diminished closer to her but was slowly moving up the hallway.

'Holy shit,' said Matthew. 'I vote for the other way.'

They turned and ran down the corridor. As they ran the lights blinked out. A second later the emergency lights kicked in, though it was at a lower level of brightness.

They made it to a door with a lit EXIT sign above it and opened the door. A few people were already on the staircase making their way up. Matthew looked back to see the stretching effect slowly making its way up the hall. Wide eyed, he closed the door behind him and followed the FBI lady as she started to climb.

Major Carmichael headed straight for the stairs when he left for the control room. Everyone in the complex was expected to know the evacuation alarm so he was confident that he didn't need to shepherd anyone along.

That belief was shattered a few moments later when a lady in a lab coat opened a door and stepped into the corridor. 'What's going on?' she asked as the major jogged past.

'That's the evacuation alarm. Get to the surface.'

She blanched. 'Oh no.' She tried to close the door behind her but it jammed, the side of the door nearest the control room obviously warped. She started at it for a second, puzzled as to what was happening. She reached her hand out to touch the door and then screamed as her arm stretched to almost twice its normal length.

The major looked back to see what the scream was about and was shocked at the sight that confronted him. The lady in the lab coat was stretching as though she was made of plasticine. The walls around her looked to be doing the same.

The major turned ran for his life.

Inside the dome room, the professor was screaming an endless scream.

To an outside observer, he would have looked as though he was shrinking slowly. Any item that had moved into the room had stopped about a foot away from him, slowly compressing into a solid mass, all of the air spaces crushed.

The walls and floor were slowly being drawn towards the man, the solid objects no match for the gravitational force being exerted.

He was encased in a solid ball of matter that was slowly growing as more and more material was added to it.

Chapter 33

Matthew and Cathy were running up the stairs with a group of other people. They could have run faster but they were encouraging the scientists and technicians, who didn't look like they took a lot of exercise, to get a move on.

Two soldiers caught up with the group and kept on going straight past. Both Cathy and Matthew noted the look of terror on their faces. They increased their efforts trying to herd the slower people along.

'Do you think whatever that is, is still behind us?' Cathy asked Matthew.

'Judging by those two guys, I would say yes. Come on, people, we need to get out of here,' he yelled.

They heard another set of footsteps coming up from below but neither bothered to look, being too busy with the people in front of them.

The next thing Matthew knew was that he was being tackled into the wall. 'This is all your fault!' yelled the man who had crashed into him.

Stunned, Matthew found himself on his back with blows raining down, with the other man sitting on him. He tried to cover up, finally recognising Corporal Crimmons, the man with the lump on his head.

'I didn't do anything,' he managed to get out.

'I don't care.' Crimmons continued trying to punch Matthew but was stopped a second later by a stunning kick to the head, which forced him clear of the Australian.

He looked up at Cathy standing a few feet away. 'You bitch. I'm gonna kill you,' he yelled. He was on his feet in an instant, charging at her.

Matthew stuck out his leg, tripping the soldier and Cathy took the opportunity to deliver another high kick to the soldier's head which launched him over the railing.

Crimmons screamed momentarily but managed to hook his fingers over the stairs to halt his fall. Matthew and Cathy exchanged looks, wondering what to do with the man.

The options decreased dramatically a second later when Crimmons started screaming again. From their viewpoint, they could both see the soldier's legs stretching.

The screams were snuffed out a moment later when he let go, to be swallowed up by the expanding gravity field.

Matthew and Cathy turned and ran up the stairs as fast as they could. At least the people they had been pushing along had kept moving and were near the top.

They all reached the exit and went through.

Matthew found himself in a cow milking shed, the exit door disguised by what looked like milking equipment.

He glanced around. The times he had come through here had been at night and poorly lit. Now he could see the scope of the operation in front of him properly, he was impressed. The smell, though, was unmistakably cow shit.

Matthew looked at Cathy and smiled, waving a hand back and forth in front of his nose. 'Excuse me.'

Cathy rolled her eyes at the crude humour but found it hard not to smile. She looked and saw there were about twenty people gathered near their exit. Fifty metres away near the other end of the milking shed there was a similar sized group. She calculated that less than half of the personnel working here had escaped.

She started waving to attract attention. 'We need to move further away,' she yelled. 'Whatever that effect was, it's still coming.'

People started to move quickly, then at the exit at the other end of the shed, Major Carmichael burst through the door. 'What are you all doing standing around?' he yelled at the people. 'Get out of here. Now.' That was when he looked across to the other group and saw Matthew. 'Shit.' The major grabbed a soldier by the arm and pointed at Matthew. 'That man there caused this. Don't let him get away.'

Private Ben Mitchell shrugged off the major's hand. 'I don't think so. Sir.'

The two soldiers who had run past Matthew and Cathy in their wild flight up the stairs, turned to Matthew with hostile looks. One of them drew a pistol from a holster on his hip. 'I didn't do anything,' said Matthew, holding up a hand, slowly backing away from the men.

'Don't you move.'

Matthew continued to move backwards. 'It wasn't me.' Unfortunately, he didn't notice that one cow had left a mess behind that hadn't yet been cleaned up and when he stood in it his foot slipped out from underneath him. The soldier was already spooked and the sudden movement tipped him over the edge. He fired his gun.

Matthew's world dissolved.

Matthew returned to consciousness on his back, a man sitting astride him, punching at him. A kick to the head of his attacker gave him a moment of respite.

The man, Crimmons, was up in a flash, glaring at Cathy. 'You bitch. I'm gonna kill you.' He charged at her but Matthew stuck out his leg and tripped the soldier. Cathy launched another kick to the head of the man and he flew over the staircase railing, screaming. His scream was cut short when he managed to grab the edge of the stairs and arrest his fall.

Matthew already knew what was coming. 'We need to go now and when we get to the top of the stairs turn right and stay out of sight. Trust me.' Cathy nodded her agreement.

They ran up the stairs ignoring the short-lived scream behind them. When they reached the top, Matthew turned to the right, relieved that the people there were looking in the other direction.

Followed by Cathy, he ran for the door of the shed and stepped behind it. Now outside, Cathy asked, 'What are you doing? We need to help these people.'

'We're not going to be able to help anyone if we're dead. Have a look if you want but stay out of sight.'

Cathy squatted as low as she could and looked around the door. She was just in time to see Major Carmichael burst through the door near the far end of the shed. 'What are you all doing standing around?' he yelled at the people. 'Get out of here. Now.'

People at his end started running away from the shed. Those at the exit Cathy and Matthew had run through started moving towards the far end and had made it about halfway when the floor in front of them started to collapse.

In the dome room, not that it was recognisable as such, more and more matter was being drawn into the mass surrounding the professor. The material was becoming so dense that it appeared to be completely solid and more was being added to it by the second.

In the middle of the mass, Professor Windsor was shrinking, his body becoming denser as he became smaller. The screaming had stopped but the pain was still intense.

Eventually, he became microscopic, so small that he was no longer able to transfer oxygen molecules from his lungs to his blood and the professor suffocated.

When he expired, the effect that had been occurring suddenly stopped.

Professor Windsor had wanted to go down in history and his final achievement was worthy of being noted for its destructive force, but few people would ever hear of his work and no-one would ever find his body or mourn for him.

The major stood and watched as people tried to get out of the newly formed hole. He half expected them to start stretching like the woman near the control room but nothing happened. Whatever had caused the effect seemed to have stopped.

'It's over. Calm down!' he yelled at the group of people in the hole. He turned to some of the personnel nearby. 'Come and help me.'

Those above ground assisted those below as they climbed out of the hole. The major spoke to the two soldiers once they were on solid footing. 'Did you see anyone else get out?'

Both men shook their heads. 'No, sir.'

The major looked around thoughtfully then, his decision made, turned back to the group. 'We're abandoning this site for the time being. Private,' he said to the soldier, 'load everyone into transportation. We're heading back to the States.'

Chapter 34

Matthew and Cathy had remained hidden while the facility was being evacuated. Both had stayed quiet, not wanting to draw any attention to themselves but once the last truck had driven off, Cathy turned to the Australian.

'Now would you mind telling me just what is going on?'

Matthew looked seriously at the FBI agent. 'What I say might shock you.'

'Listen. I've just escaped from a facility whose primary objective appears to have been time travel. I watched solid objects bending like they were rubber and people stretching like they were made of Play-Doh. I don't think anything you say is going to shock me.'

'I can travel back in time.'

'Maybe I was wrong.'

'It's true. I can travel back in time. It's been happening to me ever since I accidentally stumbled into this area a couple of months ago.'

Matthew went on to tell Cathy his story from the time of his trip to the Murchison Shire up until she was standing outside his door a short while ago. Cathy blanched when he told her about her dying in the plane flight to Australia.

'Wow. What a story. So that's how you knew to warn everyone on the plane. And that's how you knew to turn right when we reached the emergency exit.'

'That's right. I'd been through it once already and that occasion didn't work out too well. I got shot.' He paused for a second. 'So now it's your turn. Why are you here?'

Years of training were overcome by an instinct to trust the man in front of her. 'I probably shouldn't be telling you this but I'm investigating the deaths of two men from about four years ago. I think that Major Carmichael had something to do with it and I was undercover trying to gather evidence against him. With your testimony, I could make sure that he goes to prison for a long time, even if it's not for the original crime that I was looking into.'

'If it helps put that psycho behind bars, I'm in.'

At that, Cathy smiled at him and it was the first time in months that Matthew could remember being happy.

Cathy was still smiling. 'How about we see if they've left anything around here that we can drive. I don't feel like walking.'

'I hope whatever we find has keys in it or they teach you how to hot-wire cars at FBI school. Otherwise, I'm not going to be much help, I'm afraid.'

Cathy smiled again at the Australian. The men she normally worked with wouldn't have shared that with her. They would rather be shot than admit they didn't know how to do something. It was refreshing that a man was happy for her to be the capable person. She was beginning to like him.

They scouted around the farm, but it seemed that any vehicle that was useable had been taken in the evacuation of the site.

Matthew pointed to a large shed. 'Let's look in there.'

A few moments later they had the doors open and were looking inside. 'I guess it's better than walking,' said Cathy. 'I'll toss you to see who drives.'

'As long as you remember what side of the road to drive on, it's all yours.'

Three hours later a big, green, John Deere tractor pulled into the Murchison Roadhouse. Despite the enclosed cabin, it hadn't been a quiet or comfortable ride. There was only one seat, so Matthew had to position himself awkwardly to allow Cathy access to the controls.

Initially, Cathy had to concentrate to move the strange vehicle, but after a short while she was able to let her mind wander and think about other things.

'Matthew, I need to talk with you about something really important,' she had said, almost having to yell to make herself heard.

'You have a captive audience,' Matthew had yelled back.

'Just before it all went wrong back at the complex there was some really disturbing news.'

'I've just about had my fill of disturbing news for a while, but for you, I'm prepared to hear a little bit more.' Matthew smiled but realised that Cathy couldn't see him. 'Sorry. Bad joke. What's wrong?'

'I ran into Private Mitchell. He told me that there had been a nuclear attack on the US but he didn't have any more details.'

'Wow. Yes, that is disturbing. You don't know anything else?'

'Nothing. Not where it happened, how big it was, how many were killed. Nothing.'

'So, I suppose being in the FBI, that you'll want to head back and work on the case.'

'Matthew, this is going to be the single biggest case ever in the country's history. Everything that we've ever done before was just for practice. This is going to be the crime-fighting Superbowl.'

'Well, that's really bad timing. I would have thought that this was a big case and I was kind of looking forward to you being around to, you know, tidy up loose ends.'

In spite of the seriousness of what they were discussing, Cathy smiled at his clumsy attempt at flirting. 'Matthew, I'm going to ask you something really important and I hope you're going to agree.'

'So, out with it then.'

'Will you come to the States with me?'

'What for?'

'Your ability to go back in time could prove invaluable in our efforts to solve this case.'

Matthew looked quizzically at Cathy, who turned her head to study him. 'I'm serious,' she said. 'Look at what happened to you any number of times in the last few months and I've seen it myself. If something goes wrong, you have the ability to do it all again and get it right.'

'It's a one-off thing though,' he replied. 'I only get one shot at doing it again and if I get it wrong, it's all over.'

'Well, that's one more shot than most people get. We could be talking about saving millions of lives here. If there's one nuclear attack that's happened, there could be more.'

Matthew pondered that for a moment. 'You saved my life back there by getting me out of that room. I guess I trust you. As long as I'm working with you, I'll do it.'

'Great.'

'But I need to do one thing first.'

'What's that?'

'I need to give my mum a call and make sure she's alright. Then, I guess, I need to let her know that I'll be out of town for a while. Again.'

The mood in the roadhouse was sombre. The mainly male audience was staring at the television. The station was a twenty-four-hour news channel. The only thing being shown was the nuclear explosion off the coast of San Francisco. Both Cathy and Matthew looked at the screen.

The networks had been spoiled for choice of footage to show off the mushroom cloud rising in the distance. Thousands of cell phones had caught the image and after that the professional cameramen had caught up, being able to zoom in a lot closer and show much finer detail. Then the scene switched to the carnage on the roads and to the thousands who had flooded into the hospitals.

Cathy was shocked at the attack on her country. Instantly, she resolved to stop this from ever happening again.

Matthew could only imagine the devastation that would have been caused if something like that happened in Perth. He looked at Cathy and saw the determination on her face. He was glad he had agreed to help her, though he still didn't know how that was going to work.

The ticker tape display at the bottom of the screen was showing local headlines. One of these was of a minor earthquake in the Murchison region measuring 3.7 on the Richter scale. Matthew shook his head when it came to him that the last few months of his life had ended with a blip on some scientist's monitor. If it wasn't important to them, then he was glad he had agreed to go with Cathy.

Cathy and Matthew both made calls from the payphone in the roadhouse. Matthew was as relieved to talk with his mother as was she to talk with him. 'Oh, Matty. I was so worried about you. Why didn't you call?' His mother always had a way of making him feel guilty about the time between visits or calls, but this time she just sounded relieved to hear from him.

'I'm sorry, Mum, but I've been at a special training camp and I wasn't allowed to call anyone.'

'Hmmmm.'

'Anyway, it's finished now.'

'So you'll be coming to see me soon?'

'Look, Mum, I've met someone and I'm going to go and visit.'

'A girl?'

'Yes, Mum. A girl.'

'Oooh. What's her name?'

'Cathy.'

'Is she pretty?'

'Yes, Mum. She's pretty.'

'Where does she live?'

'In America.'

'America? I suppose that means it'll be ages before I see you again?'

'Maybe not. Look, Mum, my lift is here. I have to go.'

'Matthew.'

'Yes, Mum?'

'I love you.'

'I love you too. Speak to you soon.' He hung up before the goodbyes dragged out any further and looked for Cathy.

With her call, Cathy was able to arrange transport for the both of them to the US, starting from Perth. She also issued an order for the arrest of Major John Carmichael.

After that, they asked around the people in the roadhouse and were able to hitch a ride with the driver of a road train which was heading to Perth. Cathy didn't understand what a road train was until she stepped into the cabin of a truck with two trailers behind it. She was surprised to hear they can be even longer.

Chapter 35

Ahmed Barazani was a worried man.

His options for going to ground had been seriously curtailed now that al-Qaeda had tried to kill him. He had thought they would be his main source of aid once the bombs started exploding.

He was also doubting the approach of al-Qaeda in trying to build the terror of the Americans by staggering the explosions. He had initially wanted them to all go off at once but had been told the effect would be greater if they had time to think between explosions, as the Japanese had done in World War II. They had folded like a deck of cards after the second explosion. Imagine if there were three.

He cursed his bad luck. If only the bomb had gone off in the intended location in Las Vegas. He had no idea why the device was still on board the ship off the coast of California when it exploded but there was nothing he could do about it now. At least then, the Americans would have taken a much longer time to fit the pieces of the puzzle together and perhaps his erstwhile allies in al-Qaeda wouldn't have been so quick to act against him.

He looked around his dingy hotel room. Threadbare carpet, threadbare bedspread and, of course, a threadbare towel. The only good thing was that the poor lighting didn't show up all the dirt and dust on every surface. Ahmed looked at himself in the hotel room mirror, glad that the spots that showed on his face were actually fly specs on the glass.

He was well known throughout the country, so he had not shaved since the incident with the man from al-Qaeda, and the stubbly beard he was growing was much greyer than his moustache. Despite the seriousness of the situation, he still found this annoying, a slight against his manhood. He had also stopped parting his hair on the left and tried a brushed-back look, this time irritated at finding that his hair was looking thinner than it used to be.

He thought he looked different enough to fool a casual observer, but he knew the Americans had sophisticated facial recognition software and undoubtedly his former allies had operatives clever enough to see through his amateurish attempts at disguise.

Ahmed had, over the period of a few weeks before the first explosion, drawn all of his money out of the bank, so he felt that he could survive almost indefinitely or until he was eventually tracked down. This hotel certainly wasn't a drain on his resources; the standard of care was only a step above being Spartan. Definitely not what he had become used to in his highly paid government position.

He only hoped that he remained free long enough to watch and savour the damage that was to be inflicted on America. After that, he could die a happy man.

Ahmed had purchased an old car with cash the day after the incident with the al-Qaeda operative at his house and had made his way to Karachi. Just. The car had died a few streets from where he wanted to go and he had left it there and walked the rest of the way.

He figured that Karachi would be easier to hide in, with a population of over twenty-five million people. He based himself in Liaquatabad, a lower middle-class neighbourhood, where he thought that nobody would ever notice him.

Since the hotel's facilities didn't run to room service, Ahmed decided to go out to get some dinner. There were street markets dotted through the area, so Ahmed knew he would be able eat without spending too much money.

On a whim, he turned left when he exited the hotel and joined the throng of people, enjoying the anonymity of the crowd. It seemed that every moment in Karachi was rush hour, people jammed together in a procession through the streets, the colourful ethnic clothes of many people counteracting the dull Western styles of others. Modern stores and cafes competed with the street vendors' carts, some selling food, some selling clothes or any other item to make a few rupees.

The scents from the food vendors' carts set Ahmed's tastebuds watering.

The first vendor he passed was offering broasted chicken, a crispy fried chicken that was popular fare in the city. The next was selling bun kebabs, spicy, slow-cooked beef in a sweetened bun, but Ahmed couldn't go past the stall promising the best chicken chutney rolls in all Karachi. The chicken tikka pieces in a paratha roll were a favourite of his since boyhood.

As he ate, Ahmed strolled along, feeling at peace for the first time in days. As he wiped away the chutney running down his chin, thoughts of nuclear weapons or al-Qaeda didn't enter his mind.

Ahmed turned down a narrow alley, wondering what sights he would see at the other end and looking forward to the surprise.

His delight turned to concern a few seconds later. Two men stepped out of the shadows. They were dressed in jeans and grubby t-shirts and seemed to be holding clubs of some sort. Ahmed decided on discretion and turned around to go back only to find his way blocked by another two men, similarly dressed and similarly armed. They were both much younger and bigger than he was, though the one on the left was a bit smaller than his friend and had a patch over his right eye.

Ahmed cursed his stupidity. He had heard about street gangs operating in the area. In fact, it was one of the reasons he chose this area to lie low in. Hopefully nobody would expect to find him in such a place. Now, though, it looked as if the decision was going to backfire.

Ahmed looked both ways. Neither was appealing, but at least the way he had come from had more people who might help, if only they saw him.

He charged at the man with the eye patch, but he may as well have run into a brick wall. Ahmed rebounded off the man and then his world went dark when a cricket stump crashed into the back of his head.

Salman Umrani had no doubts about the guilt of Dr Ahmed Barazani but if anyone did have any, they would have been quashed when they read his bank statements. Barazani had systematically cleaned out his accounts over the past few weeks and now he was on the run with a substantial amount of money.

His station chief had told Salman that Barazani was suspected of now being in Iran. A man matching his description had been seen at Teheran's Mehrabad International Airport. All possible resources in the country were looking for him.

Nothing was being left to chance, however. Other nearby countries were also on full alert as were the major cities in Pakistan. Salman was assigned Karachi.

Without any definite information to guide him, Salman tried to get into Barazani's head. Where would he go if he was America's most wanted man? One tactic employed by fugitives was to pick expensive hotels, not expecting that anyone would look for them in elegant surroundings. He figured that since Barazani was well known, rich hotels would be too risky.

So, even if he eliminated those areas, the city was just too big for one man to find another man without help.

Salman decided to make contact with a series of informants he had cultivated over the years and make the search a lot easier. With the reward he was offering, if Barazani was here, he would be found.

Chapter 36

Matthew and Cathy were in a plane approaching Dulles airport in the early hours of the morning. It seemed to be an unnecessarily complicated journey, flying within Australia from Perth to Brisbane, then changing planes for the flight to Los Angeles and a final flight to Washington.

At least the flights had been business class. To Matthew, this was an immeasurable improvement on the standard of comfort he had experienced flying with the US Army. For a start, there was in-flight entertainment that didn't involve soldiers swapping war stories about their recent exploits. He watched a couple of movies, staying clear of sci-fi.

He had also been able to catch up on some sleep. It was restful and refreshing as it was the first time in months that he had felt free.

Matthew looked at the beautiful woman sitting next to him. She was breathing quietly, eyes closed, with the seat reclined, allowing her to be almost in a lying position. *A romance movie sounds better*, he thought, just before Cathy snored noisily. Almost as loud as a starter's pistol. Matthew grinned to himself.

The captain's voice came over the loudspeaker letting them know they were about to begin their descent. Cathy stirred in her seat then stretched and yawned. She looked at Matthew and smiled. Matthew returned the smile. 'Hello, sleepyhead.' Then as she realised where she was, he watched the curtains being drawn on her expression and Cathy was all business again.

'How long till we land?'

'We've just started our descent.'

'Good.'

They were met at the airport by two of Cathy's colleagues, Ted Branson and James Cummings. To Matthew, they looked interchangeable. Both were the same build and height, an inch or so shorter than himself. They had similar facial features and wore the same dark suit and polished shoes. The Aussie and the female FBI agent were whisked off the plane before anyone else was allowed to exit. If Matthew's presence was an issue, the men didn't show it.

'Poor suckers,' said Branson, or was it Cummings, as they walked through the terminal, looking at the long lines of people waiting to go through security screening. 'They'll be here for hours.'

'At least they're being allowed to fly around the country,' replied the other one. 'If it was me, I'd be grounding all flights till we have this guy in custody and are sure there aren't any more bombs.'

'So, we know who it is then?' asked Cathy.

'Yeah. Pakistani national, name of Ahmed Barazani. Works for their atomic energy authority. CIA identified him and to say there's a massive manhunt underway would be an understatement.'

Matthew listened in to the conversation between the three agents, dismayed at the thought that there could be more bombs out there and more than a little nervous at the thought of being vaporised by a nuclear device. *Oh well. I'm here now*, he thought. *I'll help if I can; not that I know anything about atom bombs.*

Matthew couldn't help himself and had to change the topic of conversation to something a little less disastrous. 'Did you guys manage to catch up with Major Carmichael?'

Branson turned to face Matthew. 'We traced an army flight which ended up at Laguna Airfield in Arizona. We detained everyone on the flight. They'll all be answering questions for weeks about what they were doing in Australia, but Carmichael wasn't on board. He might have decided to stay in Australia or he might have other ways to get back to the States. It doesn't matter. We'll get him eventually.'

Matthew was unconvinced at the last statement and turned to Cathy, who looked at him apologetically and shrugged.

Matthew had officially been to the United States before when competing in triathlons and much more recently as an unofficial guest of the US Army, but he had never been to Washington. He was a bit disappointed that it was night and he didn't get the full tourist treatment, but he still stared out the car window, keen to see everything he could that the city had to offer.

He caught sight of the brightly lit Washington Monument and was amazed at how tall it was and how it stood out over the surrounding area.

They pulled into the carpark at the FBI headquarters around five in the morning and Matthew was surprised at how busy it was at that time of the day. He mentioned this to Cathy.

She gave him a look a teacher would give a slow child. 'Nuclear explosion.'

'Oh. Right.'

Despite the mystique associated with the organisation, the outside of the building didn't impress him that much. It was like a huge stone block with doors and windows carved out. There were five floors above ground level but then it seemed someone had placed a lid on the top of half the structure. It protruded over the building like a visor on a cap. Not what he had expected. Huge concrete planter boxes served as protection against vehicle attack around the entrance. Matthew looked up to see the name above the door. It proclaimed it as the J. Edgar Hoover FBI Building.

Now he started to feel a sense of the power in the building. Even in Australia, the name of the former director was respected, maybe even feared.

Inside, apart from enhanced security, it was like any other office building, but somehow it was more than that. The people moving around the foyer were people who were dedicated to bringing the worst of the worst to justice. There on the wall, in letters six inches high, was their mission statement: "To protect the American people and uphold the constitution of the United States."

He noticed a sign pointing to a gift shop. 'Do you get tourists coming through here?' he asked.

'We do at the moment. It was stopped for a while after 9-11 but we're back open for business.'

After checking in at reception, Matthew was given a visitor's badge and they made their way to the fourth floor. There was cubicle after cubicle in the centre of the massive space and offices lined along the walls. Branson and Cummings left them to go back to their own duties.

'Do you have an office or a cubicle?' asked Matthew.

Cathy pointed. 'That's my office there.'

'It's not very big.'

'It's better than a cubicle.'

Matthew nodded. 'Now what?'

'Now we go and see my boss and try to convince him that having you work with us on this is a good idea.' Cathy knocked on the door.

'Enter,' boomed a voice from inside.

Cathy opened the door and they walked in. The biggest man that Matthew had ever seen stood up to shake his hand. 'Special Agent in Charge Arnold Wilson,' said the giant as they shook hands. A friendly, gap-toothed smile made the Aussie a bit more comfortable.

'Matthew Fraser.'

Wilson sat down, then turned to Cathy. 'So, Special Agent Owens, perhaps you will enlighten me as to why you thought it was necessary to bring Mr Fraser halfway around the world.'

Cathy swallowed at the formal tone of the question. 'Sir, I believe that Matthew can help us with our investigation into the nuclear explosion off the coast of California.'

'I'm aware of where it happened, just not of how this man can be of any assistance.' He glowered at her. He turned back towards Matthew. 'Aren't you a triathlete?'

'Yes, sir.'

'No nuclear physics training I don't know about?'

'No, sir.'

Cathy earned another hard stare. 'Well, Special Agent Owens?'

'Sir, this is going to sound ridiculous.' The glower became even more intense. 'Matthew can travel back in time.'

'What? What kind of ridiculous statement is that?' Arnold Wilson's voice was now reaching decibel levels that was rattling the ornaments on his desk. He seemed to be growing bigger while sitting behind his desk.

'Sir, it's true.'

'Now you listen to me,' he said pointing at Cathy. 'I think you are seriously delusional if you think I'm going to buy—'

'Your middle name is Carroll!' yelled Matthew.

It was as if someone had pressed the pause button on a remote control. Arnold Wilson stopped in place, stunned. After a few seconds, he turned to look at Matthew.

'What did you say?'

'Your middle name is Carroll.'

'And just how do you know that?'

'You told me.'

'I told you?'

'Yes, sir.'

'When did I tell you?'

'About five minutes ago.'

'About five minutes ago?'

'That's right. About five minutes ago you were yelling at Cathy just the same as you were a moment ago, when I asked you to tell me something that nobody else knew so that we could prove what we're saying is true.'

'What? And then you travelled back in time to tell me my middle name is Carroll?'

'That's right.'

Wilson placed his elbows on the table, brought his hands together and rested his chin on his closed fists. 'What else did I tell you?'

'You said that your mother had dated a Pom.' Wilson looked questioningly at Matthew. 'Limey was your exact word. Anyway, she dated this guy when she was in college. His name was Carroll. Apparently, she liked the name.'

'Well, then, I probably told you something else as well.'

Matthew nodded. 'You did threaten us with bodily harm if we ever breathed a word of this to anyone.'

'Hmmm. And just how long have you had this miraculous ability to travel back in time?'

'A few months. I was in the wrong place at the wrong time when your army was conducting some type of experiment at a secret base in Western Australia. Ever since then I have been moving back in time when under extreme stress but recently, I have been able to do it at will.'

'And just how far back in time do you go? Can you go back and stop the bomb from exploding?'

Matthew shook his head. 'No. Somewhere between five and ten minutes. That's it.'

Wilson looked down and shook his head then turned to Cathy. 'Let's say I buy this whole time-travel thing. Just how is this going to help us? We may have other devices entering the country or, God forbid, already here. How is this going to stop a nuclear disaster?'

'Sir, even five or ten minutes could make all the difference. If Matthew can give us an extra few minute, it could save millions of lives.'

Wilson pondered for a few moments. 'I don't know if I buy all of this but maybe you're right. I'm assigning him to you as a consultant. I'll take care of the paperwork. Don't tell anybody what you just told me. Got it?' Cathy nodded. 'Keep him out of harm's way for goodness sake. Now get out.'

'Yes, Ca…'

'Don't even think about it,' snapped Wilson, raising a finger at Cathy.

'Yes, sir.' She smiled, turning to open the door.

Once they were through, with the door closed behind them, Matthew turned to her and said, 'Hey, Cathy?'

'Yeah?'

'Do I get a gun?'

Cathy rolled her eyes. 'Not a chance.'

Chapter 37

Ahmed Barazani regained consciousness slowly. His head felt as if it was about to burst. He couldn't breathe. He tried to lift his head and was rewarded by foul-smelling air entering his lungs and another burst of pain in his skull. He tried to move his arms to cradle his head but wasn't able to do so. He struggled and realised his arms were pinned beneath him.

Ahmed wriggled around, each movement bringing another stab of pain. Eventually he was able to move his arms enough that he could push himself up onto hands and knees. He steadied himself while the dizziness eased. The stench was unbelievable. He looked around to find he was in a big rubbish skip.

Unsteadily, Ahmed climbed out of the bin. He was covered in filth and smelt terrible. He grabbed hold of the side as a wave of nausea struck but managed to stay on his feet as the feeling passed.

Panic struck at Ahmed as he took stock. Where was his money belt? Where was his wallet? Both were gone. So apart from a small amount he'd left in the hotel room he was broke.

He looked down at his feet. He was in his socks. They had even checked in his shoes. Ahmed looked in the bin. There they were. Gingerly he reached in and picked them up. He brushed the muck off them and put the shoes on.

He realised that his situation was now desperate. He had very little money. He would be lucky not to be recognised in the state that he was in, despite the darkness. He couldn't stay here any longer.

Ahmed put his head down and as quickly as he could, made his way back to the hotel.

The early morning light shone on Salman Umrani as he wandered the streets of Nazimabad, another middle-class area of Karachi. He had many contacts searching for Barazani, but he wasn't going to sit back with his feet up, waiting. One more set of eyes might make all the difference.

Salman was checking any place that offered accommodation and he knew that the cash he was offering would bring him results if Barazani was around. He was walking towards a low-cost hotel when his cell phone rang.

'Yes.'

It was one of his contacts in Liaquatabad, a neighbouring area. A street thug thought he recognised the picture of the man they were looking for.

Thirty minutes later, Salman was standing with the two men outside a café. His contact introduced him to an unsavoury looking character with a patch over one eye. He could well imagine the man was a member of a street gang. Salman showed him some pictures which headquarters had doctored to show Barazani in various forms of possible disguise.

With no hesitation, the man pointed to the photo of Barazani with a beard.

'So, exactly where did you see him?' Salman asked.

'He bought some food from the stall just up the road,' the man said, pointing.

Salman knew he wasn't getting the whole truth. 'If you want your money, you'd better tell me what happened.'

The man considered this for a moment. 'My friends and I relieved him of all his money and left him in a bin around the corner.'

'Is he still there?'

'No. When I saw the pictures Abdul showed me,' he said indicating Salman's contact, 'I checked, but he had gone.'

'So, you and your friends robbed him and threw him in a bin?'

'Yes,' replied the man, nodding.

'Good.' Salman reached for his wallet and took out some notes which he gave to the two men. 'There'll be more if you can give me a current location. And I want him alive.'

Both men nodded. Salman could see they would definitely cooperate if they knew where Barazani was. The two men walked away.

Salman reached for his cell phone.

Chapter 38

Cathy had taken over a conference room as a temporary headquarters for the mission. She was giving Matthew a crash course in nuclear weapons. She drew a picture on the whiteboard showing the blast radius with expected damage and casualty rates as they moved past ground zero. Her recent studies had refreshed her knowledge and Matthew found her to be an excellent teacher. Like everyone else in the world with a television he had seen a nuclear explosion, but he was staggered to hear it all in minute detail.

'Why in the world would anyone in their right mind make one of these things?' he asked.

'No argument from me,' replied Cathy. 'I suppose the idea was to never have to use them but they've worried people for decades now, wondering if their leaders were going to wipe them off the face of the earth. Now we have to worry about one nut job doing it instead.'

'Do we know why this guy's doing it?' asked Matthew. 'Maybe we can reason with him.'

'At this stage, we don't even know if there are any more devices other than the one that's already exploded. Until we are sure we're going to assume there are more on the way or already here and waiting. This man certainly has the knowledge and the contacts to be able to put more than one device together. As for motivation, that normally comes down to ideology.'

'You mean religion?'

'Yes, but in this case, not necessarily. From what we've discovered, Barazani isn't a particularly religious man.'

'Money?'

'Doubtful. He must know that if you attack the US with nuclear weapons, you are going to be found. No amount of money is going to save you. No, for him, it has to be something personal, some sort of revenge. But without knowing what his drivers are, we're never going to be able to reason with him. As for the people helping him, we suspect al-Qaeda. For them, it's spreading their particular brand of religion across the world.'

'I don't care what religion people follow,' said Matthew. 'Why can't they just live and let live?'

'Let's hope we get to ask one,' Cathy replied. 'That's enough for tonight. Let's head out. I'll drop you at your hotel. It's on the way.'

They checked out of the office, picked up a company car from the garage and drove a short distance to a hotel that had a room reserved for Matthew.

At reception, Cathy signed all of the necessary forms. 'How about a nightcap?' asked a smiling Matthew.

'I think we both need our wits about us and a good night's sleep sounds like a better idea.'

'Okay then. I'll guess I'll see you in the morning.'

As Cathy walked away, Matthew cast one last admiring glance and then turned and walked towards the elevators.

The next morning, he was up early, ready to go for a run. He was grateful to the FBI for the new clothes they had supplied him and was determined to put them to good use. The first few minutes was a bit of a struggle due to the jetlag, but then he started to loosen up and was able to put on a bit more pace.

Matthew looked around in wonder at the sights, amazed at the history that was packed into this area compared to his home city. Perth was relatively modern, being less than two hundred years of age but most of the historical buildings had been torn down and replaced as they became old.

An hour after he started, he was back at the hotel, ready for a long shower. Afterwards, Matthew went to the dining room for breakfast and thought to himself that in one way or another the US Government had been supplying his meals for some time now. He smiled to himself as he let Uncle Sam shout him yet another one.

When Cathy pulled up outside the hotel a little while later, Matthew climbed in the car, feeling as good as he had in a long time.

'You're looking happy,' she said, not looking quite as alive as Matthew felt, but to his eyes, still beautiful.

'What a great day to be alive.'

'Well, if we don't catch Barazani and see if there are more bombs out there, that might only be a temporary condition.'

'I'd almost forgotten about that,' said Matthew, a lot less happy than he had been a minute before.

'So, apart from chasing some angry Pakistani nuclear scientist around the world, what are you doing to see if there are any more bombs in the country?' Matthew asked Cathy once they arrived back at the FBI headquarters.

'We have people tracking every ship and every container from every ship that passed through Pakistan and arrived in the US in the last two months.'

'How many ships was that?'

'Eighty-seven.'

'How many containers on a ship?'

'The largest ships can carry eighteen thousand containers.'

Matthew tried to do some calculations in his head but the numbers were too large. 'Wow, that's a lot of containers.'

'There are literally thousands of agents working on this right now,' said Cathy. 'We aren't overlooking a single thing, but this is a massive task and it's going to take time, time we may not have.'

'Are there that many ports in the US?'

'Hundreds. Don't worry, we can narrow our search down to just thirty-five. That's where the container ships docked.'

'You know,' said Matthew, 'if I was a pissed-off terrorist, I wouldn't bomb something in the middle of the desert that only meant something to two people. I'd be bombing something that made a statement.'

He had Cathy's attention. 'Like what?'

Matthew said the first thing that came into his mind. 'Like the Washington Monument or something big like that.'

'Well, that's a good call. I suppose it might narrow things down a little bit. I'll pass it along the line. Any other ideas?'

Matthew shrugged. 'No.'

Only a few blocks away, President Bright had just met with the members of his security council in what had become a daily ritual since the explosion off the West Coast.

The president had been reassured that each intelligence agency was doing everything that they could to ensure there would be no further threat from any more bombs. Despite these assurances, he felt less positive when the meeting finished than when it had started.

The FBI and Homeland Security were chasing hundreds of thousands of containers of equipment around the country trying to sight every item on every manifest. That was a job that might take years and he was certain that if there was another bomb, they wouldn't have anywhere near that amount of time.

Despite all of their combined might, the armed services seemed impotent. They could smash anything in the world if they were pointed at it but finding a needle in a haystack wasn't what they were good at. President Bright even suspected that the Chairman of the Joint Chiefs was holding something back and heaven help the man if that proved to be true.

As far as he was concerned the only good news had been from the CIA with the positive identification of a suspect and a possible sighting of the man. *Fucking Pakistan. They're supposed to be allies.*

The Chairman of the Joint Chiefs, General Risley, was indeed holding something back. Not long before the meeting started, he had been informed of the destruction of the facility in Western Australia and the subsequent arrest, by the FBI, of every member of the team who had escaped and made their way back to the States. As well, his old friend General Sam Morgan was missing, presumed dead. Morgan's aide was also missing but known to be alive.

Until a couple of days ago, he had been blissfully unaware of the project. Now he was in charge of a shit-storm. With a mixture of shame and guilt, he felt somewhat relieved that there was a much bigger problem to deal with right now and maybe he and the army might be able to fly under the radar and escape unscathed.

Damn, he thought, looking up. The CIA prick Connors was heading his way. The director's bland appearance couldn't hide the intensity in his eyes.

'General, a word please.'

'How can I help, Director?'

'You didn't muck around after our last discussion regarding that facility in Australia,' said the spy chief.

General Risley hated these games. Was the CIA boss aware the base had been destroyed in an accident or did he think the army had shut it down on purpose? Why couldn't the man ask a straight question? He decided to be non-committal in his response. 'The army cannot be part of any illegal activity.'

'Of course not, but I'm sure Sam Morgan has some interesting findings he'd like to share with his fellow patriots. How about you set up a meeting and we can make sure that all the information is used wisely and that way we avoid embarrassment all round.'

Risley looked at the director. At least he didn't know the full picture. 'As soon as I hear from him, we'll do just that.'

The spy chief smiled and nodded. 'General.' He turned and walked away.

Fucking spies, thought the army man. If that asshole wanted to know what's going on, then it must be valuable. It was time to do some investigating, but it needed to be done quietly. He knew just the man.

Chapter 39

It was a long day at the FBI headquarters. Matthew felt largely useless. He could pick out the United States on a map and maybe even a few states but he didn't have that specific knowledge that a native of the country was likely to possess. He also didn't know the bureau's systems and he had no authority within it anyway.

He watched Cathy as she analysed bits of information as they came in and would have liked to get more involved. But time-consuming investigations seemed to be her speciality, not his.

Still, Matthew hadn't become an elite athlete by giving up. He managed to get access to a computer and thought he would try to familiarise himself with the geography of the country and see if anything jumped out at him. Maybe an outsider's viewpoint could help. After all, he reasoned, the terrorist was an outsider as well.

His research showed him that the United States was a massive country. In size, the third largest country in the world, at over three million square miles or eight million square kilometres. Without Alaska and Hawaii, it would still rank number five. Matthew checked the map many times, comparing mainland America against Australia, and he wasn't so sure that the US was bigger even if Wikipedia said it was.

Aware that he was getting off track, Matthew focused on the task at hand. There were so many important cities and iconic landmarks that it was almost impossible to know where to begin.

Matthew had seen many disaster movies over the years and as he recalled, the most destroyed of the landmarks in the country was the Golden Gate Bridge. Movie directors seemed to dislike it for some reason. However, because it was in California, not too far from the scene of the original nuclear explosion, he guessed it might be safe this time. Hollywood was in the same boat, so Matthew decided to move up and then eastwards across the country.

He prided himself on being a well-informed man with good general knowledge, so he was going to ignore any place or thing that he had never heard of, as he assumed a terrorist was only going to be interested in the big-ticket items.

Seattle with its Space Needle received a tick. The Grand Canyon, though a magnificent spectacle, seemed unlikely. It was too far away from a major city. A cross. Las Vegas seemed more likely. He figured that city represented everything a terrorist might find offensive about America. Another tick on his list. Hoover Dam wasn't that far away and would certainly be spectacular if blown up but, in the end, it was left off the list. Mount Rushmore would have made his list if it wasn't out in the sticks. *Was that an Australian or an American expression? Doesn't matter.*

Matthew worked his way across the country and came up with a list of twenty items that included Niagara Falls, Disney World, The Alamo and New Orleans during Mardi Gras. Cities like New York and Washington that had numerous landmarks and large populations also made his list.

He waited until Cathy was heading to the coffee machine before he asked for some of her time. She had been so involved with her own work that she had forgotten all about the Australian. 'Sure, what's up?'

'I tried, as a foreigner, to come up with a list of places where a terrorist might set off a bomb and this is what I have come up with,' he said, handing her a piece of paper.

Cathy looked at the list, rather quizzically. 'It's a lot smaller than the list our guys have come up with. What's the reasoning behind your choices?'

'I was trying to pick places or things that are known around the world, that a terrorist might attack. I only picked things that I thought were symbolic of the United States.'

'I see the Gateway Arch isn't on the list.' Cathy was referring to the six hundred and thirty-foot monument in the city of St Louis, Missouri.

'Never heard of it.'

'Never heard of it?'

Matthew shook his head. 'No. Maybe it's famous in the US but I figure that if I didn't know it, maybe a terrorist wouldn't bother with it.'

'What about Mount Rushmore?'

'Yeah, that's very symbolic but it's too far away from anything else.'

Cathy looked at the sheet of names again. 'That's a well-thought-out list that you have there. I like your thinking. Maybe as locals we put too much importance on some places because we grew up with them, but they don't necessarily mean anything to people who aren't from here.'

Matthew smiled at the praise. 'Thanks.'

'I'll see what I can do about concentrating on these items. There's lots of other people looking at other places.' Cathy picked up a cup. 'Coffee?'

The next morning, Cathy thought she would pick Matthew up early and get some breakfast with him on the way to the office. She parked at the hotel, made her way to reception, showed her badge to the concierge and asked after Matthew.

The concierge pushed a few buttons on his computer and said, 'He's at the indoor swimming pool right now.' He gave Cathy directions and a key card and she strolled off to meet the Australian.

Cathy opened the door to the pool just as Matthew was climbing out. She was in the shadows, though, and he couldn't see her.

Yesterday she had admired how he had reasoned through his list of landmarks and had the courage to back up his thoughts. Today was different. Today it was an almost animal attraction that she felt.

Years of training for the triathlon had left Matthew supremely fit. There wasn't an ounce of fat on his frame. He had a sculptured body. He was tall, well-muscled but not bulky. His wide shoulders tapered down to narrow hips and running from his hips towards his groin was a V-line that Cathy found hugely attractive. Cathy couldn't help but look down at the swimsuit to notice that any girl he was with wouldn't be disappointed.

He had obviously pushed himself hard in the swim as his chest heaved, trying to pull in deep breaths.

Matthew picked up the towel from the edge of the pool and started drying himself. The muscles in his arms rippled as the towel moved across his body.

Cathy swallowed hard while running her eyes over the man standing at the edge of the pool. *God. What was I thinking when I said no to a nightcap?* Silently she backed out of the door, exhaling quietly, and hurried back to the reception desk to drop off the key card.

An hour later, Cathy stopped her car outside the hotel and Matthew climbed in. 'Hi, Cathy.' He beamed at her.

Cathy mumbled something back.

'Are you OK?' he asked.

'What? Oh yeah, just a bit distracted this morning.'

'Well, I don't blame you. Someone just set off an atomic bomb and you're worried there could be more. That's a good excuse.' He smiled at her again.

Cathy returned the smile. 'I'm glad you understand.'

Chapter 40

This time it was Captain Ray Kingston who was kept waiting outside General Risley's office. The captain wasn't overwhelmed. He'd had some dealings with the chairman previously, having handled a rather delicate matter involving a prostitute and a private investigator with a camera and a penchant for blackmail. It had all been handled discreetly and General Risley had never been bothered by either person again. In fact, nobody had ever been bothered by either person again. That's what happened when you played with the big boys.

The general's secretary had checked out the visitor when he arrived and now stole glances at the captain while he sat with his eyes closed. He was about thirty, six feet tall, had jet black hair and the most piercing blue eyes. She had met this man before and he unnerved her. She had always thought she was attracted to "bad boys" but despite this one's good looks, there was an air of menace about him that she wanted little to do with. It was with some relief that she was finally able to send him in.

The captain saluted as he entered but didn't even receive a perfunctory one in return. 'Sit down, captain.'

He sat. He was passed a folder and barely had time to pick it up before the general asked, 'Are you aware of a special project being carried out in Australia?'

Kingston made it his business to know as much as he could about anything the army was doing but, on this occasion, he drew a blank. 'No, sir.'

'General Morgan was in charge.' The name was familiar to the captain. It must have been top secret. 'In a nutshell, the project was trying to give us controllable time travel.' Kingston found it hard to contain his surprise. 'I know. It sounds ridiculous. But they are having some success with it. Well, had some, anyway. As far as I know, the base has been destroyed in some sort of incident. It seems Morgan is dead, as is the chief scientist along with half the people involved. The survivors were put on a transport back to the States but were detained by the FBI the moment they landed.'

'So, what would you like me to do, general?'

'Do what you do best. Find out what happened. See if we can salvage the project somehow. Some details are in the folder. You are to report directly to me. Understood?' A nod from the captain. 'Dismissed.'

Kingston stood, saluted, and made his way out of the office. *That was interesting.* He found it hard to believe what he had been told by General Risley, but a reliable contact had just informed him this morning about a group of people having been detained by the FBI in Arizona. The army had been cut out.

Kingston flicked through the folder. With the confirmed death of the commanding officer, General Morgan, the suspected death of the chief scientist, Professor Windsor and disappearance of the head of security, Major Carmichael, known to him personally and a real pain in the ass, Captain Kingston had lost access to a lot of solid intelligence.

Luckily, he had a name to go on. That name was of the FBI agent who blew the whistle on the project. Cathy Owens.

Chapter 41

Pakistan was nine hours ahead of Washington, which made it late in the afternoon in Karachi. Dr Ahmed Barazani had almost survived another day. Now he had to worry about another night.

He was hiding out in his hotel room, thankful that he had paid in advance and at least had a place to stay. He hadn't eaten in almost two days because he was afraid to go out. He was afraid because he had been beaten and mugged but more so because he didn't want to be recognised and detained before the other bombs exploded. Just three more days and it would all be over. The two explosions would happen only two days apart, tearing the heart out of America. Now that was something they would remember.

His head still hurt from the mugging, which made it difficult to think. Surely, he could get something to eat without being recognised. That wouldn't stop the bombs from exploding but it might stop his head hurting. The Americans would pay for that.

Ahmed tried to reason out what he should do but he was really having trouble putting things together. It was hard to focus on the one topic. Maybe if he lay down for a few minutes he might feel better.

He woke up the next morning, clear-headed. There was a dull ache behind his eyes, but it was bearable. He figured that crack on the head must have been pretty hard because it had certainly knocked him around.

He was famished. He had to risk going out to get something to eat. He would rather that it was dark but he couldn't wait much longer. He pulled some scissors out of his toiletry bag and cut as much of his beard and moustache away as he could and then shaved.

It had been many years since he was totally clean-shaven but even so, the man who stared back at him in the mirror was a stranger, with sunken cheeks and black circles around his eyes. Ahmed wouldn't have trusted this man if he was introduced to him.

He put on a jacket with a hood and pulled it up over his head and put on some sunglasses. That was the best disguise he could think of.

He exited his room, intending to get something to eat from the first vendor he saw and take it back to his room to eat.

Matthew didn't have anything official to do for the rest of the day. Once again, he found himself looking for potential terrorist target sites but he didn't find any new ones, so he tried to research the ones he had suggested in a bit more detail.

Cathy was still working through lists and had seemed a little distant during the times he had tried to interact with her, so he had mostly left her to do her thing.

Matthew looked over at the desk where Cathy was working and saw her close a notebook, stand and stretch. He whistled silently to himself. If she was trying to fit into a man's world, she was doing a great job, but she was anything but a man. He looked away before he could be spotted staring and pretended to be looking at something on his desk.

He heard her footsteps as Cathy approached the desk. 'Hey, Matthew. I'm going to leave the tracking down of the all the containers to others. I liked the list that you came up with yesterday. I've checked and many of the places on your list have actually received shipments in the last couple of weeks. I've forwarded this data to agents in the locations.' She paused. 'I think we need to be at the pointy end of any search, so I picked one.'

'What?'

'I picked a place on your list.'

'Which one?'

Cathy smiled. 'The Alamo.'

'Really?'

Cathy nodded. 'That's one of the places that's received an overseas shipment. So, let's pack our bags. We're going to San Antonio.'

Chapter 42

They touched down in San Antonio less than four hours after they had taken off in an FBI charter jet. Cathy had conscripted two more agents to be with her and another two had come along to work through their own leads, but the small plane had enough room to seat them all comfortably.

Matthew was very aware of Cathy sitting next to him. She smelled amazing. He didn't know if she realised the effect that she was having on him. To distract himself he tried to read all he could on Texas. His competitive nature caused him to compare the Lone Star State with his own, Western Australia. He saw that his home state was nearly two and a half million square kilometres, so that Texas could fit into WA two and a half times. Even if Alaska was added to Texas, it would still be smaller. *One for the good guys.*

Then he saw that Texas actually had a population of around twenty-eight million people, which was more than the whole of Australia. Oh well. He read that the City of San Antonio itself had a population of around one and a half million, which made it the second biggest city in the state.

It was after midnight when they landed but there were still two agents from the city there to meet them with two vehicles. The local agent asked Cathy what they wanted to do. 'It's late, so drop us off at the hotel and pick us up around eight in the morning.'

After a short drive, they arrived at some hotel in a chain that Matthew didn't recognise. He was surprised to find that they had already been checked in and one of the local agents gave Cathy six keys, which she distributed.

Matthew was given the key to a room on the second floor. *It's the level above the ground floor anyway*, he thought to himself, comfortable enough with that and not wanting to debate about things like floor numbers when there were a lot more important issues to worry about.

Cathy and one other agent walked up the stairs with him while the other three agents were on the ground level. He looked at his key number at the top of the stairs and the sign pointed him to the left to room 209. The others followed him. Matthew saw they had consecutive rooms with Cathy in room 208 next to him and the other man on the far side in room 207.

'Let's all meet at seven for breakfast in the restaurant and plan our day,' Cathy said.

'Sure thing,' replied the other man. Matthew nodded his agreement, opened his door and walked in.

He dumped his bag on the floor near the cupboard and looked around. It was a basic hotel room, but it was clean and it had everything he needed—a bed and a bathroom and some other amenities such as instant coffee and a kettle. He thought to himself that it was missing the one thing that would have really made it a wonderful place to stay. Unfortunately for him, she was next door.

Matthew unpacked some toiletries in the bathroom, brushed his teeth, pulled on a pair of shorts and climbed into bed. The lumps in the mattress seemed to be in the right place and it was comfortable enough even if the pillows were a bit thick and firm. The neon lights from the vacancy sign were shining light into his room despite the curtains being drawn but he had stayed at worse places over his career.

He was tired and thought he should have been able to fall asleep easily, but he couldn't stop thinking about the beautiful woman in the room next door. If only she had given him any indication that she was interested, he would be banging on her door right now. He sighed, tried to punch his pillow into some sort of comfortable shape and resigned himself to a restless night.

What was that tapping noise? The cockroaches must wear heavy boots in Texas. There it was again, a bit louder. Quicker than an Olympic sprinter out of the blocks, Matthew was at the door.

There was a whisper from outside. 'Matthew. Open up.'

He opened the door. A hand reached in and pushed him back into the room. He staggered back a couple of steps.

Cathy stepped through the doorway and turned and locked the door. She was wearing a pair of shorts and a T-shirt. In the dim light, Matthew drank in the sight before him. She had long, shapely legs which merged into the curves of her hips and waist. Her breasts pushed out the T-shirt, mesmerising him as she stepped forward. With an effort, he lifted his eyes to look at her face, which was framed by her dark blonde hair. God, she was beautiful.

'How long were you going to make me stand out there?'

'Well, uh, I…'

Cathy stepped forward, reached out and placed a finger on his mouth. 'Shhh.' She moved in closer and replaced her finger with her lips, lightly brushing his own.

He moved his arms around her, running his hands up and down her back, hearing her moan softly while still joined in the kiss. Her tongue pressed into his mouth, surprising him at its insistence.

Cathy held the kiss for a few more seconds then softly broke away. She eyed the bed and smiled at him.

Matthew looked at the beautiful lady beside him. He felt completely content and her expression told him that she felt the same.

She gasped. 'That was amazing.'

Matthew just nodded in agreement. He didn't know if he could speak just yet. He gulped down deep breaths, waiting for his heart rate to return to normal. It felt as though he had run in a triathlon.

A few moments later, Matthew was lying on his back, staring at nothing on the hotel room ceiling. He was amazed that this had happened to him. Cathy was curled up against him with her head on his chest, lightly running her fingers up and down his stomach.

Wow. I could just hop back…

'Matthew.' Cathy interrupted his musings.

'Yes.'

'Don't take this the wrong way but I don't want you doing your thing, going back in time and then making love to me again.'

'Oh. I wouldn't…'

'Because I want you to do it again, now, in our time.'

The next morning on the way down to the restaurant, Cathy extracted a promise from Matthew. 'If you ever want what happened last night to happen again, then don't tell anyone. Especially my colleagues. Right?'

'Cross my heart.'

Chapter 43

The entire group met for breakfast in the dining room to discuss the day's plan so that they were ready when the local agents came by. Two FBI men went with the locals in one car, while Cathy, Matthew and two others, agents Brown and Jensen, decided to leave their car in the hotel car park and walk the five minutes it would take to reach the Alamo. Parking was scarce nearby as this was the most visited landmark in Texas with more than two and half million people coming to see the former mission each year.

This time, the two male agents once again wore the same dark suit and shoes but that was where the similarities ended. Ironically, Agent Brown was a good looking African-American with a huge smile he had trouble controlling. He could have played professional basketball, judging by his height. Agent Jensen was about six feet tall, medium build, with fair hair with a cowlick projecting out over his forehead. Despite the hair not being government issue, he looked all business, not a hint of a grin from him.

As he walked, Matthew looked at the scene around him. Dominating the nearby landscape was the tallest building in San Antonio, the Tower of the Americas, the over two-hundred-metre-high observation tower and restaurant, which was built to be the showpiece for the 1968 World's Fair. It looked impressive but it hadn't made Matthew's list of potential targets because he had never heard of it prior to becoming involved with this case. Cathy had found that hard to believe but realised she was born and raised in the US and he wasn't.

They walked the cobbled footpath up to the Church Entrance of the Alamo. Matthew was struck by a sense of reverence as he gazed upon the old mission for the first time. He could feel the history, the sacrifice and the glory that this place represented to the American people.

The walls looked to be constructed of irregularly shaped limestone blocks, not in neat rows as might be found in modern buildings. There were four stone columns, two on either side of a heavy door. Standing empty were four pedestals for statues, built into the walls. Matthew wondered which saints may have looked down on those people entering the church when it was first built.

It was still early but there were already people milling about the entrance. *Definitely the type of target a terrorist would pick,* Matthew thought to himself.

Two gardeners were on the lawn to the right of the entrance holding clippers of some sort and pushing wheelie bins but to Matthew they didn't appear to be doing much. It didn't matter because the grounds were in immaculate condition.

'Hey, Cathy,' asked Matthew, 'what was delivered here that you want to check out?'

'It's supposed to be a new interactive display of some sort. I don't have any other details. I just want to see it for myself.'

'There are definitely worse places to investigate, I'm sure.'

Cathy had already checked online and the only fees for the Alamo were for those people who wanted the guided tours. Since there was no charge to just walk around and no tours were scheduled at that early hour, there was nobody manning the gates.

'Let's ask one of these guys where to go.' Agent Jensen said, pointing at one of the gardeners.

To Matthew it looked as though the man who had been pointed at nearly dropped his clippers when the four of them started walking towards him, but he straightened himself up and was smiling by the time they arrived. He was of Middle Eastern appearance as was his co-worker.

Agent Jensen got down to business. 'We're with the FBI,' he said, as the three agents flashed their badges. Matthew felt a bit unimportant when he didn't have one to show and had to restrain himself from getting out his wallet and showing his driver's licence. 'We're looking for whoever's in charge here.'

Matthew looked at the other gardener who had stopped to watch the exchange. He appeared to glare at them with some hostility.

The first gardener was still smiling. 'Certainly. Through the church and slightly to the left you will find the gift shop. The administrator is in there.'

'Thanks.' The four turned and walked towards the entrance.

When they were far enough away to not be overheard, Matthew asked, 'Did those guys look suspicious to any of you?'

'You're a fast learner,' replied Agent Brown.

'Just keep walking casually until we get out of sight,' said Cathy.

Matthew felt a bit conspicuous walking casually, but thought he was doing alright until there was a yell from a member of the public. 'He's got a gun!'

The four of them turned around to see the gardener they'd been talking to lifting some sort of automatic weapon to line up on them. His co-worker was reaching into his wheelie bin.

'Run!' yelled Cathy.

They sprinted the last few steps and were through the door as bullets started bouncing off the stonework around them.

The second battle for the Alamo had begun.

Half a world away, Ahmed Barazani was counting down the hours. He paced around his dingy hotel room, full of nervous energy, constantly checking his watch. In less than an hour, the Americans would have another reason to "Remember the Alamo".

'Surely, nothing can go wrong now,' he said aloud. There was so little time left. He was almost a nervous wreck wondering what was going to happen.

He lit another cigarette, the last one in the pack, drew the smoke deep into his lungs and exhaled towards the ceiling. Within two minutes, he was stubbing it out in the ashtray on the coffee table. He was never going to get through the next hour with nothing to smoke so, against his better judgement, he decided to make another trip out of his hotel room and get another pack.

Ahmed let himself out the door and walked down the hallway to the stairs. He was passing through the door when four men burst out of the doorway at the other end of the hall. Instantly, he had no doubt about what the men were doing there.

Silently, the doctor closed the door behind him and made his way quickly down the stairs and out onto the street.

Matthew, Cathy and the two other agents made it through the church doorway with bullets pinging off the stonework around them. People were screaming and running every which way to get away from the hail of lead. Many ran through the same door Matthew and the agents had entered and kept going, past the information desk and out the exit on the left-hand side and into the gardens.

The four of them split into pairs after they were inside, Matthew and Cathy ending up on the left. The agents had their guns out in an instant and Cathy had her phone to her ear in seconds. 'Agent Owens at the Alamo. We are under fully automatic weapon fire. At least two suspects. Possible Icarus Event.' She had the phone away and her gun out in a flash.

Matthew had been in a combat situation only recently, but he had been half expecting it the previous time. This had come as a complete surprise and really shocked him. He was breathing heavily. He looked at Cathy and was amazed at how calm she was. He took a few seconds to compose himself. 'What does that mean? An Icarus Event?'

'Remember how Icarus got too close to the sun?'

'Oh.' Matthew was in no doubt now that he had made a good guess as to a possible terrorist target, but he wasn't patting himself on the back—not with bullets coming through that door frame and smashing into the stonework. 'How long before we get back-up?'

'It shouldn't be longer than five minutes. Don't worry. These walls are solid. They won't be getting in here.'

During a lull in the fire, Agent Jensen poked his head around the corner to see what was happening outside, but he quickly pulled it back in when bullets struck dangerously close. Pieces of stone were chipping off, hitting him on the cheek and drawing blood.

'Shit,' he said, raising his hand to his face to wipe the blood away. 'I think I'll stay in here where it's safe.'

As if the gods of law enforcement were having fun with Agent Jensen, a man stepped through the door at the other end of the building, raised an automatic weapon and started firing on the group.

Fortunately for the agents the shots started high and the recoil from the gun lifted the stream of bullets away from them.

Cathy snapped around and lined her own gun up on the man and fired twice. The second shot proved to be redundant as the man crashed back against the wall with a bullet in his chest. The second bullet was only inches from the first. The man was dead before he slumped down on the floor.

'How many more of them are there?' yelled Agent Brown.

'I'll check. You and Jensen keep those two outside busy. Matthew, you're with me.'

'Do I get a gun?'

Cathy gestured towards the dead man. 'Help yourself. It's obviously ready to fire. Just point and squeeze the trigger. Aim low. Those things have a tendency to track up.' She looked hard at Matthew. 'Are you sure you're up to this?'

Matthew swallowed and then nodded. 'Yeah. Sure. Things could get hotter than they are now, so let's do this.'

Trying to stay out of the line of fire from the terrorists outside they made their way to the dead man. Matthew picked up the gun.

'Just don't point at me,' Cathy told him.

'Okay.' Matthew looked down at the terrorist, wondering what would motivate a person to do what he had done. He now thought of the man and his accomplices as terrorists and he was sure that Cathy and the rest of America would think the same.

Cathy held up her left arm when they reached the door to the garden. Matthew recognised the gesture and stopped. Getting as low as she could, Cathy looked around the door and was greeted by more automatic weapon fire. Fortunately, it was once again high. 'Christ,' she said. 'How many of them are there?'

'Is that the only way out?'

Cathy looked around. 'Try that window behind the information counter.' She pointed to a shuttered window.

Matthew put down the gun and ran over to the counter, aware he was crossing in front of the open front door. Once there, he felt a bit safer. He moved to the window and heaved the shutters open. 'It's got bars.'

'Of course, it has. It looks like the front door and this one are the only ways in or out,' Cathy said. A look of grim determination came over her face. 'We need to get out there. Let's find some portable cover.'

They both looked around what was once the church. Agents Jensen and Brown were still trading fire with the terrorists outside. 'Everything looks like its bolted down,' said Matthew.

'Try the counter top. It looks pretty solid. It should stop a bullet.'

Matthew looked down. The counter top was an inch and a half thick piece of wood. It did look solid. He grabbed it with both hands and lifted. It didn't budge. *They don't make them like that anymore.* He dropped to the floor, on his back and pressed his legs against the timber. He strained as hard as he could. Nothing. 'Crap.'

'How's it going over there, Matthew?' yelled Cathy from the doorway.

'Any second now.' Matthew pulled his legs down towards his chest and kicked out. This time he was rewarded with a small amount of movement. He kicked out again and again.

On the sixth kick, the counter top parted ways with the supports and clattered to the ground. The piece was about two and a half metres in length. Startled, Cathy spun around, training her pistol in a two-handed grip on the shape of Matthew climbing up from behind the counter. 'Don't shoot,' he yelled, raising his hands in the air.

'About time. What are you waiting for? Bring it here.'

While Matthew lifted the obviously heavy piece of wood, Cathy glanced at the other two agents at the entrance. They seemed to be keeping the terrorists at bay.

Matthew held the piece of timber up and moved as quickly as he could back towards Cathy. As he was crossing the floor a bullet struck the counter top, nearly tearing it from his grip. 'Fuck.'

He staggered over to Cathy and they both looked at the effect of the gunshot. 'Good test run,' said Cathy. The bullet had penetrated about halfway into the timber.

'Not how I would have picked to test it if I was given a choice,' Matthew replied. 'Now what?'

'Here's where I need your trust, Matthew.' Cathy said, staring intently at the young Australian.

'You've got it. So, what's the plan?'

'You hold the counter top in front of you and run out the door and head slightly left to draw the fire of whoever's out there with the gun. I think the shot came from the right side of the gift shop. So, I come out after you, see where they're firing from and take them out.'

Cathy could see the gears whirring inside Matthew's mind. 'Good plan,' he finally said as he manoeuvred the counter top around to face the door. 'Ready when you are.'

'Go.'

Matthew dashed out of the doorway and veered towards the left. It didn't take long to draw the fire of the terrorists, as almost instantly, bullets thudded into the counter top and all around him. Wooden splinters struck his right hand, almost causing him to drop the piece of timber but he held on and kept going.

A shot came from behind him. Then another.

Matthew flinched, expecting to feel a bullet thudding into his back. Nothing.

The firing from the front had stopped so Matthew stopped as well. He turned to see Cathy standing there, coming out of the shooter's stance. He glanced around the side of the counter top to see what Cathy was looking at.

Slumped down between two large plants that looked like cacti, near the corner of a building, was the man who had been shooting at him.

Matthew dropped the counter top to the ground, brought his right hand up to his mouth, bit down on the large splinter sticking out just above his little finger and pulled it out. It hurt like blazes but he wasn't going to show any discomfort in front of this amazing woman who had undoubtedly save his life again.

'Yeah. Good plan,' he said spitting the splinter onto the ground.

'Why, thank you. One of my better ideas I think.' Cathy smiled at him briefly but quickly reverted to the professional agent. 'We need to be careful. There may be more terrorists and we need to find that item that was shipped here.'

'Where do you think it might be?'

'The Bowie Exhibit would be my guess. The website says there are interactive displays there.' She pointed to the right. 'That way.' They could hear sirens getting closer. 'It won't be long before the cavalry arrives.'

'I hope it works out better than the last time the Alamo was under attack,' said Matthew.

'Me too.'

'Wait a sec.' Matthew trotted over to the dead man and relieved him of the gun. 'Just in case.'

Cathy looked at the building in front of them. 'That's the gift shop. Let's check it out first. I don't want to leave any potential terrorists at our backs.'

With the sirens now screaming, the two of them walked towards the gift shop. It was another stone building made to look of the period, with carved columns either side of the ornate wooden door. An intricately carved frieze and then a bell, recessed into the wall, stood above the door.

'Pretty nice for a gift shop.' commented Matthew.

'That's Texas for you. Let me go first.' Cathy walked up to the door. 'FBI,' she yelled.

'Oh, thank God.' came the reply from inside, a female voice, obviously terrified.

Slowly, Cathy then Matthew made their way inside, Cathy with her gun at the ready. Twenty or so people were in there, hiding behind counters and memorabilia displays. A woman was on the floor, sobbing while her husband comforted her and two small children hugged her. A few teenagers were talking on phones, excited and seemingly unconcerned at what was happening around them. Others showed obvious relief at the entry of people with authority.

Cathy addressed the crowd. 'Has anybody seen anyone carrying weapons?'

A teenage boy put his hand up. 'There were three guys in here a few minutes ago. They ran out and we heard shooting.'

Cathy looked at Matthew. 'That means there's at least one more out there somewhere.' She turned to the crowd again. 'Please stay inside. More FBI and police are arriving and we'll soon have this situation under control but you are safer in here than outside.'

Members of the crowd murmured their assent.

'Come on, Matthew.'

They turned and walked out of the gift shop, leaving the civilians behind.

Chapter 44

Matthew and Cathy slowly made their way along the footpath, past the courtyard, towards the Bowie Exhibit. The exhibit was only recently opened but had proved to be tremendously popular with members of the public who could discover everything they would ever want to know about James Bowie and his famous knife.

Cathy walked carefully, her gun held in a two-handed grip, swivelling from side to side and ready to fire at any sign they were under attack. She could still hear sporadic gunfire from outside the Alamo but blocked it out, concentrating instead on her immediate surroundings.

Matthew walked slightly to the rear, knowing full well which of the two of them was better equipped in their current circumstances. He carried some sort of machine gun. He had no idea what type it was or how he would perform if he needed to but felt a bit better knowing that he was at least carrying some sort of weapon into battle.

Cathy held up a hand and they both stopped at an intersection of the footpaths. She pointed at a low stone wall at the end of the courtyard and then indicated to Matthew that he should circle around to the left while she came at it from the right. Matthew nodded his understanding. 'And don't shoot me,' Cathy whispered.

Matthew followed a path off to the left which led towards some bushes and a large tree. He was careful as he came up to the foliage and found himself holding his breath as he rounded the corner. He exhaled noisily when he discovered no-one lurking behind the greenery. He looked over to see Cathy making her way past trees and bushes, towards the wall.

Suddenly, Matthew knew he would do whatever it took to make sure she was safe.

He moved around the tree, poked out his head and could see behind the wall. Nobody was there.

From her angle, Cathy wasn't yet able to see behind the wall so Matthew stepped out and waved to attract her attention. She looked up and Matthew shook his head to indicate the coast was clear. Cathy nodded and they both walked a little more quickly towards the wall.

When they came together Matthew almost hugged Cathy with relief. 'I don't know if I'm cut out for this secret agent stuff.'

Cathy looked him in the eyes. 'Matthew, just a few minutes ago you did just about the bravest thing I ever saw, running out against a man armed with a fully automatic weapon, when you only had a bench top. I think you're doing just fine.'

Matthew accepted the praise with a smile. 'Which building is the Bowie Exhibit?'

Cathy pointed. 'That one on the right.'

In his peripheral vision, Matthew sensed movement from behind a hedge. He spun to face the threat and seeing him, Cathy started to react as well, but they were both too late as a man dressed in a maintenance uniform appeared with his gun already raised.

He opened fire. The bullets flew towards them.

'That means there's at least one more out there somewhere,' said Cathy. She turned to the crowd. 'Please stay inside. More FBI and police are arriving and we'll soon have this situation under control but you are safer in here than outside.'

'Come on, Matthew.'

'I hate to say this Cathy but that didn't work out too well for us last time.'

'Oh. Tell me what happened.'

Matthew explained the events that they had been through just minutes before. 'At least we're prepared this time,' she said.

'Yeah, but that was the only mistake we can make. Now we need to get it right. We can't do it a third time.'

'Okay, then here's the plan.'

Cathy took a circuitous route towards the hedge that she believed the terrorist was hiding behind. She kept low and quiet. She could occasionally see Matthew as he made his way towards the large tree but hearing him proved to be much easier. He seemed to rustle or crunch with almost every step.

Cathy slipped quietly through a handrail at the front of the Alamo Hall building and up behind bushes on the corner of the structure. She watched as Matthew stepped behind the tree.

A burst of automatic weapon fire came from behind the tree and there was a loud cry of 'Allahu Akbar' and another burst of bullets.

There was a triumphant cry from behind the hedge just a few yards in front of Cathy and a man holding an automatic weapon stood up. 'Freeze. FBI!' she yelled.

Rather than choosing to surrender, the man spun around while, desperately trying to line up his gun. Cathy fired from almost point-blank range and the man collapsed to the ground.

Matthew ran over to where Cathy now stood. 'Thank God you're okay.'

'I'm fine,' Cathy replied while eyeing the dead terrorist. 'Now let's go and see if we can find that interactive display. From what we've seen so far, I think that we aren't going to like what we see.' Cathy turned towards the Bowie Exhibit. 'And keep your eyes open, just in case.'

In the background, Matthew could still hear sirens and sporadic gunfire. 'Do you think the bomb squad will be coming?'

Cathy was walking forward with her gun moving back and forth in front of her. 'I hope so since neither of us has ever disarmed a nuclear device before.'

Up until Cathy had mentioned it by name, the threat of a weapon of mass destruction hadn't seemed quite real, but now the truth of the situation hit home. 'Oh God, let's hope we're not too late.' He hurried along after her, constantly scanning his surroundings.

As they approached the door to the exhibit, Cathy said to Matthew, 'I'll get you to open the door but don't go in. Okay?'

Matthew nodded and crouched down. He reached out with his right arm and pulled the wooden door towards him, half expecting to hear bullets flying past. Silence. After a few seconds, Cathy rushed past, gun at the ready. A moment later she called out, 'Clear.'

Matthew stood and walked inside. Apart from the two of them, the building was empty.

At any other time, he would have been impressed by what he saw. Even as an Australian male he had heard of Jim Bowie and his famous knife and there were lots of them on display. Today, however, his mind was crowded with other thoughts.

Cathy found what she was looking for and walked over to it. Matthew followed. They stood in front of what looked to Matthew almost like a carnival attraction. A forest scene was displayed on the background and at various heights on trees and bushes were targets. On the counter were what looked like knives, but with a bulbous magnetic end instead of a sharp tip. Matthew surmised that people threw the "knives" at the targets from behind the lines and scored points when they hit the rings in the targets. Digital displays at the top of the attraction showed the score of the knife thrower.

'Let's have a look at the back,' said Cathy as she stepped over the line. The display showed FOUL and made a beeping noise but Cathy was oblivious. 'Help me try and move this thing out so we can get behind it.'

Matthew moved to the left side and Cathy to the right. They braced themselves. 'On three,' he said. 'One, two, three.' They both heaved and were rewarded when the display moved forward about six inches. 'Again. One, two, three.' This time it went about a foot.

After two more heaves, they had turned the display almost sideways and had enough room to easily walk in behind. They found an electrical panel with a sticker on it warning of potentially lethal voltages and that only authorised people should have access inside.

Cathy wasn't put off by the sign. A second later she had some sort of tool off her belt and was opening the door. 'Oh shit!' She dropped the tool and reached for her phone.

With a sinking feeling, Matthew stepped around so that he could see what had shocked Cathy. On the floor of the panel was a metal cylinder about the size of a barrel of oil. It certainly didn't look like it belonged in there. Neither did the display that was counting backwards from seven minutes and thirty-two seconds.

Chapter 45

Cathy's initial phone call warning of a possible Icarus Event had almost instantly been passed on to Brigadier General Heather Atkins at Joint Base San Antonio (JBSA).

The base was a huge military post, the largest in the USA, under the jurisdiction of the US Air Force. In 2005, three adjoining facilities had been consolidated into one base—the US Army's Fort Sam Houston, the Air Force's Lackland Air Force Base and Randolph Air Force Base. With a workforce of over eight thousand, JBSA was the largest employer in San Antonio. General Atkins was the base's first female commanding officer and the highest-ranking woman in the US Air Force. She was a striking-looking woman, full of confidence and incredibly capable, as any woman in a predominantly man's world has to be.

As she hung up the phone, she looked anything but assured. General Atkins walked to her office door. Two captains occupied desks outside. 'Initiate the Icarus Protocol,' she told them. 'And heaven help us all.'

At Sheppard Air Force Base, about five hundred and sixty kilometres to the north, a red phone in the air control office started to ring. First Lieutenant Martha Tobias shared a startled look with Senior Airman Jay Paris. Neither was aware of the emergency phone ever ringing before, let alone had heard it for themselves. 'Shit,' she said, picking up the handset. 'Tobias.'

Paris watched the lieutenant blanch as she listened to the other end. She hung up and looked at him. 'JBSA is closed. Icarus Protocol. Everything military in the air is being diverted to here, possibly civilian aircraft as well.'

Paris looked at the radar screen. 'Fuck.' Already the display was showing multiple contacts at their outer air traffic boundary, many without a military designation. 'We're gonna need more people here, Lieutenant.'

Air traffic control at San Antonio International Airport went into meltdown. Jarred Larkham, the senior controller, took the call. 'What?' he yelled into the phone, attracting the attention of everyone else in the tower. He pressed the button for the speaker phone so the rest of the crew could get it first-hand.

A female voice blasted out. 'The airport is closed. The FBI has just reported a possible terrorist attack. Nothing lands or takes off until further notice.'

'What do we do with the planes on approach?'

'You're the senior controller. You decide.' There was a click and the speaker went quiet.

Jarred turned to face the room. 'You heard the lady. Get to it,' he ordered.

At JBSA, all training operations in progress were instantly cancelled and the base was placed in lockdown. Nobody was getting in or out without the express authorisation of General Atkins.

Next, Fort Sam Houston, as a major medical training post, had its medical staff ordered to stand by, ready to mobilise at a minute's notice to support any relief effort that may be required.

Lastly, within five minutes of the notification two uniformed men were climbing into a helicopter. The doors were barely closed before it lifted off, on its way to the Alamo.

'Matthew.' No answer.

Again. 'Matthew.'

'Huh?'

'You don't have to stay. You can try to get as far away as possible.'

'I think we both know that you can't outrun an atomic bomb.' He reached out and put his hands on Cathy's upper arms. 'You're not going to leave and if you're not going, then neither am I.'

'Well, then, we'd better see what we can do to stop this thing.' Cathy smiled wryly while holding up her multi-tool.

She squatted down to have a look at how the display was attached to the bomb. It seemed as though there was a push-in plug with a locking collar holding the mechanisms together.

'I suppose I could just disconnect the plugs.'

'You've had some sort of experience with bomb disposal that tells you that's a good idea?'

'I sat in on a seminar a few years ago.'

'You're the expert then. Do what you think's right.'

Cathy took a deep breath and reached for the connections. 'Here goes nothing.'

'Please don't do that.'

At the sound of the voice behind them, both Matthew and Cathy spun around to see a tall, hard-faced man in army fatigues standing at the door to the exhibit. A shorter man, similarly dressed, stood behind him with the same expression. They were both of very solid build and looked capable of causing a lot of damage to anyone who stood in their way. Each man had a bag of tools hanging off a shoulder. They both stepped into the room followed by Agent Jensen.

Cathy stood to face the new arrivals.

'Cathy, Matthew, meet Chief Warrant Officers Cross and Albertson,' said Jensen. The taller of the two men nodded at the first name so perhaps he was Cross, but neither stopped to swap pleasantries with the attractive female FBI agent or her companion. They were all business as they approached the panel, placed their tool bags on the floor and opened them to reveal an impressive array of hand and power tools.

Cathy turned back to Agent Jensen and looked quizzically at him. Jensen shrugged. 'Reinforcements from the office and local police arrived and we were able to subdue the terrorists. Just as we were mopping up, an army chopper landed in the garden outside and these two guys got out. Apparently, among other things, they run training courses at the local army base on arming and disarming nuclear weapons.'

'Well, I hope they're good at it because they have,' Cathy looked at her watch, 'about three minutes before we're toast.'

All the colour drained from Jensen's face. 'Fuck.'

Cathy turned to the two chief warrant officers who were busy at the bomb. They were blocking her view of what was happening. 'Can you guys work and talk?'

The tall one answered without stopping what he was doing. 'Yes, ma'am. We're in the army.'

'Are you going to be able to disarm this thing?'

'Ever since the bomb detonated off the coast of California, every soldier who does what we do has been boning up. We were told it was probably a Pakistani design, so we have a pretty good understanding of what's required. We would have liked a bit more time, though. Now, if you'll excuse me.'

Cathy looked at Matthew, who grimaced and held up crossed fingers. She nodded at him then looked at her watch. Two minutes left.

'Where's Agent Brown?' Matthew asked Jensen.

'He was shot in the arm. I don't think it's too bad but he's gone off in an ambulance.'

'The further away from here, the better.'

'You can say that again.'

Matthew switched his gaze towards Cathy. She was like a caged lioness, full of energy but with no way to expend it. She paced about, constantly checking her watch. She looked up at him. 'One minute,' she mouthed silently. The seconds ticked past.

Suddenly there were two popping noises.

Matthew and the FBI agents spun around to see that the chief warrant officers had just opened two cans of beer and were toasting each other.

'Twenty seconds to spare,' said the short one raising his beer to the three of them. 'It's a good thing that we've spent a bit of time looking at these recently or else...' and he made a gesture by opening an upturned fist, indicating an explosion.

'Well, thank heaven for the army,' replied Agent Jensen, enthusiastically.

Matthew felt just as relieved but his recent experience with the military had dampened his respect somewhat. 'Thanks, guys,' he managed. He turned to Cathy, hoping to share the moment with her but she was all business.

'It is perfectly safe, isn't it?' The short one nodded. 'Then can you show me exactly what you did to disarm this thing?'

For Matthew, the next several hours were surprisingly busy and yet quite boring.

The site was cordoned off by hundreds of local police and FBI agents. Keeping the press at bay was proving to be a challenge to them all. A terror attack at a major venue like the Alamo would have generated major interest at any stage but the speculation that another nuclear disaster had narrowly been averted had created a media firestorm.

The sight of a massive crane lifting the entire apparatus that had contained the bomb over the wall and onto the back of a military truck had only fuelled speculation. But there was no official word and the stations had to draw their own conclusions.

This time at least, based on the last explosion off the Californian coast, many of the conclusions were surprisingly accurate. Tens of thousands of people would have died instantly, with many more to follow from their injuries and radiation poisoning over the next days, weeks and months. The city of San Antonio would have become a ghost town overnight. Who wants to stay at the scene of a nuclear disaster and risk a lingering and painful death?

A convoy of media vehicles followed the truck and a number of other military vehicles back to JBSA, but none were going to get past the guards that were spread around inside the perimeter of the base at regular intervals. The base commander, Brigadier General Atkins, was taking no chances with intruders and had issued shoot-to-kill orders. The serious faces confronting the reporters convinced them that this was not the time to break the rules and they were forced to rely on stock footage and long-distance shots of the installation.

Cathy warned Matthew what was coming in terms of the debriefing they were going to receive, and they agreed to tell the truth about the day's proceedings except for the part about his being able to move back in time. About his reason for being there in the first place, he was just going to repeat that he was a special consultant and not elaborate any further, referring any more questions back to her.

The two agents and Matthew were eventually taken to the local FBI headquarters and they were each grilled for about five hours on how the day's events had gone. By the end of it, Matthew had had enough. Three different people had asked him the same series of questions and he had given the same answers.

At the end of it all, Matthew was satisfied that he had done as well as he could and he figured the people conducting the debriefing were happy as well. After all, a nuclear disaster had been averted and many of them were still alive and uninjured due to the actions of the team which had gone on the mission that morning.

It was nearly six o'clock that night when Matthew and Cathy were told they could go. They met up with agent Jensen and caught a cab back to their hotel.

The three of them had dinner in the dining room and celebrated their success by sharing a bottle of wine with the meal.

Afterwards, they made their way to the rooms. 'See you guys for breakfast,' said Cathy as she put her key into the door. When Jensen wasn't looking, she winked slyly at Matthew.

'Yeah, goodnight,' replied Matthew.

Agent Jensen mumbled his goodnights to the other two and entered his room.

Despite the long and arduous day, Matthew now felt energised. He stripped off and jumped in the shower, brushed his teeth and put on some fresh clothes. When he was dressed, he figured that enough time had passed and slipped quietly outside.

He tapped lightly on Cathy's door. One second later the door opened and there she stood, naked. 'I thought you'd never get here. I was almost going to call Jensen,' she said, smiling.

'That'll be the day,' smirked Matthew as he gently pushed Cathy towards the bed, taking his own shirt off as he walked.

Suddenly, he was the one on his back, on the bed. *You don't want to get in a fight with this girl,* he thought.

Chapter 46

Ahmed Barazani was again running. *Thank the heavens that I smoke*, he thought as made his way down the street, hunched over, trying to look as inconspicuous as possible.

Despite the threat, he found a place to buy his cigarettes and had one lit in almost no time.

Who were the men at the hotel? He surmised that it didn't matter. There was no doubt in his mind that the Americans would be after him by now as well as the people he thought were his allies in this whole enterprise.

He was about to reap more destruction on the US than had ever been done before. He should be a hero to al-Qaeda even if his motivation was selfish. At least their goals aligned. Unfortunately for him, there weren't many Moslems aware of what he was about to do on their behalf so that they would sell him out for even a small amount of US dollars.

How ironic that the US, the great Satan, so despised by so many, could still buy their way throughout the world.

Ahmed looked at his watch. Half an hour to go. Only some sort of miracle could save them now. Maybe Mexico would appreciate what he was about to do. The destruction of the Alamo and a large part of San Antonio would be some sort of payback to the Americans for stealing their land all those years ago. Everywhere he looked, he could find more justification for what was about to happen. The thought cheered him momentarily.

Now he had to try to find a place to bunker down for a short period of time, at least until his handiwork was completed. A small café would do, somewhere he could have a cup of coffee, smoke his cigarette and be anonymous. There was a place now.

Ahmed entered and picked a seat at the back of the café. It was hot and stuffy, even at this late hour in the afternoon. The ceiling fan did nothing other than circulate the cigarette smoke better. Ahmed lit another, contributing to the atmosphere. He drank his coffee; chain smoked and constantly checked his watch.

Finally, it was time. He exhaled a long plume of smoke and slumped down in his chair. Now he would wait for the excitement that the news would bring. It would travel the world in minutes.

One cup of coffee and two cigarettes later, Ahmed began to see the signs. People were hurrying down the street, obviously excited. Now was the time to see the Americans suffering, though this would pale in comparison to what was coming in two days. The thought gave him comfort.

Ahmed stood and made his way through the café and out the main door. Almost instantly someone running crashed into him, knocking him to the ground. The pig didn't even bother to slow down to see if he was alright. Then from a distance up the road the man slowed, stopped and turned around.

Recognition hit both men at the same time. It was the man with the eye patch that Ahmed had run into in the alley when he had been bashed into unconsciousness. As quick as he could, he was on his feet and running for his life in the other direction.

Salman Umrani manoeuvred his car through the traffic. He knew Barazani was around here somewhere. The cigarette butts in the ashtray had still been smouldering when he and his men had kicked the hotel room door open, so the terrorist had been gone for no more than a few minutes.

The CIA operative had just received word of the failed bombing in San Antonio. Thank goodness for that. Who knows how many people would have died.

Now he was driving around looking for the mass-murdering piece of scum, phone on the seat next to him, waiting for anyone to call in a sighting.

It didn't take long.

'Yeah. What you got?'

'Your man's been spotted.'

'Where?'

'Near the big supermarket.'

'Keep me informed,' Salman said as he spun the wheel and headed his car towards Super Market Liaquatabad, about half a mile to the east.

Up until a few days ago, Dr Ahmed Barazani had been a wealthy, respected and influential member of Pakistani society. Now he was hiding behind two large rubbish dumpsters at the back of the markets and he was the most wanted man in the world, even if not that many people knew about him.

Another woman came up to the overflowing bins and tipped her smaller load on top of what was already there. Stinking bits of vegetable peel and goodness knows what spilled down on him; he managed to stay quiet despite almost retching from the stench.

Ahmed had managed to lose the man chasing him in the crowds and had headed towards Super Market Liaquatabad, where he hoped would be even larger numbers of people.

Under normal circumstances he would have enjoyed spending hours walking around the market, checking out the beautiful clothes and delicious foods that were on offer. Instead, he was huddled, like a coward, behind a stinking rubbish bin.

Despite the smell and noise, exhaustion claimed him and he drifted off into a restless sleep.

It was light when Ahmed awoke. It sounded like a large truck was coming towards him. He suspected it was a rubbish collection truck, which meant he was about to lose his hiding spot. Awkwardly, he climbed to his feet and walked away.

He took stock as he moved. He still had a little money and half a packet of cigarettes, but he stank just as badly as the dumpsters he had hidden behind. He was going to draw attention to himself unless he could clean up quickly. Time to look for some new clothes and somewhere to wash the stench away.

A shout from behind drew his attention. One local man was pointing at him, calling to two companions.

Ahmed started to run. He didn't have to look; he knew the men were after him.

There was a loud crack and something pinged off the wall near his head. *Now they're shooting at me!* He turned around a corner, temporarily out of range.

Salman Umrani sipped on his coffee, munched a pastry and wiped the sleep out of his eyes. He had slowly cruised around the area the entire night hoping for a sighting of Barazani, but the fugitive had managed to elude them.

Finally, Salman had succumbed to exhaustion and hunger and pulled over for some much-needed rest, caffeine and food. Even so, he had carried his breakfast back to the car and had it there, just in case he had to move at a moment's notice.

What the hell was that. A gunshot?

Salman started the car and pulled onto the road, the pastry forgotten and the coffee spilling onto the floor.

Even with the car going he heard a second shot. 'Fuck!' he said out loud. They needed Barazani alive. He had made it clear to those idiots. Alive. Now they were shooting at him.

He turned the car around the corner. There was Barazani now, staggering up the road towards him. He was holding his hand to his left side and Salman could see blood seeping through his fingers. Damn it. Salman stood on the brakes.

Three men were chasing Barazani and even as he watched, one raised a gun and fired again.

The shot went wide of the fleeing man and struck the bonnet of Salman's car, sounding like a hammer blow. 'Idiots!' He took his own gun from the door pocket and fired.

The shot sprang off the road in front of the three men, who immediately dove to the ground.

Barazani looked up to see who his saviour was.

'Quickly, Brother, we must get you away.' Salman yelled.

Barazani lurched ahead and around the car to the passenger door. He opened it and tumbled inside.

Salman looked across at the doctor. It was an ugly exit wound in his left side. The CIA agent had seen enough gunshot wounds in his time to know that this one was fatal. He swore to himself.

Salman trod on the accelerator pedal and peeled away. 'Don't worry, Brother,' he said to the terrorist next to him. 'We will get you to safety.' He knew of a safe house nearby where hopefully they could get some answers from the man before he expired.

Barazani gasped. 'You, you know me?'

'Of course, Brother. You are a hero to our cause.' Umrani nearly choked on the words.

'A hero, yes. A hero.' Despite the agony, Dr Ahmed Barazani smiled. Salman leaned closer as the terrorist spoke. 'I haven't heard…' A grunt of pain interrupted the sentence…'about the Alamo.'

You piece of shit, Salman thought. Instead, he said, 'San Antonio is decimated. At least a hundred thousand dead. You have brought America to its knees.'

Ahmed smiled again. 'Good. Now just one to go.'

'Yes, Brother, one more. Where will it be?'

'New…' The scientist's voice trailed off.

Salman looked away from the road again towards Barazani but he wouldn't be getting any more answers. The terrorist was staring into the distance through sightless eyes.

'Fuck!' screamed Salman as he bashed the steering wheel.

There was another bomb.

Chapter 47

Cathy was only half awake, staring at the ceiling, smiling dreamily. Matthew had gone back to his own room after they had spent some time snuggled together in bed. She preferred that they not fall asleep together, just in case, and he had reluctantly agreed.

Cathy reached out and grabbed her phone, looked through her email then had a quick shower and readied herself for the day. She went and banged on Jensen's door and then Matthew's. 'Time for breakfast.'

The two men arrived together, five minutes later. 'What's up?' asked Jensen. 'Couldn't you sleep?'

'I slept just fine, thank you. But I think we need to consider the possibility that wasn't the only bomb.'

'Shit. You think there's more?'

'I don't know. But we'd be kicking ourselves if one went off and we had stopped looking.'

A waitress came to the table to take their breakfast orders, which killed the conversation for a minute. The clinking of cutlery on plates and the scents of the meals on the nearby tables seemed to give Matthew quite an appetite this morning, Cathy noted with a smile. She was a bit hungry herself now that she thought about it. Jensen, though, settled for coffee.

They talked as they ate, Jensen looking on in amusement, as his two companions tucked into bacon and eggs with toast.

'You know,' said Matthew, 'this has to be the best bacon and eggs ever.'

Cathy seemed to choke on a bite of her breakfast just then, but Jensen didn't appear to notice. 'I guess saving thousands of people from a nuclear annihilation will make things taste better,' he commented.

'So, Jensen,' asked Cathy, 'what's your best guess about the next place we should go?'

'Based on yesterday it's going to be some place significant. They don't care how many people they kill. The more people that die, the happier they are. So, a large city with a significant landmark. Seattle maybe with the Space Needle.'

Cathy looked at her list. 'Something has been sent there. Matthew, what do you think about Seattle?'

'I've watched reruns of *Frasier*. It's a famous place. Sounds as good a bet as any other.'

Cathy looked at the two men. 'Okay. Let's get ready to catch a flight. I'll make some calls as we head to the airport.'

They didn't get to stand up before Cathy's phone rang. 'Owens here.'

'Cathy, Arnold Wilson.' The voice boomed out of the phone. Both men could hear the conversation despite the phone being pressed up to Cathy's ear.

'Yes, sir.'

'Well done yesterday at the Alamo. Great work.'

'Thank you, sir.' Cathy beamed at the praise.

'Well, you can't rest on your laurels.'

'Sir?'

'We've just received word from the CIA in Pakistan. There's one more bomb.'

Matthew and Jensen looked at each other and sighed.

'Where?'

'We don't know for sure. We managed to get the word "New" but the suspect died before they could get anything more useful from him. We are throwing everything at this. Agents are going everywhere with "New" in the title, New Hampshire, New Mexico, New Jersey. I want your team to go to New York to help there. Check your email for the details.'

'Thank you, sir.' Cathy looked at the two men. 'I guess you heard all that?' Both nodded. 'We're off to New York then.'

They all stood to make their way back to the rooms.

Matthew had hoped to have a few private moments alone with Cathy but the look on her face was all business. Reluctantly, he followed the other two up the stairs.

Cathy had been busy making calls throughout the trip to San Antonio Airport and had then told her two companions that they would be heading to the FBI office in New York once they landed.

After the four-hour flight, they caught a cab from LaGuardia airport to FBI headquarters at 26 Federal Plaza and made their way through security checks. Cathy made a query at the reception desk. She spoke with the lady at the desk for some time then was handed a sheaf of papers before turning to Matthew and Jensen. 'We're in conference room three. This way.' She pointed and then walked off. The men followed.

They walked along a hallway, found the sign for the right room and walked in to find almost thirty people seated, facing a lectern at the front of the room.

When they were noticed, the group in the room started to applaud. Matthew realised that these people were aware that they had just come from the Alamo and were congratulating them on a job well done.

Jensen smiled, looking a bit embarrassed and raised his hand in acknowledgement. Matthew thought about bouncing back in time just to avoid the whole spectacle but decided to just go with it. The two men took vacant seats near the front. Cathy appeared like she was unaware of the clapping and went straight to the lectern to speak with the man addressing the room. He wasn't as tall as Cathy but was extremely powerfully built, so much so that his jacket looked about to pull apart at the seams around his shoulders. Closely cropped grey hair gave him an air of authority. After a minute of conversation, she sat beside her two colleagues.

The man at the front started to talk. 'Thank you to everyone for being here on short notice. I'm Special Agent in Charge, Dan Walters. The newcomers are Special Agent Cathy Owens, that's Special Agent Jensen,' he waved his hand towards Jensen, 'and that's a consultant, Matthew Fraser. I believe everybody's been given a copy of the list of landmarks that correspond to some sort of container delivery. The logic is sound because that's how we found the bomb at the Alamo.' There were a few cheers at that. 'Other teams are focusing on other places around the country pretty much anywhere with the word "New" in the title. We've had a look and New York gives us almost fifty landmarks with delivery matches. There's thirty-two of us here so that's eight groups of four. After the experience the team had in Texas, I feel more comfortable with bigger teams than normal.'

Cathy looked down at the papers in her hand. Dan Walters continued. 'You have all been assigned a team and a list of places.' He looked at the clock on the wall. 'It's three o'clock now so each team should be able to check at least two or three places before we finish tonight and then continue in the morning. Any questions?'

There were a few comments about kicking ass and busting heads from the crowd but no questions. Walters spoke again. 'Call it in when each item is checked off. Let's do it.' People started shuffling out of the conference room.

Cathy checked her lists again. 'My team has been assigned Special Agent Arturo,' she called out. A lady in her early thirties waved and made her way over to them. She was an attractive lady of medium height with olive skin and long dark hair, held back in a ponytail. She stuck out her hand.

'Linda Arturo. Nice to meet you.'

They all introduced themselves. Cathy handed her the list. 'You're the local here, so which place should we visit first?'

After a quick scan, Arturo replied, 'Let's try One World Trade Center.'

Captain Ray Kingston put the phone down.

His contact had come through with useful information. FBI Special Agent Cathy Owens was in New York.

Apparently yesterday she had been responsible for San Antonio not being turned into a nuclear wasteland. While he was grateful for that—he had friends who worked there—it wasn't going to stop him from doing his job. Cathy Owens and he were going to spend some quality time together and he was going to get some answers as to what had happened in the Australian Outback and the truth about the time travel experiments.

Chapter 48

The team followed Arturo to the carpark and after a few minutes in her vehicle they were at the World Trade Center precinct. They made their way to the One World Trade Centre building and entered the lobby. The building, colloquially known as Freedom Tower, was now the primary structure in the World Trade Centre complex, the site which housed the Twin Towers destroyed on September 11, 2001.

They walked up to the white marble and steel reception desk. While they were waiting, Matthew turned to admire the huge splash of colour on the wall opposite the reception counter—a mural that had to be close to thirty metres long. He had no idea what it was supposed to represent and before he had a chance to ask Cathy was showing her identification. 'Special Agent Owens. FBI. We need to speak with the duty manager please.'

The young lady behind the counter didn't seem phased by the request and picked up the phone and pushed a button. After a few seconds, she was speaking. 'Yes, Mr Sutton. There are people here from the FBI who would like to see you.' A few more seconds and she put the phone down. 'He'll be here in a few moments.' She smiled at Cathy and then the four of them might as well have disappeared as the receptionist moved on to the next customer.

Two minutes later a well-dressed man in his thirties strode towards them. 'Are you the FBI agents?'

Cathy nodded. 'I'm Special Agent Owens,' said Cathy showing her ID again. 'These are Special Agents Jensen and Arturo.' Each nodded in turn. 'This is consultant Matthew Fraser.'

'Richard Sutton,' replied the man. 'How can I help the FBI today?'

'We need to look at an overseas shipment that came in within the last two weeks. We can supply a consignment number.'

'Any particular reason?'

'We're checking the correct import tariffs are being paid on this type of goods and want to sight the consignment,' Cathy replied.

Sutton made a show of looking at the four people in front of him with a clearly sceptical look on his face. 'If you'll follow me, we'll go and see the building services manager. He'll be able to take you straight to it.' He about-faced and walked off. The four visitors quickly followed.

They went through a door at the end of the counter and into an office space full of desks with a person busy at each one. Matthew guessed that a building this size needed a lot of people to make it work.

They pursued the fast-moving Sutton to an office with the appropriate title on the door underneath the name "Gene Milton". He knocked but didn't bother waiting for an answer before opening up.

'Gene. These people are with the FBI. Could you offer all assistance please?' With that done, Sutton turned and strode off without another word.

Cathy moved to the door and Matthew heard a friendly, 'Please come in.'

They filed into the room. There was a neatly arranged desk against the wall. A short, balding, slightly overweight man with an open face rose from his chair. 'Gene Milton. What can I do for you?'

Cathy showed her ID yet again as did the agents. 'Cathy Owens.' She didn't bother with the other names but Milton smiled at them all anyway. 'Mr Milton, we need to sight an item to determine if the correct import tariff has been paid.' She pointed to an item on a piece of paper she pulled from a folder.

Milton took the paper from Cathy and sat back down at his desk. He made a few mouse clicks, typed in a number and looked at what appeared on the computer monitor. 'That's a new sump pump that is scheduled to be installed tomorrow. It's down in the lower basement level.'

'What's a sump pump?' asked Jensen.

'They are water pumps generally installed at the low point in a building in case of seepage or flooding. They pump out the water, keeping the level dry.'

'Could we see it please?' asked Cathy.

'Certainly. Please follow me.' Milton stood and walked back the way that the duty manager had come a few minutes previously. Once back in the foyer he made his way to a lift marked "Service Elevator" and pressed the call button. The door opened instantly and they all entered.

Matthew couldn't quite see all the buttons from where he stood but there were lots of them. Milton pushed B3.

The lift dropped from underneath them; in a few seconds they stopped and the doors opened.

Matthew felt he had been underground enough of late, enough to last him a lifetime, but he took a deep breath and stepped out with the others. They followed Milton through a brightly lit space full of columns and a procession of service vehicles that looked like golf carts and the things that towed luggage trailers at airports.

They seemed to be going down slightly as they approached the far wall. Next to the wall was a pit surrounded by a handrail and on the ground next to it was a wooden crate.

The three people who had been at the Alamo looked at each other with worried looks. The crate appeared to be of a size capable of holding a bomb despite the contents label attached to it.

Milton walked to a nearby storage locker, came back with a pry bar and worked at opening the lid of the crate. It came with a squeal as the last nail pulled out and there were smiles of relief from the two men and Arturo as the contents were revealed, a pump and motor assembly as advertised.

Matthew could tell Cathy was disappointed because they hadn't had instant success. 'Thank you, Mr Milton,' she said. 'Very generous of you to spare the time to help us. Let's call it in.'

Their next stop was the New York Stock Exchange located at 11 Wall Street in Lower Manhattan. To Matthew, hardly anything said "America" like the centre of world capitalism. By the time they arrived, it was well after the four o'clock bell for the cease of the day's trading, which was a bit disappointing, but he consoled himself in the fact that he was going to see something that was now closed to the public.

Since the 9/11 attacks the trading floor was off limits to most people as it was considered a critical piece of national infrastructure, too important to put at risk.

Cathy had made phone calls on the way and they were met by a man who introduced himself as Samuel Tyler, Superintendent.

Cathy had given Tyler the cover story and he had led them through some corridors to a modest office.

Matthew was discouraged as he didn't see any differences between this and any other office building. They had been nowhere near the trading floor.

Tyler opened a filing cabinet drawer, pulled out a folder, found the sheet he was looking for and compared it to the piece of paper Cathy had given him. 'That part has already been installed. It's a digital display above one of the trading floor kiosks.'

Matthew couldn't help himself. 'I think we'd like to see it anyway, Mr Tyler. Just to be on the safe side.'

Jensen and Arturo both gave Cathy a bemused look, but she had a little smile on her face and nodded at them. 'Thank you, Mr Tyler,' she said.

They followed the superintendent through a couple of doors and they were on one of the trading floors. It had a huge American flag on one wall and any number of the fluorescent blue logos of the NYSE spread around the trading kiosks.

The kiosks were round, about two metres in diameter and three metres tall. They were covered in computer monitors and digital displays. They looked like where a street vendor would sell food to the public. Matthew half expected a window to open and someone to pop their head out and ask him what he wanted on his hotdog.

The monitors were all blank, but they could all imagine the numbers flashing and cries of "buy" and "sell". It was a place where fortunes were made or lost.

Tyler understood the mood of the group. 'There used to be over five thousand people in here every day taking orders and buying and selling stocks. These days we do it with about seven hundred. Technology has made it a lot more civilised, but it is still a cut-throat business.'

He moved around the floor to the kiosk he wanted and then pointed to the display on the top. It was a long thin item that would scroll a stock price or news item. 'That's it.'

Definitely not what the team was after.

'Thank you, Mr Tyler. Let's call it in.' Cathy checked her watch. 'It's nearly seven now. Let's call it a day.'

'Where are we going now?' asked Matthew.

'A Holiday Inn in the Chelsea District, not too far away. The FBI has an arrangement with the place. Hopefully our bags have been taken there already.'

Agent Arturo took them to the motel and went her own way after they all agreed to meet at the FBI headquarters around eight the next morning for an update prior to heading to the Empire State Building.

The bags had been dropped off and it turned out to be a comfortable place, though somewhat disappointing for Matthew. Cathy had whispered 'Not tonight' as they had finished their meal in the restaurant and headed up to their rooms.

Chapter 49

While Matthew, Cathy and Jensen were in the air on the way to New York, a tall man with a newly cultivated beard wandered down Fifth Avenue on the island of Manhattan in the city of New York. He was having the time of his life. He had never been to New York as a tourist before, only for work. Now, since his early retirement, which left him with a nice little nest egg, he'd decided to see and do all of the things he had never had the chance to see and do in his own country.

He decided that New York would be the place where he would start his grand tour. There was just so much going on here. In the last three days, he had visited the Statue of Liberty, the American Museum of Natural History, something he enjoyed much more than he expected and finally, One World Trade Centre.

The trip to the observation deck of One World Trade Centre followed by a visit to the 9/11 Memorial and 9/11 Museum was a much more emotional experience than he had imagined it would be. Terrible sadness, rage and pride had welled up within him as he paid his respects to the spirits of those who had died there, especially those who had put themselves in harm's way to save those who couldn't save themselves.

Today, he was going to do a little shopping. It was time he spoiled himself. With stores like Macy's, Barneys, Bergdorf Goodman and Saks Fifth Avenue he was sure he would be able to find himself that expensive suit he had always wanted as well as the smart casual clothes he had never had the time to wear. The thought of buying some golf clothes entered his mind. Despite never playing, he was naturally athletic and a few lessons should see him hitting the ball long and straight.

The daydream almost made him miss the face of the Middle Eastern man who passed him walking the opposite direction. He was around fifty years old, about five ten, with a slim build and the graceful walk of an athlete. A broken nose which had never been straightened spoiled what otherwise would have been a handsome face.

He had seen that face before. But where?

The name refused to come but the bearded man felt it was important. He let the face move from his consciousness. It would be sorted and processed in the back rooms of his mind and an answer would be presented soon enough.

He casually turned around and began to follow the mystery man. In the absence of a name, a destination would be important. His previous thoughts about new suits and golf clothes were trivial things of the past. Old instincts had surfaced and he was once again a dangerous man.

To a casual observer he was strolling along Fifth Avenue, taking in the shops and sites, but there was no way the mystery man was going to lose him, despite the crowds.

The two men walked south, separated by distance and knowledge, towards the entrance to Bryant Park. Another four men, unsurprisingly also of Middle Eastern appearance, were seated on benches. They all stood and nodded greetings to the first. There was a brief exchange of words and the five men continued south, a few steps between them so as not to appear to be together.

The bearded man didn't recognise the new companions, but he wasn't reassured at all when four more men joined them a few moments later after leaving two sandwich shops along the way. His threat assessment went through the roof.

The men continued south until they crossed West 34th Street and then they were at 350 Fifth Avenue, the Empire State Building. They all entered the lobby one by one; if the bearded man hadn't followed them there was no way he would have thought they were a group.

The bearded man hadn't had lunch yet so he ordered at a nearby burger joint and settled down at a table where he could see the entrance.

Yesterday he had been having the time of his life, but today was shaping up even better.

The afternoon greyed into night and as far as he could see it was still business as usual in the iconic building. People came and went, unbothered by the nine Middle Eastern men. Despite the peace that pervaded their surroundings, the bearded man knew a terrorist cell was in operation.

The waitress came up to his table with a coffee pot, topped up his cup and politely asked if he would like something else to eat. He ordered something light as he wasn't sure how long he was going to be there and didn't want to draw undue attention to himself. He was used to long periods of inactivity but it would look strange to the people in the burger joint. While he watched and waited, he read a tourist brochure about the building.

The Empire State Building opened on 1 May 1931, and it had been the world's tallest building for the next forty years. Millions of tourists visited the building every year, many of them looking out over the city from the 86th floor and 102nd floor observation decks.

It was a perfect terrorist target.

Finally, approaching two in the morning, closing time for the Empire State Building, the nine men began to meander out. They didn't acknowledge each other but walked off on their own, up town.

The bearded man pondered for a moment. That he had just seen a dry run he had no doubt. But for what?

Opening time for tourists across the road was at eight in the morning and he was going to be there.

He threw some money on the table and made his way out the door.

Chapter 50

It was still dark in the cheap hotel room on West 38th Street. Fahad Malek had selected it as he could walk to the target easily, not because of the comforts it offered. It was a tiny space and the bed was like the rocks he had slept on in his early days as a freedom fighter.

Malek arose early. In truth, he hadn't slept much at all. He was too wound up. Today just had to be a success. After the disasters of San Francisco and San Antonio, this was their final chance to crush the American spirit.

He thought for a moment.

Maybe the first bomb had not been such a complete disaster. It had struck fear into the hearts of the infidels and many had died as a result. However, the bomb had not reached the intended target of the casino in Las Vegas, instead detonating off the coast of California. It was ironic how the Americans' laziness had saved them.

In Las Vegas, the explosion would have wiped out at least half "the strip", as the Americans called it. Las Vegas would have become the ghost town it deserved to be. It was such a symbol of decadence that surely even the rest of the world would have rejoiced with him.

The one good thing to come of the bomb exploding in the wrong place was that he now had extra men in his team to ensure that nothing would go wrong this time. The four men who had been assigned to sacrifice themselves in that unholy place had drifted east across the country and met up with him in New York.

As for the Alamo, he didn't even want to think what had gone wrong there. The American authorities could never have figured out that a bomb was about to reduce their beloved shrine to atoms along with thousands upon thousands of the ignorant peasants who lived there. It must have been someone within his own organisation. That thought disturbed him more than anything.

A traitor.

It had to be Barazani. Malek had sent a trusted lieutenant, Farouk, to check out his loyalty but he had not been heard from since. The only possible reason for that was that his man was dead or captured. In either case, Barazani was the culprit.

Farouk didn't know the location of the bombs—only two people knew where all three were to be delivered. So, it had to be that fat little doctor.

If events went according to plan and he survived, then Malek vowed to track Barazani down and make him pay for his treachery. Little did he know that Barazani had already paid his price.

It was nearly twenty years since he had first met the Pakistani. During that meeting and subsequent contact, Malek had never doubted the nuclear scientist's zeal but now, with victory so close, perhaps his resolve had wavered and he had given them up.

During the trial run yesterday, though, there had been no sign that the authorities were aware of him or his men. The soft drink dispensing machine had still been there on the observation deck. A little scratch he had put in the bottom corner showed him it was the same one. How ironic that another symbol of the American invasion of the world would be used to strike a killing blow against them.

Malek had originally planned that his men would be in position when the bomb exploded but that he would be long gone. He was a leader within the organisation and much more important than these soldiers. They were prepared to die for the cause, as was he, but only if he had to. He could serve their brotherhood much better by leading and planning further attacks against the ungodly.

If everything looked like it was running smoothly, Malek planned to leave at least an hour before the explosion to give himself plenty of time to be clear of the blast zone. He wasn't flying; a train was going to be his method of leaving this accursed city. He didn't trust that he could slip into or out of the country undetected through airport security. He wasn't sure if his face was known or not but he couldn't take the chance.

He had come into the US aboard the freighter that carried the bomb. What a miserable trip that had been. He had been constantly sick for almost two weeks. How could anybody do that for a living? Give him the desert or the mountains and he was content. He had thanked Allah when he had finally set foot on solid land again.

It had proved to be a simpler task sneaking off the freighter than through the much tougher security at the airport. He could pick his time and so in the small hours of the night he had made his way from the ship into the wider community.

Malek knew his followers could enter the country without fear as none were suspected of any wrongdoing and so they had travelled over, in the previous two weeks, by plane.

So here they were. Today was the day.

Malek gazed out of the grimy hotel room window. The sun was rising. It was time to pray.

Two blocks away in a much more luxurious room, the bearded man had slept well. In his previous life, he had been used to knowing that the next day was going to be something out of the ordinary, so he had trained himself to sleep when he could. A good night's sleep could be the difference between success and failure and in his line of work, failure generally meant death.

There was a knock on the door. 'Breakfast.'

He let the porter in with his meal and gave a generous tip, something he was getting used to doing. The aromas from the tray set his tastebuds watering.

He took his time over the meal, savouring the flavours, knowing that he might need the energy that this meal would provide. It always paid to be prepared.

He looked out of the gleaming hotel room window. The sun was rising. It was time to get ready.

Despite taking a long time to drift off, the days of excitement he had experienced lately had caught up with Matthew and once he went to sleep, he slept well.

He woke up feeling refreshed, but the habits of a lifetime meant that he felt a need to do some exercise. Since the hotel had a reasonably well-equipped gym, he worked out for half an hour and ran a few miles on the treadmill. He felt mentally better for the effort.

The young Australian went back to his room and took a long shower. He dressed in his best FBI imitation clothes. Room service delivered a light breakfast.

He was looking forward to today. He had only seen the Empire State Building on television and at the movies—he'd seen the original 1933 *King Kong*—and to see it up close himself was going to be a real thrill. Maybe he could even take in the higher of the two observation decks. That would be something.

It was a symbol of American enterprise and know-how and it still had that special feeling, even now, years after it had been superseded.

The thought suddenly disturbed him.

A reflection of the sun from the building across the street shone through his window. It was time to go and check on the others.

Chapter 51

The man with the beard and glasses used his crutches to propel himself up to the security station on the second floor of the Empire State Building. The guard looked at the bandage wound around the man's left foot and felt sorry. He had recently returned to work from a broken leg and knew how frustrating it was to not be fully mobile.

The guard smiled at the bearded man. 'Can you get through the metal detector without the crutches, sir?'

The bearded man considered for a moment. 'I think so, officer.' He passed the guard the crutches and with his left leg held out to the side, did a funny sort of hopping motion through the electronic equipment.

Satisfied, the guard moved around the metal detector and handed the bearded man back his crutches. 'You have a nice day, sir.'

'Thank you, officer,' replied the man as he tucked his crutches back under his arms and moved off. He had pre-printed tickets so there was one less line to join, though at this early hour, the lines were short. Once he showed his ticket, he made his way past the Sustainability Exhibit that showed how the building had undergone renovations in order to save energy costs and reduce carbon emissions. A figure over four million dollars was prominently shown off as the annual savings the structure had made since the retrofit which started in 2009.

The bearded man browsed around the displays, nodding at all the right items, and then made his way to the men's restroom. Once there he locked himself in a stall and sat down. He propped the crutches against the wall, then brought his left leg up and unwound the bandage. It had looked bulky but there was only a couple of wraps which covered a layer of padding and a boot underneath. He wriggled his foot around to get some blood flowing.

Once happy with how his foot felt, he reached for the crutch with the blue-taped hand grip. He undid the wing-nuts holding the top and bottom parts of the crutch together then turned the bottom half upside-down. A number of packages, wrapped in plastic to deaden the noise and stop random movement, dropped into his hand from the hollow tubing. The bearded man repeated the procedure with the second crutch, the one with the red-taped handgrip, and then unwrapped each package.

Thirty seconds later he had assembled a SIG Sauer P320-M17 handgun, specifically designed as the personal sidearm for the US Army. He had obtained a unit of the gun during its test phase and had been very happy with its performance. He hadn't felt the need to return it afterwards. The gun was tucked into his belt in the small of his back and the extra ammunition clips into his pants pockets.

The bearded man took off his white jacket, turned it inside-out and put it back on. He was now wearing a black jacket. He took off his glasses, pulled a blue baseball cap out of his back pocket and put it on.

He was now a different man.

He opened the stall door slowly and looked out. He was alone. He walked over to the trash receptacle and dropped the pieces of the crutches in along with the glasses, then went out to join the crowds.

He looked around. So far there was no sign of any of the men that he'd seen yesterday. Wait. There was one now waiting outside the security checkpoint. And here comes one of his friends even if he doesn't look like one of the men from yesterday.

It looked like the day was going to be very interesting.

Fahad Malek walked into the lobby of the Empire State Building.

His initial thoughts had been to keep his men there, in the lobby, in order to be ready for any eventuality but when he had researched the place, he realised that would have generated too much notice. It wasn't like a five-star hotel with huge open spaces and bars and dining rooms that they could spread out in. One Middle Eastern man loitering here would be suspicious; seven or eight of them gathered in the one spot would be like waving a flag or shooting a flare into the sky on a dark night, especially now that tensions were raised after San Antonio.

The problem he had was getting his men from the office section of the building, past the security checkpoint which led to the observation decks, with their weapons so that they could react if they had to. He wanted them spread throughout the building just in case the authorities showed up and attempted to defuse the bomb. If the US federal agents didn't show up within an hour of the planned detonation he would disappear, leaving his men to keep watch. Of course, they didn't know that he wouldn't be coming back.

Sometimes sacrifices were necessary.

All of his men were prepared to die for the cause, as was Malek, but firstly he wanted to do a lot more living before he arrived in paradise.

Malek was lucky in that he had plenty of time to plan this particular part of the mission. He had sent a trusted lieutenant to the city three months ago with a view to renting office space in the building.

Posing as a member of what was a legitimate organisation, the United States and Middle Eastern Trade Development Association, the man had carried out his task and leased an office on the forty-ninth floor of the building. The man had nothing to do with the association but the Empire State Realty Trust was paid, so they didn't bother to investigate further. He had to take the minimum six-month lease term, which meant that three months' rent would be wasted. Oh well, he could live with that. Malek smiled at the thought.

For much of the time, the office was empty; however, with a presence in the building, deliveries could be made and, over time, weapons could be smuggled in, hidden with other deliveries. Now there was enough firepower sitting in the office to invade a small country. Malek knew the US wasn't a small country and that it could respond quickly but he hoped that they wouldn't need to use the guns at all.

Malek knew he could cover the tenant area of the building by having half of his men visit the office they had rented then spread out from there, but he had to make sure that weapons were distributed to his other men covering the visitors areas.

The problem that had to be overcome was the separation of tenants and visitors. Both parties did not enter the building the same way. Visitors gained access via the 33rd or 34th Street entrances and use different elevators. If tenants wanted to visit the viewing platforms, they had to enter via the same security checkpoint as tourists.

Malek decided to overcome his problems the old-fashioned way. Through violence and extortion.

The man renting the office space, Hisham Nasry, had observed the staff on his many trips through the security station and had become friendly with one man in particular, Ted Watson. Not much information was needed from him, just an approximate location of the area that he lived in and his wife's name. The next step was to trawl through social media until her Facebook page was found. After that, a little bit of detective work was required but it didn't take too long before they had an address.

Malek engaged a couple of fringe members of his organisation from New York to take care of the rest this morning. Ted Watson was going to have quite a surprise in a few minutes and not the happy kind.

Nasry appeared in the area leading up to the security station. An almost imperceptible nod was the only sign that he saw Malek. He pulled his cell phone from his pocket and swiped his way around the screen. The stony expression became a lot more relaxed as he found what he wanted. He scanned the security station quickly and spotted the man he was looking for. He waved.

Smiling at one of his regular customers, Ted Watson walked up and asked Nasry how his day was going. By way of a reply, Nasry held up his phone and showed the security guard the screen.

Malek could see the man blanch from where he was standing but as expected, he didn't show too much outward emotion. He seemed to realise quite quickly that the life of his wife and his young daughter, who he could see on the screen, tied up with guns pointing at their heads, depended on him remaining calm.

'What do you want?' Watson asked the man in front of him.

'Some of my associates will be coming through the security station very soon. It would be best for your family if the metal detectors showed nothing as they pass through. You can arrange that, can't you Ted?'

Watson's mouth was almost too dry to speak but he croaked out an affirmative reply.

'Good. I will wave to you when I am ready, and you will let me and my friends through and then forget we ever met.'

Watson nodded and Nasry turned and walked away.

Malek watched as Watson walked back to the screening area. He spoke to one of the other guards. The second man nodded and walked away leaving Watson on his own manning the metal detectors. The compromised guard made some adjustments on the control panel.

Malek nodded his approval. The day was going well.

He knew that Nasry would be heading back up to the office space, collecting a mail cart and bringing it back down to ground level. He would wheel it around to the tourist entrance where he would meet up with the other men as they entered the building. Of course, there was no mail in the cart, just a number of backpacks containing fully automatic weapons which he would distribute to the men as far from the public view as possible. They would then have to enter the building one at a time, so they didn't draw too much attention. After that, two men would drift around the environmental display and the other two would go to the viewing platform. At least, their last sights would be spectacular.

He would be up there himself for a short time but he intended to be gone long before the fireworks.

The bearded man watched unobtrusively as the scene before him unfolded.

He shook his head. How could he be the only one who knew something was happening here? What good did it do to have an alphabet soup of intelligence services in the country if not one of them knew something about a plot at the Empire State Building? The thought disturbed him.

What was the plot? What was their end game?

Suddenly, he knew.

The bearded man considered leaving but quickly realised that he couldn't abandon a lifetime of discipline. He had wished for a chance to get at these bastards and here it was. If he had to, he would take out all of these fucks by himself and if it all went to shit, well, he wouldn't be around to worry about it, would he?

He watched for a few minutes. One by one the terrorists made their way through the security checkpoint. The sullen-looking guard manning the detector was either in on the plot or had been coerced somehow. Either way he was a traitor.

He contemplated calling in the authorities but dropped the thought as he scanned the crowd again.

Now there was someone he never expected to see again. And who was that with him?

Today *really* was going to be one of the most interesting days ever.

Chapter 52

The update at the FBI headquarters hadn't shone any new light on their investigation, merely eliminated some of the possibilities.

Matthew could see the frustration on Cathy's face as each entry checked had a line drawn through it. He knew it meant a lot to her career to be right but even so, it was hard for him to want there to be a bomb in this amazing city.

'Cheer up. It's a good thing if an atom bomb doesn't blow up New York.'

With a rueful smile, she replied, 'I know. I just can't help but think that it's here. Somewhere. We've got to find it.'

He nodded his agreement.

Cathy continued. 'Anyway. One thing's for sure.'

'What's that?'

'We aren't going to find it here. Let's go. Oh, by the way, this is for you.' She tossed him a small wallet.

Matthew caught it and opened it up to see a picture of himself with the letters FBI prominently displayed. 'Thanks.'

Agent Arturo drove them all and parked in a garage not far from the historic building. She placed a sign indicating they were on official business on the dash and they walked off.

When they reached the pavement, Matthew looked up but his view was blocked by other buildings.

Jensen noted Matthew rubbernecking and laughed. 'Don't worry. I think we'll be able to find it from here.'

Matthew smiled back at the FBI man. Jensen had accepted him as one of the team and the young Australian appreciated that. It couldn't be easy for a career agent to suddenly have an outsider thrust upon him. As for Arturo, she didn't share the same history and so was a bit more reserved. Hopefully nothing much would happen today and Matthew wouldn't have to try to prove himself again. That was getting dangerous.

Arturo looked at Cathy. 'How do you want to handle it? Two each for the visitors and the tenants?'

'We've only come to see one particular consignment for ourselves so let's stick together to start with and see if we need to split up after. We'll go to the security station and they can direct us from there.'

They all nodded their agreement as they approached the entrance to the historic landmark.

As they entered the lobby, Matthew gazed in wonder at the grandeur before him. He had read that about ten years ago the area had been restored to the standard of the original build. It was amazing what the builders had achieved in the 1930s—the lobby restoration had taken longer than it had originally taken to construct the whole building.

His eyes were drawn along the corridor to the display behind the reception desk. An anemometer was built into the wall. It resembled a clock face with its big and little hands, but this device was connected to a sensor positioned towards the top of the structure and measured wind speed and direction. The small hand showed the wind direction and the larger one displayed speed. The building was originally designed to have an airship mooring station near its pinnacle, so wind speed and direction were important. Despite this, Matthew knew that the idea had been abandoned after a couple of nearly impossible attempts to dock the unwieldy crafts.

He looked up at the ceiling and the stunning art-deco mural, with its gold and aluminium leaf, representing the heavens but with 1930s machine parts representing the celestial objects. He wondered how much effort had gone into this work.

He looked back down. Cathy seemed oblivious to the splendour. Maybe she had seen it before. He had never asked. Now he felt like a bad boyfriend. *Is that what I am?* he thought. *Oh, for God's sake, Matthew. Focus.*

The man standing at the desk saw the FBI logos on their clothes and realised these visitors were here in some official capacity.

'Security please,' said Cathy. The man waved them through.

The four of them basically followed the crowd up to the security screening station. Jensen pointed to the left at a door that was clearly labelled and they walked after Cathy as she turned the handle and entered the office.

The man sitting behind the desk looked up from his paperwork at the unannounced entry. If he was surprised by visitors wearing FBI jackets, he hid it well. 'How can I help the federal government today?' he asked.

Cathy took point. 'Special Agent Owens. FBI,' she said holding up her ID. She glanced down at the nameplate on the desk. 'Chief Constantine, we're part of a special unit tracking that correct import tariffs are being paid. We have a consignment number and we hope you can physically show us the item.' She held out a piece of paper.

Constantine shot her a sceptical look. 'That's not really my area but let me make a call to admin and hopefully they'll be able to help. If it gets me out from behind this desk, I'd be happy to show you personally.'

He picked up the phone on the desk and pushed a two-button combination. A few seconds later he was engaged in conversation with someone on the other end of the line. He wrote something down, thanked the person and put the receiver down.

Constantine looked back up at them. 'Have any of you ever been to the observation deck before? Every one of the four visitors shook their heads. 'Well, you're in for a treat then because that's where your consignment is.'

'What exactly are we looking for?' Cathy asked.

'It's a Coca-Cola dispenser,' he said, standing up. 'So, if you'd like to follow me, we'll head up and have a look.'

Opening the door, he turned and looked at Cathy. 'If you don't mind me saying, Agent Owens, four people to look at a Coke machine seems a bit excessive. Is there anything I need to be worried about?'

'Let's hope not, Chief,' she replied.

Kasim Abidi was going to die today. He had made his peace with Allah and he knew that he would be travelling to paradise soon. To know you were going to die and to realise your death meant nothing would be the most terrible thing; more than anything else, he needed his death to be significant.

Kasim was twenty-five, but a life in the desert made him look older. He was barely five and a half feet tall and looked slim in the Western clothes he was wearing, but his upbringing had ensured he was stronger than he looked. He was all wiry muscle.

Some years ago, not far from this very spot, his brothers-in-arms had achieved such a death as to strike fear into the hearts of this Godless country and today he was going to do the same but in an even more spectacular fashion.

Kasim swallowed hard. Just because he was about to terrorise this most unholy of places, didn't mean that he was unafraid. His stomach was in turmoil and he felt that he was about to shit his trousers. That was not how he wanted to enter paradise. He swore quietly and told himself to relax. He looked around, hoping to see one of his brothers to gain some of their strength.

What he saw instead chilled him to the bone.

The FBI were coming out of the security office.

Kasim shrugged out of his backpack and rummaged around inside. He quickly found the handle of what he was looking for and pulled out a Heckler & Koch MP7. It was just over sixteen inches long with the stock collapsed and had been chosen so it would easily fit into a backpack.

Kasim started to raise the MP7 into a firing position but he had hardly begun to lift it before there was an ear-piercing scream.

A woman tourist, visiting New York with her husband from their farm in Kansas, suspected that all men of Middle Eastern appearance were terrorists. She had been keeping a watchful eye on the nervous-looking foreigner and her worst fears were confirmed at the sight of the gun. With a voice that her sons could hear calling from half a mile away at dinner time, she made everyone in the area aware that something bad was about to happen.

All of the people walking out of the security office instantly looked towards the source of the scream. Years of training kicked in with the FBI agents and they were reaching for their sidearms within a fraction of a second.

The sound of the scream startled the already spooked Kasim and he pulled the trigger of the MP7 before it was even halfway to horizontal.

As a result, the floor around the security station was torn to pieces as the rounds exploded into the tiles in a line that rapidly streamed towards the group.

Unfortunately for Special Agent Arturo the last three rounds in the magazine struck her in the hip, chest and throat and she was thrown violently back into Matthew, whose world dissolved in a blinding flash.

Chapter 53

'We've only come to see one particular consignment for ourselves so let's stick together to start with and see if we need to split up after. We'll go to the security station and they can direct us from there,' said Cathy.

Matthew tapped her on the shoulder. 'We shouldn't do that.'

'Now what do you mean by…' She saw the look on his face. 'Oh.'

Jensen and Arturo shared a questioning look. 'What's the matter?' Jensen asked.

'There's a man in there with a machine gun.' He looked at Arturo. 'I don't know what type it is but you don't want to get hit by those bullets.'

Arturo screwed up her face at Matthew and turned to Cathy. 'What is this shit? Does he think he's a psychic or something?'

'You can believe him or not but I trust Matthew with my life. If he says there's a man in there with a machine gun, there is.' She looked at Jensen. He seemed to be considering what she said and then he nodded his agreement.

'I go with Matthew,' he said. 'I've seen him in action.'

Arturo gasped in frustration. 'Fine then. Is there anything else you can tell us?' she asked, voice dripping with sarcasm.

Matthew closed his eyes, trying to remember what he had seen. He had been a bit like a kid in a candy store, not knowing where to look. 'The man was to our right, through the screening station, looking at a display of some sort. He's Middle Eastern, has a blue sweat shirt, a green baseball cap and he's wearing a backpack. There's another man further over to the right, Middle Eastern, not too tall, grey shirt, no cap but he has a bushy moustache. I think we are after a Coke machine on the observation deck. That's all I know.'

Arturo looked at Matthew like he was from another planet but then saw the other two agents were willing to go along. 'Right then.' She looked at Cathy. 'What's the plan?'

'Let's turn the jackets inside out and hide the logo. I don't want to spook these guys.' Matthew nodded and gave her a small smile. 'Matthew and I will go in together and try to alert the security team. Wait till we call, then follow us. Try to look like you're a couple. We'll try to get past them and then we can catch them between us. Hopefully, without gunfire.'

'Let's do it,' said Jensen.

Matthew and Cathy held hands as they walked towards the reception desk. The anemometer held no interest for Matthew this time. Cathy discreetly showed the attendant her ID. 'We need to speak with your head of security.'

The man showed surprise at the request but answered quickly. 'Straight through the entrance there and over to the left.'

'I know,' said Matthew.

Arturo looked at Jensen. 'What's going on with the Aussie? He's only a consultant and it looks like he's running the show.'

Jensen considered his response. 'You know, I'm not quite sure but he was right in the thick of things at the Alamo. Everything he seems to do and say is right. Maybe he is psychic. I don't know. But he helped stop a nuclear bomb going off and killing God knows how many people, so I'm going to stick my neck out and go with him.'

Cathy looked around as they walked. She spotted the two men that Matthew had spoken about but didn't have time to look any further before she and Matthew had another guard intercept them. Once again Cathy quietly explained that they were with the FBI and needed to see the security chief. The guard escorted them to the door, knocked, let them in and then backed away and closed the door.

With a solid barrier between them and the people outside, Cathy felt a bit more relaxed. She flashed her ID. 'Chief Constantine, we have it on the best authority that there are at least two men on the other side of the security screen with fully automatic weapons in their backpacks.'

'What? They have to pass through a metal detector.'

'Then one of your men is involved or has been compromised.'

The security boss pointed to one of half a dozen monitors in a bank of screens on the wall. 'That's the area around the detector. It looks like Ted Watson on station.'

Constantine reached out and pushed a button on the intercom unit on his desk. A voice responded instantly. 'What's up, Chief?'

'Can you man the metal detector and send in Ted Watson?'

'Sure thing.'

Constantine looked up. 'I guess we'll find out what's going on in a minute.'

A few seconds later there was a knock at the door and a man entered. To Matthew, he had the look of a guilty man. He wondered what Cathy saw when she looked at him.

That question was answered straight away. 'Why did you do it?'

Watson looked from one face to another. His shoulders slumped and tears started to roll down his face. 'They have my family.'

'How many have gone through?'

'Five. I think three went to the viewing platform.'

Constantine looked at Cathy then at the crying man. 'Sit down, Ted.' The guard did as he was asked.

Cathy looked at Matthew then pulled out her phone. 'It's all confirmed now. I can call it in.'

Matthew nodded. 'I get it. You had to have something tangible to report.'

'Thanks for understanding, Matthew.' Cathy pressed a couple of buttons and a few seconds later was talking to the local headquarters.

Matthew moved around the office trying to look around the edges of the venetian blinds at the area outside. He heard Cathy say the word "Icarus". He knew what she was talking about this time, so he was tuning it out, instead wondering how he had managed to get so lucky, or was it unlucky, to be close to two nuclear bombs. 'Sometimes it doesn't pay to have good instincts,' he mumbled to himself.

Cathy hung up then made another call. This time Matthew heard her talk to Jensen. She explained that the situation had been called in. Jensen and Arturo could come in now. She and Matthew were going to try to get on the other side of the gunmen and hopefully they could be disarmed without anyone being injured, or worse.

'Let's go, Matthew.'

Kasim Abidi was contemplating his death, wondering if it was going to be significant. He was prepared to die but still scared shitless about what was going to happen. He tried to distract himself but it was proving difficult.

He studied the people in the display area. The couple walking past him were obviously in love. No wonder. The woman was very beautiful. He wondered if they would still be together in the afterlife but he doubted it. Surely the Godless would not be with him in paradise.

Another couple were entering. They were holding hands but they didn't look like they were in love. They looked uncomfortable. In fact, they looked like cops.

Kasim shrugged off his backpack and started rummaging around inside. He had just placed his hand on the grip of the gun inside when he was crash tackled from behind.

Matthew knew what the man in the blue shirt and green hat was capable of and when he saw the man reaching for his gun, he decided to act. In only five steps, he had reached a significant speed so when he smashed into the terrorist the wind exploded out of the man in a whoosh. When they hit the ground, the man's head made solid contact and he went limp. *Not bad for someone who never played rugby*, thought Matthew as he brought the man's arms up behind his back.

Cathy moved over to assist Matthew, getting out a pair of handcuffs from within her jacket. Just as she was about to snap them on the air around them erupted with the sound of automatic weapons fire. 'The other terrorist!' yelled Matthew as he and Cathy ran to the cover of a display.

Matthew watched as the man he had tackled slowly regained his feet, picked up his weapon and ran towards the security office, firing wildly as he went.

People were screaming and running to get out of his way, but one man wasn't fast enough and was struck by the bullets. He was dead before he hit the ground. A security guard finally overcame his shock and started to draw his gun. The terrorist turned his gun on the man, who was blasted back against the wall.

Blue Shirt continued to run and in a second, he was in the office screaming at the men inside.

'Matthew!' yelled Cathy. 'Can't you do anything?'

Matthew closed his eyes for a moment and focused, but the familiar burst of energy didn't happen. 'No, I can't. It must be too close to the previous time I jumped. I can't do it a second time.'

Bullets started tearing through the display they were hiding behind. They both squatted lower. More bullets passed above them. Fuck.

Then there was a single gunshot. Blam. Even to Matthew's untrained ear it was from a different gun. The machinegun fire had stopped so he cautiously looked out and saw the terrorist with the grey shirt and bushy moustache staggering away, clutching at his right arm.

Suddenly, there was a shadow over Matthew. Startled, he looked up. A bearded man wearing a black jacket and a blue cap and holding a gun was looking down on him.

'Hello, Matthew.' The man smiled.

'Carmichael.'

Chapter 54

Carmichael looked over at Cathy. 'And the last time we met you were Rachel Black. Now I'll assume that's not your real name.'

'Special Agent Cathy Owens,' she said. 'FBI.'

'Of course, you are.'

'What the hell are you doing here?' blurted out Matthew.

'Among other things, saving your sorry ass I think,' the former officer grinned.

'Yes, thanks for that,' Cathy butted in. 'But what are you doing *here*, and can you tell us what's going on?'

They all turned at the sound of more shots. The man Matthew thought of as Blue Shirt had reached the office and was firing out at Jensen and Arturo, who were returning fire.

Carmichael casually dismissed the scene and returned to his conversation with the two people directly in front of him. 'I saw the leader of this little gang yesterday. I recognised him as a member of al-Qaeda even if I couldn't quite remember the name. I think it's Malek. He was on a list of people we wanted to talk to during my time in Iraq. I followed them here. They were obviously carrying out a rehearsal of what was going to happen today. I decided I would stop them.'

'How many of them are there?'

'Nine. But I think they have one more inside man here who has provided all the weapons, so I hope you have more help on the way.'

Cathy nodded. 'In ten minutes, this place will be swarming with federal agents.'

'If we have ten minutes,' Matthew added.

'Shit.' Cathy looked at Carmichael again. 'Do you have any idea why we're here?'

'It took a while but eventually I got there. There's a nuclear device somewhere in the building, isn't there?'

Cathy nodded again.

'Any idea where?'

'Matthew thinks it's in a Coke machine on the observation deck.'

'Well, that could be a problem.'

'Why?'

'There are three of them up there now as well as five or six throughout the rest of the building. We're going to have to fight like hell against a heavily armed enemy in an advantageous position just to get to the deck. And if we do get to it, then what?'

'Now just what do you mean by "we"?' Cathy asked. 'You're lucky that I don't arrest you right now.'

Just then two more men ran through the entrance from the lobby. They were carrying the same type of guns as the other terrorists. They ignored the civilians streaming past but when they saw Jensen and Arturo they opened fire. Both of the agents hit the floor, though neither Cathy nor Matthew could see if they were hurt as they dropped behind the conveyor used to move goods through the screening station.

Carmichael fired and one of the terrorists went down, causing the other to duck for cover behind a corner.

Carmichael, Cathy and Matthew took a step back till they were behind the display. Matthew wasn't sure how much protection it offered but at least they were out of sight. He was really getting sick of being shot at.

'Well, I think you need all the help you can get.' As if nothing had happened, Carmichael picked up the conversation with Cathy where it had left off.

Cathy ignored him. 'Jensen! Arturo!'

Jensen yelled back. 'I'm okay. Arturo's taken a hit in the shoulder. It looks pretty bad.'

'Can you help her?'

'I'll do what I can, but this other asshole is blocking the way out.'

On cue, the other asshole stepped out and started firing again in Jensen's direction; a snap shot from Cathy forced him back around the corner.

They all looked around as a security guard crawled along the floor towards them. He was obviously terrified. 'What's happening?' he cried.

It was the man who had escorted Carmichael through the metal detector. The ex-army man shot him a withering look. 'What do you think? Armed terrorists are trying to take over the Empire State Building.'

'What should I do?' the man pleaded.

'Sit still and stay out of our way.' The man nodded his understanding.

The door of the security office opened. Both Cathy and Carmichael snapped up their guns to take aim but held fire as they saw the guard Ted Watson and Chief Constantine walking out with their hands raised. They had only gone a few steps when, from within the room, a stream of bullets hurled the two men forward.

Shocked, Matthew tried to calm his breathing and focus. He closed his eyes but again nothing happened. 'Damn.'

Cathy looked at the guard, now wide eyed with terror. 'How many of you are left?'

'Uh, uh,' the man stammered, 'there were four guards and the chief on duty.'

'So, there's another guard somewhere. Any ideas where?'

The guard stared vacantly into space for a few seconds. 'Uh, I think he was over at the elevators.'

Carmichael spoke. 'I think the one I winged went in that direction.'

'Great,' said Cathy. 'There's at least one guy blocking the front entrance, one in the office and probably another one over at the elevators.' She looked at the guard again. 'We need to get up to the observation deck. How do we get there?'

'Why do you need to go there?' The question was met with stony silence. The guard tried to fill the space. 'The elevator.'

'Is that the only way? There's more of them waiting for us at the top.'

Yeah. No. Wait.' The guard's eyes were like slot machine reels, rolling in his head. Finally, they came to rest but there was no pay-out. 'The only way to the observation deck is the elevator on this floor.'

'No stairs?'

'Uh, yeah, but it's eighty-six floors. We don't let the public use them.'

Cathy turned to Matthew. 'Feel like running up eighty-six flights of stairs?'

The Aussie shook his head. 'I don't think I'd be good for much once I reached the top.'

Cathy looked at Carmichael. 'You're right. We need your help.' The ex-officer nodded. 'But first we need to take out the guy in the office. We can't leave our friends trapped on two sides. Any ideas?'

'How about I work my way towards the door? I get into position; you fire through the window to distract him and I do the rest.'

'Okay. Let's do it.' With that, Carmichael moved away. Cathy watched as he moved easily from one place of cover to the next towards the office door. *Glad he's on our side*, she thought to herself. A short time later he stopped and nodded back towards them.

'Here goes,' she said to Matthew, standing up and then firing at the window. She ducked down as a hail of bullets came blasting back out towards her.

Coolly, Carmichael stepped out from the corner he was behind, over the dead bodies of the security officers and into the office. He fired twice. He turned and nodded at Cathy.

'Jensen,' she yelled.

'Yeah?'

'We need you to hold this position while we get to the elevator. Can you do that?'

'Sure.' He fired off a shot at the corner the terrorist was using as cover. 'Why not? I'm not doing anything else today.'

Cathy looked at the guard. 'You've got a gun. Can you help him?' The man nodded but didn't move. 'Well, get going.' She watched as he scurried off to where Jensen and Arturo were hiding then turned to Matthew and Carmichael. 'Let's get to the elevator.'

The three of them carefully made their way to the lift. They were worried about the terrorist that Carmichael had wounded. Cathy paused at the corner and cautiously poked her head around.

The worry proved to be unfounded, but at a cost. The terrorist had bled out and was slumped against the wall in front of the lift, blood pooled around his lifeless body. The security guard who had been looking after this area was also lying on the floor, a pattern of bullet holes stitched across his chest.

Matthew looked at Cathy. 'There'll be more of them waiting at the top. As soon as the doors open, we'll end up like him,' he said, pointing at the dead guard. 'We need a plan.'

Carmichael spoke up. 'I think I have an idea.'

Chapter 55

Up on the observation deck, people were having a marvellous time viewing the spectacular sights of New York. At three hundred and twenty metres, the viewing platform circled the building, giving tourists three hundred and sixty-degree views.

One young father held a laughing boy up to the metal lattice that crisscrossed diagonally above the stone wall, so that he could point out the Statue of Liberty off in the distance. His mother stayed back as far from the edge as she could, wondering what had possessed her to want to come up to such a high place.

People had their phones out, busily snapping pictures of the views or selfies of themselves with the views of other famous buildings in the background. Others were looking through the telescopes that were regularly spaced around the deck.

Generally speaking, the people on the platform were happy but Fahad Malek's day had just taken an unexpected deviation. He had received a call on his cell phone a few minutes ago from Kasim Abidi. The call had been cut short by gunfire. He had to assume that Kasim was dead.

Straightaway he had phoned one of the other men waiting around the office at the United States and Middle Eastern Trade Development Association. He had been instructing the man to gather the others and head down to the security station when he realised, he was talking to dead air. He had redialled but couldn't get through.

Malek looked at his phone. There was no signal.

This was a standard tactic from the Americans when so-called terrorist events occurred. They would shut down cell towers to disrupt communications between the individuals or to stop remote triggering of any explosives by cell phones.

Their own tactical radios weren't affected and the authorities could communicate freely.

Malek wondered what had happened. It had to be that traitorous Pakistani, Barazani. What had made him betray their cause, he couldn't imagine. Then he thought that it didn't really matter. What it did mean, though, was that he, Malek, was going to die today, one way or another.

Malek had been about to tell his men that he was going down to the ground level to check on how things were going when Kasim phoned him. He had really been going to leave the city altogether but they didn't know that. Instantly he knew the call was bad news. It couldn't be anything else. His team had strict instructions not to call him except in emergencies.

So that was that. If the American authorities had shut down the phones, they would be coming. His focus now had to be making sure the bomb went off. He checked his watch. There was just less than one hour. Fifty-nine minutes until the country that had murdered his family would be made to pay. He would show them what collateral damage really was.

Malek contemplated his surroundings. There were three ways the Americans could assault his position. The first way was to ride the elevator up from the ground. The second way was to use a helicopter to drop men higher up at the 102nd floor observation deck who would then come down via another elevator or perhaps abseil down. The higher deck was closed for renovations now, but the Americans wouldn't care about that as long as it could be done.

Finally, they could try to get take out his men from choppers hovering off this observation deck or lower men onto it somehow and take the fight to his men that way. Any of the methods he contemplated were possible if the Americans had enough time.

Personally, he would bring up a helicopter and spray the area with the machine guns mounted on them. Sure, it would kill all of the civilians, but it would kill the opposition too and then they could ride the elevator up here and disarm the bomb. But he doubted the Americans would do that. It would be political suicide for the president to give the order to open fire on their own citizens. Even if they succeeded, he would be the villain and that would be the end of him.

So, it would probably be the elevators, most likely the one from the ground but they would keep an eye out for choppers flying too close to the top of the building.

He looked at the sightseers. Some of them were holding their cell phones up in the air trying to get reception. It wouldn't matter what angle they held them at, there wasn't a signal any more. It was time to let these tourists know who was in charge here and round them up to use them as human shields. He signalled his men.

At that moment, President Bright was in an emergency meeting of his National Security Council. His chief of staff, Rebecca Smart, was seated on his right.

He looked at all the faces before him. 'Are we even sure that's where the bomb is?' he pleaded.

Timothy Scott, the national security advisor, and CIA Director Ash Connors looked at each other. Connors shook his head. 'No, sir.'

'How about, how much time do we have?' The president's voice was getting louder with each question. There were just head shakes this time.

'Well, that's just great.' He turned to the Chairman of the Joint Chiefs, General Colin Risley. 'How would you handle it?'

'I'd take up half a dozen choppers, hose down the observation deck and ride the elevators up and look.'

'Fuck. I'd be the president that kills his own people. Even if the bomb is there I would be a pariah. Does anybody have an idea we can use?'

Director of the FBI James Benson spoke up. 'We need to storm the observation deck. Sure, we might take some collateral damage but you'll be able to ride that out. That's an accident, not a deliberate action. If we throw enough men at it, we'll get the job done.'

The president looked at his chief of staff, who nodded back.

With a sigh he said, 'Get it done.'

Malek looked at the display for the elevator. It was slowly rising. *Here they come.*

He signalled his men. One, Behram Abbasi, had his gun trained on the more than twenty tourists lined up along the edge of the platform. They were providing some protection in case the Americans decided on his preferred option of killing everyone up here.

His other man, the twin brother of the first, Ghulam Abbasi, stood to the side of the elevator doors, ready to blast anybody inside the second the doors opened. The Abbasi brothers were only fraternal twins but may as well have been identical. People who had only just met them had trouble telling them apart. They were average height, with lean builds. Both had grown bushy moustaches under prominent noses. The expression on Ghulam's face left the tourists in little doubt that he was prepared to shoot them if they gave any trouble.

Slowly the display moved up until it stopped with a chime. There was a half-second delay and then the doors moved apart. Ghulam took a step to the left and emptied his magazine into the lift.

Finally, the gun clicked on empty and the racket from the firing ceased. The screams and whimpers from the sightseers against the edge of the platform continued. Behram yelled at them to be quiet and the noise diminished.

Malek stepped forward and looked inside the elevator.

It was empty. A trick.

He looked back towards the tourists, now expecting some sort of attack from that direction. All was quiet.

Malek went to step away but a noise from behind brought his attention back to the elevator. A man had suddenly appeared. A bearded man in a black jacket.

Ghulam lifted his gun and pulled the trigger. Nothing. He hadn't reloaded since firing into the lift when the doors opened.

Malek and the stranger both lifted their guns and fired towards each other; a single shot from the pistol of the intruder but multiple rounds from Malek's machine gun. Malek was smashed backwards with a bullet in the chest. As his life faded away, he saw the other man, bloodied, lying on the floor. The man lifted his gun and fired towards the roof of the elevator.

Chapter 56

Matthew found himself with Cathy and Carmichael standing on the roof of the elevator. The last thing he remembered was the military man shooting at him from the floor. That prick.

'Carmichael.'

The major turned around and had no time to react before a fist crunched him in the face. He slammed back against the wall before slumping to the floor.

The ex-major sat there for a few seconds, then rubbed his jaw and smiled. 'Should I ask what that was for?'

'That was for about five minutes from now when your plan didn't work out. I think we need to tweak it a bit.'

Cathy glanced at the two men. 'If you two are quite finished.' She looked down at the guard who was standing by the elevator control panel with a key in his hand. 'Send us up then go back and help Jensen.'

The guard turned the key and the doors slid shut. Cathy dropped the access panel back into position and turned on her flashlight. Despite the lights dotted up and down the elevator shaft, the extra brightness gave her some comfort, helping her to feel less closed in.

They started to ascend.

'What was wrong with the plan?' asked the ex-soldier as the lights passed by.

'It ended up with you shot to bits and then turning the gun on me.'

'Any suggestions on how we can improve it?'

'They shoot the shit out of the lift as soon as the doors open. After that, we need to wait a bit longer before we drop down onto the floor. We don't get a third try.'

'You tell me when.'

Malek looked at the display for the elevator. It was slowly rising. *Here they come.*

The doors opened and Ghulam took a step to the left and emptied his gun into the lift.

Finally, the gun clicked empty and the noise stopped.

Malek stepped forward and looked inside the elevator.

It was empty. A trick.

He looked back towards the tourists, now expecting some sort of attack from that direction.

He walked over to Behram. 'Keep a close watch. The Americans might try to land men from helicopters.'

Behram gripped his gun even tighter. 'I hope so.'

Those were the last words Behram Abbasi ever spoke. A sharp crack from the direction of the elevator coincided with Behram being flung forwards towards the sightseers. Screams erupted from the tourists, both men and women.

Malek instinctively ducked. There was another shot and he felt the bullet actually pass through his hair as he scuttled away around the viewing platform, putting as much space and cover as possible between him and the mystery shooter.

Ghulam Abbasi had just seen his brother shot dead. Rage filled him as he turned back to the elevator. A man was charging towards him.

Ghulam raised his gun and pulled the trigger.

Nothing. It was empty. The man smashed into him like a battering ram. Ghulam was lifted off the ground and then hammered into the floor, his head making sickening contact.

'Maybe I could get a contract with the Rabbitohs,' said Matthew as Cathy rolled the unconscious man over and cuffed his arms behind his back.

'I don't even want to know what that means,' Cathy responded.

'They're a rugby league team.'

'Football?'

Matthew nodded.

'Well, I bet they don't have people shooting at them when they try to tackle the opposition.'

Matthew shook his head.

Carmichael stepped up to them. 'There's one left. He went that way.' He indicated with a nod.

Cathy turned to Matthew. 'Get these people out of here. Carmichael and I will try and flank this guy.'

The young Australian looked reluctant but nodded. He raised his voice over the sobs of the people huddled at the edge of the platform. 'Please come with me,' he said, waving towards the elevator. He pressed the call button and the doors opened.

There was no movement for a few seconds then it was as if the dam burst as the people flooded towards the way out of their nightmares.

Matthew wasn't sure how many people the lift was licensed to carry and none of the tourists cared; they managed to cram themselves in. Clearly, they all wanted to be out of there as quickly as possible. Nobody was waiting for a second trip.

Despite all of the bullet holes, the doors closed and the display above the elevator started to go down.

Matthew turned around. He was alone.

Cathy pointed. 'You go that way. I'll go the other and we'll catch him between us.' The ex-soldier nodded his agreement and they slowly went in opposite directions.

Malek was mentally kicking himself. He had let the Americans outsmart him. It didn't matter. He checked his watch. In less than half an hour, this place was going to be radioactive dust. Every second of time he bought now was going to ensure that his plan succeeded. His passing would bring death and desolation to millions of these Godless people. Sweet revenge.

He huddled down behind one of the viewing telescopes waiting for the attack he knew was coming. It was going to come from both directions; he just wasn't sure how many there were. He knew there weren't many—there wasn't enough noise. Apart from the wind, which was a constant at this height, he couldn't hear anything.

Cathy moved slowly counter-clockwise around the observation deck. The man looked to have a HK MP7, which could unleash a storm of lead, so she wasn't going to rush into anything. Holding her gun, arms extended, ready to shoot, she stepped around a corner.

Malek's eyes were constantly moving, trying to cover both directions at once, his gun swinging back and forth, in synch with his eyes.

A woman stepped around the corner. In a fraction of a second, he squeezed the trigger and a stream of bullets flew towards the target.

She disappeared back around the corner but Malek was sure he had hit that American bitch at least once.

He stepped out from behind the telescope. *Time to finish this*, he thought. *How dare they send a woman against me.*

Malek strode towards the spot. He could see blood on the floor. 'Take that, you cunt,' he yelled. He stepped around the corner to see the woman lying on the ground clutching at her thigh, her weapon a few feet away. She feebly reached towards it. He smiled in anticipation as he raised his gun.

Blam.

Cathy groaned in pain as she held her left leg. The pain was excruciating and blood was everywhere. She had dropped her gun as she fell back and it was lying on the ground a few feet away. It may as well have been a mile. She didn't think she could reach it but she had to try.

'Take that, you cunt,' the terrorist yelled as he stepped around the corner.

A malevolent look crossed his face as the man raised his gun.

Blam.

The terrorist's head exploded in a cloud of red mist and grey matter and the body slumped to the ground.

Carmichael stepped up to her and surveyed the scene. Causally he bent down and pulled the dead man's belt from his trousers and started to use it as a tourniquet on her injured leg. She gasped in pain as he tightened it around the wound.

Crashing footsteps drew her attention as Matthew ran up to them. 'God. Are you alright?' he yelled.

She winced in pain as the ex-military man finished his first aid. 'I'll be okay.'

'Let me…' he started.

'Matthew. No. Even if you could, we can't risk it. Next time could turn out worse and we need to find that bomb.'

Mathew turned to the ex-major. 'Can you, do it? Can you stop the bomb?'

'Sadly, that's not my area of expertise.'

'Of course not.'

'I can do it.' Cathy grimaced. 'I just need your help to get me to that Coke machine.'

'It's this way,' said Carmichael.

Matthew bent down and effortlessly lifted Cathy, then followed the man who had been such a source of frustration for him. 'Thanks for saving her,' he said. 'I owe you for that.'

'We're on the same side, Matthew. It's in all our interest, you know.'

'Yeah. Well, all the same. Thanks.'

'Sure.'

They stopped at the drink dispenser. Matthew mused briefly at the irony, and how something so ubiquitous in this country could now look so deadly to him.

He gently laid Cathy down on the ground and moved to the opposite side to that of the other man. 'One, two, three.' They both heaved and the machine moved forward about three feet.

The rear of the dispenser was protected by a sheet of steel secured by screws to the main body. 'Use this,' said Cathy, grabbing a Leatherman multi-tool from the holder on her belt.

Carmichael took the tool and selected a Phillips screwdriver from within the handle and started to work on the screws. When he had unfastened the top row, then half on each side, he folded the steel down. He turned to Matthew. 'It's taking too long. Give us a hand.'

The two men pulled at the sheet and the remaining screws were ripped out. The ex-soldier threw it to the side. The bomb was exposed to the world.

'Shit!' gasped Matthew as he took in the digital display. 'There's less than ten minutes left. Cathy, I hope you remember how to do this.'

No answer.

He looked down at Cathy. Her eyes were closed. 'Christ.' He dropped to the ground and reached out a hand to Cathy's neck. Thank goodness. He could feel a pulse.

'I guess it's up to us,' he said to the other man.

'How hard could it be?' responded the ex-major as he picked up the Leatherman tool and moved towards the bomb.

'Please don't do that.'

The unexpected voice behind them startled both men, who turned to see a number of black-clad men with guns pointed at them. FBI logos on their clothing identified them. 'Who are you?' asked one of the men. He was at least six inches shorter than Matthew but with a very powerful build. His eyes almost matched the colour of his clothing and he looked willing to shoot if he didn't like the answer he was given.

Matthew and Carmichael both raised their hands. Matthew spoke first. 'Just let me get my ID out of my pocket.' The Australian accent didn't inspire a lot of confidence in the men watching and many of the guns moved closer. 'Matthew Fraser. Consultant for the FBI.' He showed the identification he had been given and tried to point to the logo on the inside of his jacket. 'This is Special Agent Cathy Owens,' he said, pointing to the still-unconscious woman. He turned to the former soldier. 'And this is Special Agent Carr.'

Matthew's former tormentor turned to the young Australian and nodded his appreciation.

The man who had spoken to them looked at the digital display. 'Shit. Eight minutes. Where are those army guys?'

'Here.' Two men stepped forward. They were both just over six feet tall and obviously spent a lot of time in the gym. Serious expressions discouraged any conversation. Carmichael recognised them instantly as warrant officers as did Matthew due to his recent experience at the Alamo. They moved quickly towards the drink dispenser and placed their tool bags on the ground, opening them to select the instruments they needed.

'Let's give them room!' ordered the leader of the men in black and his men moved further away.

'Cathy's been shot. Can we get her some medical attention?' pleaded Matthew.

The leader spoke into a microphone on his collar. 'Agent down. Gunshot wound. We need medics up here.' He must have received a positive response in his earpiece. 'Roger that.' He looked at Matthew. 'On the way.'

More men came up to them. 'The area's secure, sir. One unconscious man in cuffs over near the elevator. Two dead. No others.'

'Good.' The man turned to Matthew. 'Special Agent Biggs,' he said by way of introduction. 'Just what the hell happened here?'

Matthew gave him an abbreviated version of the events that had led to this point, Biggs asking a few questions along the way. When he was finished, Biggs nodded. 'How long left?'

One of his men answered. 'One minute.'

'How's it going, gentlemen?' he asked the two warrant officers.

'Nearly there.'

'I fuckin' hope so. It might get a bit warm up here otherwise.' A few nervous gulps from some of his men showed that they agreed with their leader.

'Just one thing left to do,' said one of the warrant officers.

'What's that?'

'Celebrate a job well done.' And with that he and his companion both lifted a can of beer from their tool bags, popped the tops and toasted each other.

Biggs exhaled loudly while a number of his men cheered at the news. One man made a sign of the cross and looked to the heavens.

Carmichael quietly asked Matthew if he could borrow his jacket.

Chapter 57

The medics came and saw to Cathy. Judging by their actions, Matthew suspected they had seen many gunshot wounds in the past. He was relieved to hear that they thought she would be okay.

He was about to go down with them when Special Agent Biggs decided he needed to hear Matthew's story one more time. 'Don't worry. You'll be able to see her in the hospital.'

When they were done, Biggs looked around for "Special Agent Carr" to get his description of events but he was nowhere to be found, so Matthew took the opportunity to head for the ground.

The elevator doors opened and Matthew felt like he was in Grand Central Station. Heavily armed men stood guard at strategic points. Paramedics were treating many people for shock and FBI agents were interviewing the people who had made the initial trip down from the observation deck. None of them had been allowed to leave the scene. Some of them pointed when they spotted him, the attention unwelcome on his part as he wanted to get out of there and find Cathy.

A tap on the shoulder startled him. When he turned around, he saw Jensen. 'Thank God you're alright,' the man told him, throwing his arms around Matthew, who hugged him back, equally pleased to see that the federal agent was uninjured. 'I saw them bring Special Agent Owens down on a gurney a few minutes ago but couldn't get over to her through the crowd. How is she?'

'She was shot in the leg, but they tell me she'll be okay. How's Arturo?'

Jensen blew out his cheeks. 'She lost a lot of blood. I think we might have lost her if the guys hadn't stormed the building when they did. As it is, they tell me it's touch and go.' Jensen put his game face back on. 'So, what happened?'

Matthew recounted his story again, editing out the part about Carmichael taking his jacket and disappearing.

The FBI man looked thoughtful. 'I don't know how that guy got a gun through security in the first place but it worked out well for us. I'll speak to him about it as soon as I see him.'

Good luck finding him, thought Matthew. 'Yeah, me too,' he said. 'What's the next step here?'

Jensen gestured towards one of the black-clad FBI men with guns. 'The storm troopers are clearing the building floor by floor. It's a big place, though, and it's going to take hours. These guys,' he said pointing to the agents talking with the civilians, 'are going to be interviewing everyone to make sure we haven't missed any bad guys.'

'Okay. What's it like outside?'

'It's cordoned off for a block in every direction. The networks are broadcasting about a terrorist event and they're speculating that there's a bomb, but they don't know for sure. Thank God it didn't go off. I can't imagine how many people would have died.'

'That's for sure. Hey, do you know which hospital they would have taken Cathy to.'

Jensen gave him a knowing smile. 'I would think Bellevue. It's not too far away and has a big emergency centre. The quickest way to get there would be to bum a ride in one of the ambulances. I'm pretty sure there'll be a few more people taken there soon.'

'I'll do that.'

Jensen slapped him on the shoulder. 'I'm glad you're OK. I'd better get back to work.' The agent walked back to assist another man conducting interviews.

Matthew looked around trying to see if the paramedics were about to take any patients away. He spotted Carmichael waiting unobtrusively over near the entrance. The tall man was still wearing his jacket. It was a reasonable fit despite the sleeves being a bit short. He crooked his finger at Matthew, indicating he wanted to speak with the Australian.

Matthew made his way over. 'I'm surprised that you're still here.'

'Me too. I was about to leave but I thought there was something you'd like to know.'

'And what's that?'

'Your girlfriend's been kidnapped.'

Matthew's world closed in on him. 'What?'

'I saw someone I used to know hijack the ambulance she was in. Nobody else noticed anything.'

'What? Who would do something like that? Kidnap an FBI agent?'

'His name is Captain Ray Kingston and he works for Military Intelligence. Not the kind of man you want working against you.'

'Well, you'd know about that.'

Carmichael squinted at Matthew, then relaxed and nodded. 'I suppose you're right.'

'So why would I believe you? You could be trying to turn this situation to your advantage, get back in the good books.'

The ex-soldier threw him a cell phone. 'Call the hospitals. See if she's arrived. Ask about ambulance eighty-seven.'

Matthew took the phone and walked off. Five minutes later he was back. 'No FBI agents at all have been admitted and it appears the ambulance is missing. Fuck.' He could feel his heart racing as he handed the phone back. 'Why would this man have taken Cathy?'

'Kingston is an attack dog for General Risley, the Chairman of the Joint Chiefs. I guess they're trying to salvage the time travel project.'

'But Cathy had nothing to do with it.'

'Her name would be on the FBI reports. As far as they're concerned, she could be the one with access to all of the information. They won't know that everything was sucked into a black hole. If it was me, I'd probably do the same thing.'

Matthew had to rein in his temper. He felt like lashing out at the taller man, but he had to put Cathy's welfare ahead of his own temporary satisfaction. 'Where would he take her?'

'That's the spirit.'

Matthew sat on the bed in Carmichael's hotel room. He felt decidedly uncomfortable about the course of action he was about to embark on, but he was committed to doing all he could to get Cathy back.

The taller man exited the bathroom. He was freshly shaven and once again looked the part of an army officer, especially wearing the neatly pressed uniform. 'You realise, Matthew, that what you're about to do is a federal offence? Impersonating an officer is a serious thing.'

Matthew bit back his natural response to verbally attack Carmichael. Instead, he said, 'Whatever it takes.'

He stood up and once again looked at himself in the mirror. The uniform he was dressed in was a bit long in the sleeves and the legs but didn't look too bad. The two dark bars on his shoulder meant nothing to him. 'What rank does this indicate?'

'That would mean you're a captain in the US Army.'

'Couldn't you find me a general's star or something higher instead?'

'I had to go with what I had. You're lucky I even decided to keep these uniforms. Who'd have known being sentimental would pay off?'

'Somehow, I don't think you were being sentimental,' replied Matthew.

Carmichael smiled back. 'You're probably right.'

'So where do you think Kingston has taken Cathy?'

'My best guess would be Fort Hamilton.'

He was referring to the only military base still active in greater metropolitan New York. Located on the south-west tip of Brooklyn, it was home to army engineers, provided support to Army Reserve and National Guard units and housed the New York City Recruiting Battalion.

'Fort Hamilton? Where's that?'

'Brooklyn.'

'Brooklyn? It can't be very big then. Surely there's a bigger base than that around here somewhere?'

'Well, there's Fort Drum in upstate New York about five hours drive from here.'

'Why not there then?'

'For one thing, I think that's where they're going to take the bomb, so security is going to be tight. I wouldn't let you and me on the base in a hundred years so there's no way Kingston is going to get your injured girlfriend through the gates. Getting into Fort Hamilton will be a lot easier.'

'Hmm. I hope you're not just looking for a quarter you dropped in a dark room because that's the corner with a bit of light in it.'

Carmichael stopped polishing his shoes and looked at the Australian. 'Look, Matthew, I can disappear anytime I want and live out the rest of my life touring around the world. Thanks to our little jaunt in the jungle, I have all the money I'll ever need. I'm not doing this out of some obligation to you because I think I fucked your life up. Consider my help a reward for you and your girl for saving millions of lives. It's Fort Hamilton.'

'I just don't think you're telling me the complete story. You've kept secrets for so long I don't know if you're capable of the whole truth.'

The other man thought for a moment, then smiled. 'You know, you're smarter than you look.' Matthew rolled his eyes. 'This will give me a chance to kill three birds with one stone,' Carmichael said, then started ticking items off on his fingers. 'One. I really want to help you and Cathy. Two. Being a civilian is boring. I need the action. And three, I fucking hate Kingston. That Intelligence prick sent me and my squad into the mountains in Afghanistan chasing some Taliban chief and they were waiting for us. Ten went in and only two came out. This is payback.'

Matthew contemplated the admission for a few seconds. 'Well, what are we waiting for?'

'That's the spirit.'

Chapter 58

After Matthew had discovered that Cathy was missing, Carmichael had asked what type of car they had driven to the Empire State Building. He had replied that he thought it was a Lincoln something or other, an SUV. Carmichael said it sounded fairly typical for an FBI or an army vehicle so at the ex-military man's suggestion he had asked Jensen for the keys to Arturo's car. The FBI agent had given them to him without question, expecting the young Australian to use it to drive to the hospital, rather than trying to catch a lift in an ambulance.

They made their way to the parking garage. Matthew went to throw the keys to the other man but Carmichael held up his hand. 'As the junior officer you would be expected to drive.'

'Well, I'm used to driving on the left-hand side of the road so if you find me drifting out of my lane just let me know.'

'I'm sure you'll be fine.'

Following Carmichael's directions, they crossed the Brooklyn Bridge and got onto the Brooklyn Queens Expressway.

'So, do you think you'll be able to get us into the fort okay?'

'I have a number of ID's that I've collected over the years, not all in my own name. Just remember to call me Major Carter. The one you have says you're Captain Childs. With luck, the guard won't look too closely at the picture. I don't think I ever looked as hopeful in a photograph as you look in real life. And if anyone asks, just say you're 82nd Airborne out of Fort Bragg and try to talk English.'

'What? It's the only language I know.'

'Hmm. Could've fooled me.'

Changing the subject, Matthew asked, 'Have you been here before?'

'A number of times. I've had occasion to make use of the army engineers for a few projects.'

Once again, Matthew bit his tongue.

They took an exit and a short time later they were on Fort Hamilton Parkway. Another turn and they were driving past an old cannon and then, in fading daylight, they arrived at the gates. 'Piece of cake,' said Matthew, quite pleased with himself for getting them there without incident.

'Now the hard work starts.'

Two guards came out of a little hut. One was armed with an M4 carbine and the other with a pen and clipboard. The one with the clipboard walked up to Carmichael's side while the one with the M4 stayed a few yards back, covering the first. 'Can I help you, sir?'

'Good to see security is top notch here, soldier.'

'Thank you, sir. Can I help you, sir?'

The once-again major handed over an ID card. 'I'm here to see Major Venables.' The guard made a notation in his clipboard then handed it, the pen and the ID card to Carmichael.

'Sign please, sir.'

Carmichael scrawled a signature where required and the guards moved to the other side of the car.

'82nd Airborne out of Fort Bragg,' said Matthew handing over the bogus ID card.

The soldier gave him a strange look and the ID card a cursory glance. He made a note on his clipboard then gave it and the ID card to Matthew. 'Thank you, sir. Please sign here.'

Matthew scratched how he thought Captain Childs would sign his signature and handed the board back.

'Do you know where to go, sir?'

'Yes.'

'Have a nice day, sir.' With that, the two soldiers moved back to their hut. Matthew waited for the gates to rise and drove onto the base.

'What the hell was that?' exclaimed Carmichael.

'What?'

'That voice.'

'That was my best American accent.'

'It sounded like John Wayne sucking on helium. Just try not to talk to anyone else.'

'So, I'm not very good at accents. At least we're in. Now, where are we likely to find Kingston?'

'Turn left at the end of the road. He'll want somewhere quiet so he can talk to your girlfriend in private.' Matthew gritted his teeth at the comment, then turned the car. 'So, since a large proportion of the army engineers based here are in Haiti for reconstruction projects after the latest earthquake, I figure he'll be somewhere in that section of the base.'

'Do you think he'll still have the ambulance?'

'I doubt it. He'll have dumped it. Now he'll have some bland sedan and my guess is she'll have come onto the base in the trunk.'

Matthew clenched his hands even tighter around the steering wheel. 'If he's hurt her, I'll kill that bastard.'

'Straight ahead.' Carmichael directed as they reached a turn with a sign pointing to "Engineers' Administration". 'You know, Matthew, I think you'd have made a good soldier. All you need is the right motivation. Take a right here.' Matthew turned the car as directed, passing between two large buildings. One looked like offices and the other was some sort of storage facility. A car was parked off the road between the structures. Without being asked, the Australian pulled the car over behind the other vehicle.

'It's a pity you don't have a gun,' Carmichael told Matthew. 'That means we're relying on just mine.'

'Shit. What if he has more men with him?'

'I don't think so. To people like him, knowledge is power. He won't want to share it with anyone else.' He opened the car and stepped out, closing the door quietly behind him. Matthew followed suit.

'Quietly does it and stay behind me,' commanded the soldier as he silently moved towards the entrance to the building. They were two huge double sliding doors, with a normal size door built to the right-hand side to allow personal access without the need to open the main doors. He tried the handle and found it unlocked.

As slowly as he could Carmichael pulled the door. At first, it moved without a noise but suddenly it squealed, the sound seemingly the loudest that Matthew had ever heard. They both froze and waited to see if they had been discovered.

After a minute of standing like a statue, Matthew slowly exhaled. 'Wait here,' he said. He made his way back to the car and looked on the floor well in the rear. He remembered seeing a small toolbox on the floor. He opened the box and looked inside.

Matthew was relieved to see a small can of WD40, which he hoped would lubricate the hinges on the door. He shook it and found it nearly full. He also gratefully pocketed a flashlight he found inside. The natural light was starting to dwindle quickly.

Back at the door, Matthew sprayed the hinges with the lubricant and slowly worked the door back and forward to try to make sure it reached the offending parts. 'Try again.'

This time the door opened noiselessly. 'Good work,' said Carmichael stepping through with Matthew close behind.

They were in a huge storage area full of machinery, much of which Matthew had never seen before, though he did recognise a backhoe and a bulldozer. He imagined that the gear was used for digging holes, building bridges and any other task required for shifting men from one place to another.

The main part of the building was unlit, with still enough natural light to see the machinery, though not sufficient to make out the finer details. On the far side of the building, there was a mezzanine level walkway with about six or seven offices with a staircase at either end. The offices were all lit.

Carmichael pointed to Matthew and then the stairs on the left. He then indicated he would take the right-hand steps. Finally, he held a finger to his lips. Matthew nodded.

Matthew walked as quietly as he could towards the stairs. He was thinking that it was alright for the other guy, he had a gun. He began looking around for anything he could use as a weapon. He passed an open storage locker which was full of tools. He grabbed a shovel. It wasn't exactly what he would have selected if his choices were unlimited but having something in his hands was strangely reassuring.

He put his foot on the bottom step.

Cathy was at the bottom of a dark hole with a heavy weight holding her down. She struggled to push it off and climb out but she was such a long way down and she had no strength. She slowly made her way towards the light at the top, struggling to shrug off the burden.

She opened her eyes. Where was she? It was beyond her comprehension.

A sudden bolt of pain in her leg made her gasp but helped her mind focus. Events started flooding back.

Cathy remembered being at the top of the Empire State Building. She had been shot. She could see her leg. There was a belt tied around it and her pants were covered in blood.

Then what had happened? She was going to defuse the bomb. Had she done it? Maybe she hadn't and this was hell. It certainly wasn't a hospital, which would have made more sense. She was lying on a cold floor in an office. Where was she? Was she somewhere in that famous building? It was time to find out.

Cathy tried to move but another stab of pain threatened to throw her back down the well of unconsciousness. She lay there gasping.

From behind her came an unfamiliar male voice. 'Finally, you're awake.'

Turning around to see who was talking was too much effort. 'Where am I?' she managed to croak out.

She heard the man stand up from a chair and walk around so that he was in front of her. 'Somewhere private,' he said.

Cathy managed to move her head a bit and saw a man in uniform. Was that an army captain's bars she saw?

God, she was thirsty. 'What am I doing here? Who are you?'

'Who I am isn't important. Why you're here is so that we can have a little talk and you can tell me what I need to know.'

'What? Tell you about what?'

'About the time travel experiments.'

'Huh? I don't know anything about any time travel experiments.'

'Oh, I think you do. Let me help jog your memory.' The man squatted down, reached out and poked her in the leg.

Cathy didn't have the energy to scream. She gasped and once again faded into oblivion.

The climb out of unconsciousness was just as disorienting the second time but eventually she made it. Clarity returned. This pig wanted to know about Matthew. That wasn't going to happen. No way in hell.

'You're back.' The man was back in his chair. 'That's good.' He stood up and walked over to her again. 'Would you like some water?'

Cathy managed a weak nod. 'Yes.'

He dropped down next to her and lifted her head so that she was more upright and moved a glass to her lips. She managed a few sips then he lowered her head back to the floor.

'You can't do this to me. I'm an FBI agent. Just let me go.' Her voice was barely above a whisper.

'Well, actually, I can do this. However, if you tell me what I want to know then I'll let you go. How's that for a deal?' He smiled at her but the man's eyes remained as cold as ice.

'I don't know what you're talking about.'

'That's a pity because I have plenty of time. But I'm sure we'll get there in the end.' He reached out towards her leg again but before he could touch her there was a noise that split the silence. A squeaky hinge?

The man stood up and moved to the office window.

With a bit more awareness, Cathy could now tell they were not a ground level. She could feel the man's footsteps through the floor. He looked concerned as he stared through the glass. Maybe he didn't have as much time as he said. She had to fight him.

He turned around and came back to her. 'Sorry about this.'

'About what?' she asked as he squatted down.

'This.' He punched her in the leg. Once again, her world went black.

Chapter 59

Holding the shovel like a baseball bat, Matthew slowly climbed the stairs, carefully, so as not to make any noise. Was Cathy in one of these offices? He was going to find out.

He reached a step where he could almost see the top of the walkway when there was a gunshot.

Abandoning stealth, he ran up the last few stairs just in time to see someone disappearing down the steps at the far end. Was that a woman slung over the man's shoulders? It was only a fleeting glimpse but it gave Matthew the surety that they had found Cathy.

Footsteps echoed from the far steps and across the floor as Matthew ran along the walkway. He wondered where Carmichael was.

That question was answered when he reached the end of the walkway and started down the steps at the far end. A body was lying on the ground. Matthew bounded down the stairs.

It was Carmichael. He was still alive but moaning, clutching at his stomach, his left hand covered in blood. 'Are you okay?' asked Matthew.

'What are you worried about me for? Go save the girl!' the man hissed through gritted teeth.

There was another gunshot, this time from outside the building. Matthew sprinted to the door and through it just in time to see a car disappear around the corner.

Matthew ran to the car he had driven to the base. He looked down. That explained the gunshot. One of the tyres had been shot out. There wasn't time to change it. Kingston would be long gone and Cathy with him.

Matthew started to run.

Captain Kingston was shaken. He wasn't used to being in harm's way. His job had never seen him in combat. He had killed before but never in a fair fight or combat situation. He was high on adrenaline. He took deep breaths, forcing himself to calm down, to drive at the base speed limit and not draw attention to himself.

He replayed what had happened. That was Major Carmichael back there, he was sure of it. How had that man tracked him here? That pain in the ass.

It didn't matter. They wouldn't find him again.

He took the turns back to the base's main gates. To his dismay, the boom gates stayed down. He pulled up to them.

The soldier armed with the clipboard stepped out of the guard's hut but not the one with the carbine. Evidently, they were more worried about people coming in than going out. He handed the clipboard through the window. 'Please sign here, sir.'

Kingston scrawled a signature and handed the clipboard back. 'Thank you, sir. Have a nice night.' The soldier had bent down at the last few words to give a friendly smile, just as he had been ordered by his lieutenant. Everyone should leave the base with a positive last impression he had been told.

That was when he saw the woman lying on the back seat. 'What the...' was all he managed to say before a gun was pointed in his face.

'Open the fucking gate.'

The guard lifted an arm and the gate started to rise.

Kingston looked in his mirror. His heart rate nearly doubled when he saw a man sprinting down the road after his car. 'What is this? The fucking Terminator?'

Finally, the gate was high enough. Kingston stood on the gas pedal and the car took off with a squeal of tyres.

Matthew didn't slow down as he passed the guard's station. 'That man kidnapped an FBI agent,' he yelled as he leapt over the lowered boom gate like a hurdler in the Olympics. The guards stared at him as he barrelled out of the gate and down the road.

Part of Matthew knew that this is what all of the years of training had been for. This was for something more than a medal in a race. This was for life. He wasn't going to give up. He ran even harder as the car fishtailed around the corner.

Kingston exhaled noisily. He was safe. They couldn't catch him now. He glanced at his mirror again just in time for the street lights to shine on the soldier running around the corner after him. 'What the fuck?' he said, heart pounding. He couldn't believe it. He turned his head to look over his shoulder at the man.

Robbie Caldwell was kicking himself.

He had finally talked Sandra Watkins into a date. He had wined and dined the beautiful college freshman and the night had been going wonderfully well. The restaurant was superb, the food was delicious, he was funny and had made her laugh throughout the date. To his utter delight, she had agreed to come back to his place for a nightcap.

Sandra had made the final commitment to go upstairs with him. She had teasingly removed her clothes, enflaming him with lust. When he had lain down next to her, he was sure heaven was only moments away.

Then, 'You do have a condom, don't you?'

Robbie's world came crashing down. He quickly pulled on some clothes, imploring Sandra to stay, he would only be moments. He ran out the door to his car and jumped in. He started the car and reversed out of the driveway, oblivious to what was coming down the road.

Who is this guy? thought Ray Kingston. He turned back around just in time to see the car backing out onto the street in front of him.

There was nothing he could do. At nearly seventy kilometres per hour, he hit the back end of the car before crossing the road to glance off another car and crash into a tree.

Stunned from the impact with the airbag, Kingston struggled to push the deflating device out of the way before opening the door and stepping out.

He staggered upright and turned around. Once again there was no time to avoid the collision. This time with the fist hurtling towards his face.

The second punch Matthew had thrown that day connected with the force of a piledriver. When Kingston eventually regained consciousness the next day, it was to find that he couldn't open his mouth as there were wires holding his jaw together.

Once the man was down, he was instantly dismissed from Matthew's mind. He nearly ripped the back door from its hinges getting it open.

Cathy.

She was so still. He checked her pulse. He found one. Relief.

She had hit the back of the seats in front of her when the car crashed and been protected from the worst of the impact. Carefully, Matthew lifted her from the car and laid her on the ground.

The driver of the other car came over. 'It wasn't my fault. I didn't see him. He was speeding.'

'Go away,' Matthew told him just as an army jeep came around the corner and then cruised up beside them.

'This woman's been shot. Call an ambulance.'

The guard who had been armed with the clipboard quickly pulled out a cell phone and made the call.

Matthew used his assumed rank to throw questions at the soldiers using his best American accent. He wasn't prepared to face criminal charges for impersonating an officer, so he kept up the pretext. Arrest this man he had told them, pointing at Kingston. And just how had they let this woman come onto the base and then leave it? The phrase "court martial" was thrown around.

When the ambulance arrived, the guards were only too happy to let the captain climb in and accompany the woman to the hospital.

Just before the ambulance pulled away, he told them they should call another ambulance and to check the machinery shed. They would find an injured man there.

The guards did as ordered. They found a bloodstain on the floor but despite an exhaustive search no injured man was found.

They did find a backhoe was missing and a hole in the fence.

Epilogue

When Cathy regained consciousness the next time, she was lying comfortably in a hospital bed.

'Welcome back.' Matthew smiled down at her.

'Hi,' she whispered. 'How long have I been out?'

'It's the day after tomorrow.'

'Oh.'

'Don't worry. I'll fill in the blanks for you.'

'Mmm.' She smiled and fell back asleep.

When Cathy awoke next, it was to see some familiar and friendly faces. Matthew was still there beaming at her. Jensen was there, as was her boss, Arnold Wilson.

The deep voice boomed at her. 'Special Agent Owens, it's good to have you back.'

Cathy looked around. There was a jug of water on the table. Jensen reached out and poured a glass. He held it in front of Cathy and she tentatively reached out and grabbed it before taking a swallow. 'It's good to be back, sir. How's Arturo?'

'She's going to need a lot of rehab but the doctors think she'll make a full recovery. We did manage to get her to the hospital a bit quicker than you, though, so that helped.'

'So, it's all over?'

'That's right!' Wilson boomed again. 'We went through the building and took out the rest of the terrorists. None of them were interested in being taken alive. The only live one was the man Matthew here knocked unconscious. We're interrogating him now to see if we can find anything useful. The army captain that abducted you…Kingston is his name. He's in the army's custody at the moment, though we are pressing to have him handed over. Either way, it's going to be a long time before he sees the outside of a cell.' He paused for a moment. 'You are going to be awarded the FBI Medal of Valor by President Bright himself, as soon as you're well enough to stand up. Jensen here is getting the FBI medal for Meritorious Achievement and Arturo is getting the FBI Star. You three have done a tremendous job of defending our country and preserving our lifestyle.'

'Thank you, sir. But what about Matthew?' She looked at the man she had shared so much with in such a short time. 'I suppose you'll be going back to Australia?'

Matthew gave a noncommittal shrug. 'Well, actually, your boss has offered me a permanent job and I was thinking of hanging around a bit. How would you feel about that?'

Her smile gave him the answer.

THE END